ULTIMATE
WARRIORS

Jaide Fox
Brenna Lyons
Joy Nash
Michelle M. Pillow

Futuristic and Paranormal Romance

New Concepts   Georgia

Be sure to check out our website for the very best in fiction at fantastic prices!

When you visit our webpage, you can:

* Read excerpts of currently available books
* View cover art of upcoming books and current releases
* Find out more about the talented artists who capture the magic of the writer's imagination on the covers
* Order books from our backlist
* Find out the latest NCP and author news--including any upcoming book signings by your favorite NCP author
* Read author bios and reviews of our books
* Get NCP submission guidelines
* And so much more!

We offer a 20% discount on all new ebook releases!
(Sorry, but short stories are not included in this offer.)

We also have contests and sales regularly, so be sure to visit our webpage to find the best deals in ebooks and paperbacks! To find out about our new releases as soon as they are available, please be sure to sign up for our newsletter (http://www.newconceptspublishing.com/newsletter.htm) or join our reader group (http://groups.yahoo.com/group/new_concepts_pub/join) !

The newsletter is available by double opt in only and our customer information is *never* shared!

Visit our webpage at:
www.newconceptspublishing.com

Ultimate Warriors is an original publication of NCP. This work has never before appeared in book form. This work is a novel. Any similarity to actual persons or events is purely coincidental.

New Concepts Publishing
5202 Humphreys Rd.
Lake Park, GA 31636

ISBN 1-58608-701-0
Demon Huntress: Sacrificed © copyright August 2004, Jaide Fox
With Great Power © copyright August 2004 Brenna Lyons
Heroes Incorporated © copyright August 2004 Joy Nash
Silk © copyright August 2004 Michelle M. Pillow
Cover art by Eliza Black © copyright August 2004

NCP books are available at special quantity discounts for bulk purchases for sales promotions, premiums, fund raising, or educational use. For details, write, email, or phone New Concepts Publishing, 5202Humphreys Rd., Lake Park, GA 31636, ncp@newconceptspublishing.com, Ph. 229-257-0367, Fax 229-219-1097.

First NCP Paperback Printing: 2005

Printed in the United States of America

4

TABLE OF CONTENTS:

Demon Huntress:
SACRIFICED

Jaide Fox

Chapter One

The warm summer air caressed my skin as I soared through the air, searching frantically for my house. It was difficult to find, since it was dark, and the country seemed to swallow light like a black hole, leaving me aimlessly wandering above winding dirt roads and the treetops.

My heart lodged in my throat, pounding and making it difficult to breathe. I couldn't remember landmarks near my house ... couldn't get my bearings. Fear induced adrenaline suffused me.

I'd felt fear often enough, but never so strongly. This was as close to terror as I'd ever come. Perspiration coated my skin, cooling rapidly in the air, giving me goosebumps in spite of the humidity.

He was out there, somewhere. Hunting me. And I knew he would find me. There was no stopping him.

Lightning flashed above like a strobe light, blinding me. The clouds moved, parting in a furious wind.

I dove and smacked into something, gasping as it grabbed me in a merciless grip.

There was nothing there but air and darkness and the heat of a creature from the deep. I smelled fire and brimstone. Fucking brimstone.

"Got you," a deep voice said with a growling chuckle that rumbled against my chest.

Shock raised chills on my skin. His fingers bit into my wrists, forcing my back to arch, my breasts to flatten against his chest.

I struggled against him, but there was nothing I could do to break his hold. I had nothing to brace myself against, nothing but my own powers of flight, and they were pitiful against him. Panic made my stomach flutter, my heart beat in my chest like a hip hop bass on speed.

It was with a dawning sense of horror that I realized I'd lost my clothes, and I couldn't remember how or when they'd disappeared.

"Let me the fuck go!" I screamed, gnashing my teeth, tossing my head as if it would help somehow.

He laughed again, tightening his hold. Struggling only seemed to excite him. He rubbed against me, forcing my legs to part around him, until his hard cock ground against my bare cleft.

The movement shocked me to my core. Unbidden wetness saturated my labia on the instant of that unwanted touch. My belly clenched on a spasm, and my vaginal muscles tightened reflexively with the instinct to shut him out.

"I like it when you fight me like that, Nari. How much would you buck and gnash if I fuck you here, in the open?"

I went stiff all over, breathing hard through my nostrils until they flared with each breath. It was always the same with him. He wanted me to fight. He wanted my absolute submission.

I didn't know what to do, only that I couldn't give up. I had to change my tactics.

He knew my name. I didn't know his. He felt like a man, but he wasn't. He was something else. I'd never been able to see him. How could I fight someone I couldn't see?

A helpless feeling washed over me, draining the fight from my body in slow increments. Flight had tired me, but the strain of trying to hold myself stiff to resist him wore on me.

"You don't answer. Could it be you're considering my offer this time?"

He sniffed my neck, his breath hot, moist, and then his mouth opened over it, his tongue lashing out to lave my skin.

I growled at him in warning.

His tongue traveled up to my ear, pushed inside, molten and wet … and forked. I shuddered. With revulsion, I told myself.

"I could be persuaded to let you go this time if you asked," he whispered before lapping my neck.

Asking was too much like begging. I'd never begged for anything in my life. Besides, I didn't think he'd do it anyway. I grit my teeth. "I'd never ask you for a damned thing, you fucking bastard."

He grunted and nicked me with his teeth. I controlled the wince. Pain I could deal with. I couldn't handle him trying to seduce me. That terrified me more than I cared to admit.

"Good. It's better this way. Don't you agree that pain makes the pleasure so much the sweeter?"

The world spun as he whirled us toward the ground. My house rose up before us, a pitiful facade of safety. The door burst open on a gust of wind.

Locked around my body, he flew us down the hall as if he knew exactly where my bedroom was. The door slammed open just before we hit it, and then we were inside, crashing down on the bed.

I bucked immediately, freeing a hand to go for the knife I always kept beneath my pillow.

He laughed and snatched my hand back, pinning my wrists down into the mattress, holding my legs down with his own as his weight settled over me.

He was huge, heavy enough I could barely breathe with him on top of me. I couldn't tell just how big he was, only that he seemed to be everywhere.

He held me down, but he didn't seem to need his hands. I felt him dip over me, felt his hot breath just before his mouth closed over one breast. His teeth bit into me, ever so lightly, and his tongue flicked out. Rough, it ground against my nipple, making it instantly hard.

I sucked in a sharp breath, breathing harshly. His grunt of approval was barely audible past the roar in my ears. Ripples of pleasure radiated from my nipple. He circled my distended flesh, suckling me until I knew he'd left his mark, sucking until he wrung a cry from my throat.

"God damn you," I said, my voice breaking as he thrust my legs apart with one rough hand and ground the hard ridge of his cock up against my slit.

He broke free, releasing my achy breast to torture the other with the scrape of his teeth.

"You're wet, Nari," he growled as he tugged my nipple between his lips, rocking his hips to glide against my clit. It seemed to blossom under that insistent pressure, grow swollen and achingly sensitive.

"Big fucking deal," I ground out, hissing as he rubbed against my folds as if to prove a point.

He laved the underside of my breast, nipping it, pleasure and pain mingling. "You want me to rape you, don't you?"

"No." I clenched my hands, feeling my fingers go tingly with the restricted flow of blood.

"It's not rape if you want it," he taunted, dragging himself lower, kissing the hollow of my stomach. I didn't even know how he could reach it and still hold my hands. "You want my tongue inside your tight little cunt." Something touched my slit … and it wasn't his hand or cock.

"No!" I screamed. I struggled then, fought until I was gasping for air.

He rose over me once more, his shaft riding back against my slit, slipping through my wetness to slide over my clit with unbearable roughness. My clit seemed to swell under the pressure, throb with an acute, piercing pleasure. He pressed his weight down, burying me in the mattress until my skin molded to his, my breasts bulged against his chest. My nipples felt like two rocks, so incredibly sensitive and hard the slightest touch made them burn. The pressure of his chest made me scream in unfulfilled agony. I tried to buck again, hands clenching, feet scrambling for purchase. My throat hurt from holding back a scream.

Each struggle only made him rougher. Made it hurt more as he rubbed against me like a beast that enjoyed toying with its prey. But, god help me, I was beginning to enjoy the pain. Crave it.

I needed to come so badly. Needed it with a desperation akin to madness.

A plea for surcease caught in my throat before I could utter it. I choked on it, gasping and coughing.

"Nothing you say will stop me," he said against my ear. "I'll just enjoy it more the more you resist me."

What woman in her right mind would want this? But the more he touched me, the more I wanted it. Oh god! Fuckin' help me! I screamed inside my mind, jerking to attention as the harsh slide of his cock became a prod against my vagina. My nether lips seemed to peel back for him, to stretch and grasp for the thickness of his cock.

He barely nudged me and already my belly ached, my pussy burned.

Teeth scraped my jaw line. "Join me, and I'll make it good for you. You haven't known ecstasy until my cum has been inside your womb."

"Never!"

He shifted his hips, pressing my thighs so wide apart my hip bones popped. His cockhead nudged my opening, but it would never fit without ripping me apart. My juices flowed at the threat of sensual pain, defying my mind, or perhaps because of some unconscious desire to be ridden like a whore.

"I could take this from you," he whispered.

"Fuck you!" I snarled, biting at the face I could feel but not see.

He growled furiously and shifted, pressing his dick against my anus, pushing, pushing until it hurt … so good.

I jerked against him, my inner muscles clenching. I almost came right then. I cursed at him again and again as he forced his way into me. The fight was leaving me, and I suddenly wanted him to take me. Fuck me all night long until I was broken and weak.

No. I couldn't give in. I tensed. "No!" I screamed, trying to resist the sensual lure of pain and pleasure.

* * * *

Nariko Suzaku jerked from sleep, bolting upright in bed. Tears burned at her eyes, a cry choked her throat. She could almost smell him on her skin, still feel the touch of him nudging her body's openings, his teeth on her throat and breasts. She collapsed back onto her pillows, trembling, fighting the arousal and fear that permeated her senses.

Oh, god. It was close that time. "Too close," she whispered to herself.

Nariko rolled onto her side, a hand pressed between her thighs as if it would assuage the ache there. She was wet with arousal. It disgusted her that she got so aroused about being taken by force, especially from a creature she'd never seen, who enjoyed tormenting her.

He was a monster. A demon from hell or wherever else monsters came from.

She'd run so far, so long. It had made no difference. He knew her. He'd caught her now, and his seduction tore at her control, frayed her nerves. Why did he want her submission? Why did she fight it so hard? It was just a dream.

But it wasn't. It had always been real to her. Real in a way that if she was conquered by him, she would never recover. She knew it.

Already the memory of the dream faded to hazy details, but the intensity remained. Fear. Lust. Crowding her body, seeping away willpower as effectively as a drug. Nariko knew she had something wrong with her mentally. And really, it was no wonder she was fucked up in the head.

She was a monster too.

It was why she'd been abandoned at birth, left to grow up at an orphanage. No one had wanted her, even as a baby, because they all knew there was something wrong with her. Physically, she was fine. But evil could be masked by even the most beautiful, and her face was far from that of an angel's.

Nariko climbed out of bed and walked into her bathroom, turning on the shower and slipping inside.

She still felt like she could smell him on her, and she wanted the reminder of the dream and her arousal out of her mind and off her body.

Today. Today she would see a doctor about these night terrors. If she didn't, she knew it was only a matter of time before she went completely insane. She just hoped it wasn't already too late.

Chapter Two

"The Doctor will see you now."

Nariko was nervous. She was always nervous in doctors' offices. Of course, Doctor Savage wasn't a "real" doctor. He was a sleep therapist. But she was still nervous and dreading the visit.

When she was shown into his office, he was bent over searching for something in the bottom drawer of his desk. "Just take a seat," he said without looking up.

Nariko looked around at the offerings and finally settled on the couch. The drawer slammed, drawing her attention back to Doctor Savage as he sat up in his chair and folded his hands on his desk, smiling at her and displaying a beautiful set of gleaming white teeth.

A shock of surprise ran through Nariko as she gaped at him. He didn't look like any doctor she'd ever seen. Not in real life, anyway. The actors on TV couldn't even hold a candle to this guy.

He was blond, his hair a dark gold but streaked with locks of platinum that created sun-induced highlights lovely enough to make her loathe her own drab, black hair. His bangs fell across his forehead in a way that inevitably made a person want to push them aside just for the chance to touch that silky hair, and she was not immune. He was sun bronzed, made more evident by the contrast of his white shirt, which covered a set of shoulders so broad, she knew they had to be all muscle. That he was all muscle.

His dark brows were heavy and straight over his eyes. Angry eyebrows, she'd always called them, but on him, they were just enough to offset the perfection of his face and make him truly arresting.

She couldn't figure out what it was about his face that made her want to stare at it. It seemed normal, almost average if she looked at each feature separately, but there was something there in the combination that seized her attention and made her heart gallop.

She didn't know if she could handle being around a doctor this damn sexy. She wondered if it was too late to get up and walk out the door.

"What can I help you with today Miss … Ms. …." he trailed off, searching around his desk and picked up a file his nurse had dropped there when she'd escorted her into the room. "Is it Miss or Mrs. Suzaku?"

Nariko recovered from her initial surprise. She eyed him speculatively, wondering what difference it made. "Miss. Why?"

He reddened slightly. "This is usually easier if we can form a bond of trust, and part of that is getting to know you."

She relaxed fractionally. "I'm really a lot more interested in getting something to help me sleep."

He lifted one dark, golden brow. "I don't work that way, Nariko."

Nariko didn't know what irritated her worse, his familiarity, or the fact that he just dismissed her request out of hand. She resisted frowning at him, keeping her face impassive. "How do you work then?"

He allowed his gaze to travel her length before meeting hers once more. "Drugs are for the incurable. I've found that most patients can be treated naturally, overcoming the problems that prevent them from sleeping."

Nariko studied him for several moments, lacing her fingers in her lap to keep from fidgeting. "So I'm just supposed to discuss it with you? Is that how I'm supposed to be cured from not sleeping every night?"

He lifted his hands outward and shrugged. "Why don't you explain exactly what your problem is."

Nariko couldn't help it. Blood flooded into her cheeks. "I have … dreams. They're very … real and very disturbing."

He frowned thoughtfully. "Why don't you tell me one of your dreams?"

Nariko hadn't thought it possible to blush any harder than she was already. She gaped at him, opened her mouth, and closed it several times. "I don't remember them, actually."

Something gleamed in his eyes. She was sure it was amusement. "Sexual?" he asked.

She felt really hot. All that blood pounding in her cheeks was starting to make her sweat. She cleared her throat. "Um. Sort of."

He was silent for several moments. "Ah … are you involved with someone at the moment?"

"No," she said stiffly.

"Is it possible that your dreams are related to problems you had in a previous relationship?"

"I don't think so."

"Why?"

She sighed, turning to stare out the window. "Because number 1, I've never been in a relationship at all. I'm a virgin. And number 2, the thing I always dream of is a demon."

She didn't want to look at him. She was sure he was trying hard not to laugh. Either that, or he was staring at her like she was some kind of freak because she was a grown woman and claiming to be a virgin. He was silent for so long, however, that she found she couldn't resist turning to look and see what his reaction was. To her surprise, there wasn't a trace of amusement in his expression.

"What makes you think he's a demon?"

Nariko frowned. "I'm not sure. I've never actually seen him. It's one of those things you just know."

"So you do remember the dreams?"

"I don't really want to talk about them."

"I understand that you're not comfortable when we've only just met, and believe me, I wouldn't pry if I didn't think it wasn't important, but I need to know the nature of the dreams before I can begin to understand what's causing them and help you work your way through them."

Nariko stared at him, feeling a mixture of hope and doubt, discomfort and embarrassment. It really was getting harder and harder to cope with these dreams. As uncomfortable as she felt even thinking about telling him, if there was any chance he could help her to get rid of them, she really wanted to have peaceful sleep again. She had permanent circles under her eyes. She could barely remember sleep without nightmares. "I'm just not really comfortable talking about them."

Smiling, he rose from his desk and moved to the light switch, dimming the lights. "Why don't you just relax there on the couch. Sit up if you want to, lay down if you want to. Just get comfortable. I'm going to move to the chair by the window so that you don't have to look at me. And when you feel relaxed enough, I want you to tell me about your last dream."

Nariko nodded. She thought about it a few minutes and finally decided to lay down on the couch. She heard his movements as he settled in the chair by the window.

"Before we get started, why don't you tell me how long you've been having these dreams and if you can remember anything out of the ordinary that happened in your life before the dreams started?"

Nariko frowned, thinking back. "They've only gotten really bad lately, but I've been having nightmares for about ten years I guess. Since I was fifteen."

"Did something happen when you were fifteen?"

Nariko shrugged. "Not that I can remember."

"Something between your parents?" he prompted.

"I grew up in an orphanage. I never knew my parents."

He was silent for several moments. "An accident? An injury? Did something happen to you in the orphanage?"

"No. Not really." She thought it over for several minutes. She really wasn't comfortable telling him, but he was a doctor. "I was fifteen when I got my period."

Again, there was a prolonged silence. "But you think that's along about the same time that you began to have the dreams? The nightmares?"

"Sometime along then."

"You say they're worse now? In what way?"

"Before, I used to dream that I was being chased. I never knew what it was that chased me, only that it was evil and that something terrible would happen to me if it caught me. But I always woke up before it did. Then, about a year ago, the dream seemed to change."

"How did it change?"

"He began to call my name. And somehow then, I knew that it was a demon that pursued me. And it's gotten even worse. Twice now, he's caught me."

"Why don't you tell me what you remember about your last dream?"

Nariko shivered. She felt more comfortable than she thought she would feel. His voice soothed her, and there was no judgment in it. Haltingly at first, and then with more surety, she began to describe the dream to him in detail. When she'd finished, she felt surprisingly better.

Doctor Savage had said nothing, however, and she began to have the uncomfortable feeling that he thought she was crazy.

"What do you think?" she asked, finally.

Doctor Savage said nothing. She heard him get up from the chair, however. He moved within her range of vision and reached for the light dimmer once more. She blinked and sat up as the lights in the room brightened. When she looked around, she saw that the doctor had seated himself behind his desk once more. He was studying the file, frowning.

As if sensing her nervous gaze, he finally looked up at her. A faint smile curled his lips. "I think what you need is someone to teach you how to cope with the demon."

* * * *

Stretching into the distance like a riotous sea lay a chasm of blackness, interrupted only by winks in the night like glowing eyes. It was with a sense of terror that I realized they were eyes, and they were coming closer. My stomach lurched at that unending blackness crawling toward me as if the very night lived and breathed evil.

The limits of the precipice crumbled, making me stagger backward, but a cushion of something unseen kept me from fleeing, kept me there at the edge of some unfathomable horror.

A chill wind shifted over me, tangling my hair over my face in loopy tendrils that caught at my eyes and mouth. I pushed it away, unable to look from the darkness.

"Nari," something whispered close by, raising chills on my arms and neck like an abrasion.

I wanted to close my eyes and cover my ears, to will it away. Will it all away. This was a dream. A nightmare. I knew it, and yet I was no more able to control it than I'd been able to any other time since the dreams had begun. I was paralyzed, both mentally and physically. Something held me here, wanted me to see this.

He locked one arm around my breasts, pulling me back against his chest. "They come for you, Nari. For the chance to fuck your sweet little pussy," he said, cupping my femininity for emphasis, curling his fingers into my fabric covered slit. I bit my lip, struggling not to moan. He loosed his hold and grabbed my arms, trapping me as effectively as manacles. "Do you want them fighting over you? I've held them back this long, but I can take my protection away if you crave a gang bang. Perhaps that is what's needed to break you."

I didn't struggle. The edge was too close for me to risk it, and I couldn't be sure he wouldn't throw me off if I fought him. But I would never let him break me. Never. "Why should I believe anything you say?" I said, fighting back the swarming urge to shudder at the implication of his words.

"Believe or not. You cannot change my will, wherever it may roam."

"Then why ask me at all?" I gritted out.

He laughed, tightening his hold. "Perhaps simply because I enjoy taunting you?"

He manifested. One moment, I could see nothing, and the next, I saw his hands. They locked around my biceps, black as ebony. His skin gleamed as if he'd oiled down, and each finger ended in a short claw that just cleared the end of each finger. They looked like glass. Black glass. Sharp enough to slice me open.

A strange calmness settled over me. I had to find out more about him if I was going to fight him. I knew he wasn't real, that he was some part of my subconscious fighting against me, but if I could now see just a small part of him, it told me that I was beginning to be able to face him. "Who are you? What do you want with me?"

He laughed, a deep, gravelly sound that grated on the nerves more for its cockiness than its sound, which would've been pleasant under other circumstances. "I enjoy your growing bravado, Nari," he said, stroking my skin with his thumbs. "Is my seduction so unexpected that you no longer know me?" He rubbed against my buttocks, his cock a hard insidiousness that nudged the cleft like a hot poker. His hands shifted to my breasts, squeezing them, pinching my nipples as he kept me trapped against him. He bit my neck, lips locking against my flesh, sucking at the crook of my shoulder until I cried out in pain.

He broke away, only to fierce my skin as he dragged the edges of his teeth up my neck to breathe hotly in my ear. "I am called Onyx," he whispered, grinding himself against me. "And you are mine."

"I don't belong to you or anyone else," I said, my voice monotonous. I felt drugged, even stiffer and unable to control myself than I had been before. Had he done something more than bite my neck?

I couldn't support my weight anymore. My knees gave out. He caught me as I crumpled, lowering me to the ground.

I looked at him between my lashes, but he was indistinct as a shadow, a dark outline marring the starry sky above us. I wanted to open my eyes more, but they wouldn't budge. My body wouldn't obey any of my commands. I lay, limp and malleable, for whatever pleasure or pain he intended.

Grasping my clothing, he pulled until it ripped open, exposing me until I was naked and at the mercy of his raking gaze.

He stopped a moment as if studying me. I could practically feel his eyes touching my every curve. A prolonged silence ensued, broken only by my own harsh breathing. "I far prefer your struggles, Nari, but your complacency makes our joining easier."

"Fuck … you," I managed to whisper, willing my body to move, to flee. Nothing.

My thighs parted beneath his hands. He settled between them, his skin oddly hairless and smooth, warmed within by an insatiable heat hot enough to sear me by touch alone. "In a moment, I will oblige you," he said on a husky growl, lowering himself over me.

I tensed infinitesimally, preparing for invasion. Where arousal had been before, now there was nothing but pervading fear. I was completely dry. He would hurt me.

This couldn't happen. It was a dream. A dream! I wouldn't allow myself to be taken in a dream. I couldn't.

The knowledge couldn't save me, however. Where was Doctor Savage when I needed him? How could my own subconscious deny me the hope to escape?

As if by only thinking about a savior had conjured it, a light pierced the darkness beyond my closed lids.

Onyx hissed and thrust himself away. I felt the loss of his heat replaced by the warmth of the sun. It invigorated me, broke the paralysis I'd been under. Opening my eyes, I blinked against the blinding light that surrounded me, wondering what the hell had happened.

Sitting up, covering my eyes with one hand, I reached out with the other, feeling around for the source of the brilliance. I connected with flesh and jerked back.

"Who's there?" I asked, tensing up again. Had I just gone from the pan into the fire? Those things were out there. Had they broken through whatever barrier kept them trapped in the deep?

"I am no foe for you to slay," a deep, amusement tinged voice spoke.

For some reason, it was soothing to me, eased my fear. The light dimmed enough I could uncover my eyes without going blind. Before me crouched a man--no, not a man. He was a monster, but he was more beautiful than any monster had the right to be. This was the kind of demon that could tempt saints to sin.

Hair trailed down his chest nearly to his belly, stirring in the wind created by the massive wings moving at his back. It was nearly a pure white, broken only by contrasting streaks of dark gold. His skin was gold too, almost a metallic shade and too surreal to ever be considered human. His body was all muscle, massive, hard and defined, sculpted by the hand of a master. The angles of his face were pure, beautiful symmetry, broken only by the arch of his brows as he stared at me. His eyes were gold too, a glowing gold that rippled with hints of red and orange, like metal heated to the melting point. Out of his forehead sprang two curled horns, spiraled and twisted like ram's horns but reaching toward the sky. And his wings ... they gleamed like polished ivory, marbled with golden threads as they stirred the air in a gentle current.

He reminded me forcefully of Doctor Savage. Not in form, which wasn't human, but in face. Enough so, that it startled me at first, and then I realized it had to be thoughts of him just moments before that must have put him into my mind.

There was something inherently carnal about him, aside from his near nakedness. He looked at me with a hunger so intense it radiated from his pores. I covered myself, bringing the edges of my clothes together, uncomfortably aware of how long his gaze had lingered at my breasts and between my legs. If it was possible, I'd swear my nipples and cleft blushed.

As it was, they tightened, coming to achy, needful awareness.

"Who are you? Why did you come?" I finally asked, my voice so husky it didn't sound like me.

He stood, looking around warily before turning his gaze back to me. "You need to protect yourself against him and the others. I cannot protect you."

I hadn't asked for his protection, but I wasn't about to argue with that logic. I did need to learn how to protect myself. Running had only prolonged the torment, and I couldn't escape him--Onyx--any longer. "I can't fight what I can't see."

"You cannot see him because you don't want to."

Tired of looking up at him, I stood. I still had to look up to meet his eyes. "I don't understand," I said, tightening my hold on the scraps of clothing covering me. This close, I could feel the heat of his body, breathe in his scent. There was no describing the intoxicating effect it had on me. He was more potent even than Onyx, and I wondered if it was a result of my attraction to Doctor Savage. Who knew? Not me, and I didn't really relish the idea of exploring my theory with the object of my attraction.

"This is your world. Your rules. We can but obey them." He turned to go.

"Wait!" I said, grabbing his arm, stopping him. He looked down at my hand and then back up to my face. "Could you teach me?" I asked, feeling almost breathless with the tension between us, and the strong muscles flexed beneath my hand.

Turning fully, his body rubbed against my chest. "There are many things I could teach you, Nari," he said, his voice soft, seductive. I felt the deep tone vibrate in my bones, warming my muscles, making my body heat to the point of combustion.

He inclined his head, bending even as I tilted my own to meet his lips. He stopped just shy of satisfying my sudden craving to kiss him. His breathing was harsh, warning me his control was on edge, that he felt as frantic for the connection of our mouths as I did.

"Now is not the time. Wake up, Nariko…."

Chapter Three

Nariko rolled over in bed, pounding the mattress with her fists. "Dammit!" she cursed, collapsing into stillness, squeezing her eyes shut and willing sleep to return. It wouldn't, of course, not now that she wanted it ... and wanted to begin that kiss.

She rubbed her thighs together, feeling the slippery arousal there. Who'd made her feel that way? Onyx, or the stranger?

"Damn."

Nariko rolled out of bed, wincing when her head and neck felt like they were going to seize in a charley horse. She brought her hand up to it, grimacing as she connected with tender flesh. Jeez, she felt like she'd been--Nariko stopped at that thought, jumping to her feet to rush into the bathroom.

She flipped on the lights, leaning over the sink to stare at herself in horror. At the crook of her shoulder and neck was a circular bruise. As she moved closer, she could see darker, smaller bruises within the edges of the circle. Like the marks of teeth....

The creature ... Onyx had bitten her. It'd hurt, hurt like something really happening.

She covered her face with her palms, as if it would make the bruising disappear, slowly dragging them down her face but coming up against the same sight.

"How is this possible?" she asked herself.

Dreams weren't real. How then had she been marked in her sleep?

Had her mind created the bruise? Could she die in real life if she died in her sleep? What else could happen to her?

No one knew the extent of the human mind, however. She'd heard stories of people healing themselves by the power of thought alone. If she'd been raised in the tradition of her ancestors, would she know more about this? Would she be able to protect herself?

To think that it was something else was nearly as unbearable as the thought of her own body at war with itself. It was enough to make her never want to crawl into bed again and never go outside.

* * * *

Nariko felt none of the nervousness she'd felt the first time she'd visited Doctor Savage. She was really scared now.

As soon as she took her seat on the couch, she began to fidget, waiting for him to finish glancing over the file and give her his attention.

After what seemed an interminable amount of time, he looked up. "You're still having the bad dreams?"

Nariko bobbed her head nervously. "It's worse than that, though. The dreams are worse, and this time when I woke up, I had a mark from the dream."

Doctor Savage frowned, clasping his hands together on atop his desk. "I don't understand."

Nariko dragged in a shaky breath. "In my dream, the demon bit me. When I woke up I found this mark on my neck. It looks like a bite."

Doctor Savage stood abruptly and moved toward her. Crouching in front of her, he met her gaze. "Show me."

Nariko pulled her shirt away from her neck and showed him the mark she'd found that morning in the mirror. He studied it in silence for some time. "You dreamed that you were bitten and then you found this?"

She nodded jerkily. "You can even see teeth marks."

Doctor Savage frowned. "You're certain that this didn't happen first and then you dreamed of it, and in your dream, it became the demon who had bitten you?"

She stared at him wide-eyed. "You think I'm crazy, don't you?"

"I didn't say that."

"You don't have to. You just said that you thought that I couldn't tell the difference between dreams and reality."

He shook his head. "Sometimes things happen to us and they disturb us in a way that they manifest themselves in our dreams."

She shook her head. "This did not happen to me. I know the difference. Don't you see how deep the bite is? How could I not remember that someone had bit me like this? And then think that I had dreamed it?"

He stared at her for several moments. "So maybe it's not a dream at all."

She frowned. "I don't think I understand what you're suggesting."

"I'm suggesting that maybe something is happening to you while you're asleep. Perhaps you're not fully conscious of it, but it enters your dream. It's like, sometimes the doorbell will ring when you're asleep, but you're dreaming, and in your dream you think that it's the phone ringing. It's something outside your dream, in the real world, that's intruding into your dreams. And while you're asleep, you are interpreting it as something else."

Nariko shivered. Just the implication of his words turned her stomach and sent cold chills down her arms and legs. "I live alone. I told you I wasn't seeing anyone. Are you suggesting someone is coming into my apartment? While I'm asleep?"

"I'm not suggesting that at all. I really find this disturbing, however, and I think what we should do, if you're agreeable to it, is that I should setup my equipment in your apartment and observe you while you're sleeping."

She frowned. "Don't they usually do that sort of thing in a controlled environment?"

He shrugged. "Usually, yes, but I don't think there's anything usual about your dreams. Would you like to do that?"

Nariko didn't think it over very long. She hardly knew Doctor Savage, but it made her feel tremendously better just thinking about him being there while she slept so that she wasn't alone. She nodded.

* * * *

"Do you really think you can stay up all night watching me?" Nariko asked, looking over the video cameras he'd set up around her bed. She wasn't sure how well she'd sleep under surveillance but probably better than her average night anyway. She had nothing to lose.

"I've gone without sleep before. I normally don't have to worry about it though, since I usually have technicians and nurses taking shifts as well," Doctor Savage said, adjusting one tripod.

She arched a brow. "But none this time. Should I be worried?"

His head snapped up from what he was doing, and he looked at her. "Of course not."

She couldn't help herself. She laughed. After a second, he let out an uneasy chuckle and smiled at her, making her heart skip. Damn, it was going to be hell trying to sleep tonight with him in the house. She hoped she wouldn't do anything embarrassing in her sleep.

* * * *

The bed shifted, dipping as someone climbed into it, sidling up behind me. The warmth of another person brushed against my air space--aura--heightening my awareness and bringing me from the deep blackness of dreamless sleep.

I turned my head slightly toward the movement behind me. "Doctor Savage?" I asked groggily, my voice husky with disuse.. The room wasn't completely dark. Muted light filtered through the blinds covering my bedroom window.

"No," he said softly, soothingly.

When he touched my hip, I stiffened, watching as his hand traveled down in a leisurely caress around the curve of my buttocks. He caught the sheet covering me and pulled until the edge slid over my hip and pooled on the bed, leaving me bare save for the silk panties I wore. I could've sworn I'd gone to bed in pajama pants, since I'd never gone to sleep with a man in my immediate vicinity, and I darn sure didn't want the doctor seeing me unclothed without a good reason. But having a man see me now didn't bother me as much as I thought it would.

He leaned forward, catching the fabric of my panties with his teeth. That's when I saw his horns.

I startled, tried to jerk away, but his hands were on me, trapping me, flipping me onto my stomach until I was pinned to the bed beneath him. The hot, hard flesh of his thighs closed around my legs, keeping them still while he cupped my buttocks and roamed over them up my spine. "Let me go!" I said, gasping, shaking my head until my face was clear of the pillow. I didn't know his name, but I knew who it was. I should've been fighting, and my body was in turmoil … but for a different reason altogether.

"Is this not what you crave?" he asked, leaning over me until his warm breath brushed the back of my neck. His fingers slipped under my panties, teasing the under curve of my ass cheeks, lingering near my cleft.

I sucked in a sharp breath, unable to speak for the anticipation choking me, making my heart pound in a raging gallop.

He rubbed a sensuous circle, his touch feather light, never quite roaming the direction I wanted him to go to so badly.

"Stop torturing me," I said, squirming beneath him, digging my hands into the mattress like claws.

He chuckled, adjusting himself until he'd freed my legs to sit between them. It should've been an embarrassing position, having him looking at me this way, but all thought of shame disappeared when he snapped the sides of my panties and tore them away. I jumped, shocked when he ran a finger up my slit.

"I am no more good or evil than any of my kind. We each serve our own purpose. You should not relent so easily, Nariko. You're stronger than this." He stopped at my core, fingering the edges of my tight hole.

I didn't feel strong. I felt weak and needy, and I damn sure didn't want a lecture. I was having trouble concentrating on his words. All I could think about was having him ram that finger inside me and assuage this ache I'd been feeling for what seemed like forever.

Biting my lip, I pushed back, trying to urge him to do more.

"Onyx seeks to gain power from you," he said, tormenting me with his nearness.

I growled against the mattress. "And what about you? What do you want?"

"You, Nariko," he said, and I felt his breath brush over my bare cheeks.

I froze, holding my breath, waiting for him to say or do something. Even my heart seemed to have locked into place. Anticipating. Begging. Emptiness gnawed.

Something hot and wet swiped one cheek. I jerked, trying to see what he was doing, but I could twist around that far. I didn't need to see anyway. I knew what he was up to. My body felt singed, my nerves so high strung the stroke of air could set them off.

He pried my lips apart. Cool air grazed the moistness, sending chills up my spine, and then the probe of something hot and wet slipped down the slick path, jarring me, sending me whirling into a frenzy of heat and need.

He found the entrance to my vagina, edged it, teasing, provoking me to curse him and groan, struggling to do something--anything.

He seemed to enjoy torturing me as much as Onyx. I was going to go crazy from all this want, this unappeased, unending arousal.

"Do you want my tongue inside your pussy?" he asked, muffled, his breath striking my slit.

His words were eerily similar to the other demons, but I was too far gone to care. I just wanted to come. I didn't care anymore who made me do it. "Yes. Please!"

He grinned against me, his lips a soft stretch against sensitive parts, then swiped a swath up and down my slit like he had to devour me before I melted. My muscled jumped and quivered.

He drew back a moment, holding my labia apart as his mouth hovered near. "Mmmm. Very good," he murmured, and then his tongue slipped through my creamy seam to my core, thrusting inside. It was long, longer than I had anticipated. It seemed to unfurl inside me, move like it had a mind of its own, like it could see exactly where I needed it to touch.

Almost immediately, he found my g-spot. I nearly screamed at the sharp pleasure that stabbed my inner muscles, making me push back against his face until I was sure I'd smother him.

He gripped my hips, digging his face into my slit, stroking deep inside me as he rubbed his chin against my clit.

I gasped, arching my back, the sheer uncomfortable-ness of the position did nothing to assuage my fervor.

Swells of ecstasy rippled through my muscles, churning around my clit. His tongue withdrew with a smack, and he angled his head until he could reach my clit. He nibbled the base and parted lips, not quite doing as I needed and wanted, barely touching me.

"You're killing me!" I wailed, squeezing my eyes tightly shut, frustrated beyond measure.

He smiled again, and then plucked at the bud, sucking it into his mouth as he thrust his fingers inside my vagina. I jerked against him at the sudden, intense pleasure that spiked through my body, whimpering, begging for more. I couldn't ever remember being so aroused.

I was panting for breath now. Desperate for the culmination of pleasure hovering just beyond my reach. The small, wet noises he made only increased my arousal.

He suckled my clit, moving his fingers in and out of me in a mock fucking, stroking the tender patch of my g-spot.

I shuddered violently. Overcome by the torturous pleasure rasping from his mouth, radiating from his fingers. Tingling, knee-weakening, heart stopping ecstasy vibrated through my body.

I cried out, my muscles gone limp as I jerked with each debilitating wave. I couldn't feel anything anymore, only a vague sort of numbness that left me incredibly sleepy and fulfilled.

He moved off of me, but I was so worn out, I didn't stir. I couldn't seem to even open my eyes.

He stroked the back of my neck, kissing my temple. Strangely enough, I couldn't smell myself on him. "If ever you need me, Nariko," he whispered, "Call my name, Xalen. Call and I will come."

* * * *

Nariko came awake slowly, with such a sense of well being that she was reluctant to give up the drowsy comfort. The threads of sleep refused to remain within her grasp, though. As she came at last to full awareness, she realized she still felt absolutely wonderful--rested, without any sense of sluggishness, no tension, no lingering anxiety.

It was almost like suddenly realizing a complete absence of pain when one had been suffering a toothache for days and days. Rolling from her bed, she glanced self-consciously a the cameras and scurried into the bathroom to perform her morning grooming ritual.

She found, as she showered, that she was actually humming. She didn't even recognize the tune, but it didn't matter. She felt better than she could remember ever feeling in the morning.

She glanced shyly at Doctor Savage when she reached the living room, where he'd set up the monitor station for his equipment. Her heart stammered uncomfortably in her chest, the breath rushing from her lungs as she took in his tousled look from the all nighter he'd just pulled.

He was a total hunk when he was immaculate, as she usually saw him in his office. He looked succulent now, with his heavy lidded eyes, the day old stubble of beard, his tousled hair. He'd unfastened his shirt and pulled it from his jeans. The top button of his jeans were undone, as well.

He looked like a man that had spent a night satisfying a woman, and she felt her nerves sizzle with an unaccustomed tension that had everything to do with being around an extremely attractive male.

She smiled at him tentatively when she saw that he was studying her.

"Did the demon disturb your dreams?"

His voice was husky. It sent a shiver of sensation along her nerve endings that made her heart trip over itself. Warmth gathered in her sex.

She ignored it with an effort, focusing on the real reason he'd spent the night in her apartment. "I didn't," she said with a touch of surprise. "It's the first time I haven't in--I can't even remember when I didn't." She frowned, feeling a faint blush rise in her cheeks. "Actually, I dreamed about you."

He arched one eyebrow. Something gleamed in his eyes and she was torn between a warm response to the look and a touch of irritation. It seemed to her that he was assuming the dream had been sexual in nature--which it had been-- when he had no reason to think she would be dreaming of him like that.

She moved into the kitchen. "I don't really remember what it was about," she lied, "except that it was just one of those tame sort of dreams you have sometimes. Like you're going somewhere--something like that."

When she glanced at him over the counter that separated the kitchen from the living room, she saw that he was looking amused. "Would you like some juice?" she asked with determined cheerfulness, although she felt like slapping the smug look off his face.

"Yes, thanks," he said, rising from the chair and adjusting his jeans and fastening them.

Nariko glanced away quickly as he adjusted his "package" in the snug jeans.

She dropped the first glass she dragged from the cabinet. The noise of the glass slamming into the counter set her nerves on edge. Thankfully, it was made of thick glass and didn't break. She righted it and dragged another glass out, then tossed some bagels into the toaster over before she went to the refrigerator to get the juice.

Dr. Savage was sitting at the counter when she turned around and she nearly dropped the carton. "So … you don't remember what you dreamed?" he asked conversationally.

"Bits and pieces, I suppose," Nariko muttered, recovering and heading for the counter to fill the juice glasses. "Nothing that really makes sense."

"Why don't you tell me what you do remember?"

Try though she might not to think about what she'd dreamed, she blushed again, overfilled one of the glasses and spilt juice on the counter top. She felt like kicking herself when she glanced at Dr. Savage as she handed him his glass of juice and saw the knowing look on his face.

Or was she only imagining he knew what she'd been dreaming because she felt so uncomfortable about it? And her attraction to him, for that matter.

She frowned, turning her attention to the bagels. "Just something about calling you when the demon came."

He sipped his juice thoughtfully while she put the bagels on saucers and got the cream cheese from the refrigerator.

"I told you to call me?" he prompted when she settled on a counter stool at the other end of the short bar.

That part wasn't exactly crystal clear in her mind--not nearly as clear as the things he'd done and the heat that had curled inside of her--and rose inside of her now, when she thought about it again. She thought about it for several moments. "That was one of the things that made the dream seem really weird. You told me I had powers of my own, and that if I needed you I could--summon you to me. All I had to do was call your name. The strangest thing, though, was that you didn't say 'Doctor Savage' or 'Shayne Savage'. You said your name was Xalen.

"You said that if the dark demon came after me again, I was to say 'Xalen! Come to me!' and you would come."

His brows rose, but he didn't comment. Instead, he concentrated on his juice and bagels. When he'd finished, he climbed off the stool and did an all over stretch that exposed every lovely muscle in his chest and belly. His jeans, as he pulled in his stomach in the stretch, rode low, and Nariko's eyes were drawn to the light, narrow trail of dark hair that arrowed down from his belly button.

"Do you mind if I use your shower?"

Nariko blinked, snapped from her zen meditation of his lower belly when he straightened. "Huh? Oh! Sure! Towels and washcloths in the bathroom cabinet."

When he'd left, she dropped her face into her hands, mortified. She was behaving as if she'd never seen a man before. He was going to think she'd enticed him to her apartment to try to seduce him!

It was that damn dream demon! She wasn't in the habit of looking at men and thinking sex. She had never even had sex! Up until she'd started dreaming about the demon that was chasing her, she'd never looked at a man, even an attractive one, and thought about sex. She'd been plenty attracted. She'd thought about kissing--maybe a little heavy petting.

Ok, so maybe she'd had a few very tame fantasies about . sex, but they were pretty much PG-13. She completely understood the mechanics of it. She'd read plenty of books. She'd seen a lot of sexy movies, but she'd never really associated such things with herself, and she certainly hadn't fantasized about the sort of things she did now.

And now she'd started thinking about doing those things with her sleep therapist of all things.

She shook it off after a while, deciding that she must have dreamed that because she thought Doctor Savage was attractive and knew he was in her apartment. Most likely, it would never happen again.

When Dr. Savage came out of her bathroom carrying the overnight bag he'd brought with him, it was a knee weakening jolt. Freshly scrubbed now, clean shaven, she didn't know if it was the way he looked or the cologne that nearly knocked her socks off, but she wished she had something to do besides gape at him like a love sick calf.

He didn't seem to notice, thankfully. He was all business now.

Dropping his bag beside the chair he'd spent the night in, he settled on the edge and faced her where she sat on the couch, her arms wrapped around her knees.

"I need to have a look at your records from the orphanage," he said without preamble.

Nariko blinked. "I don't understand. I know you said you thought something might have happened to me, but nothing did. I'd remember."

"Not necessarily," he said grimly. "It's possible something did, and you've managed to block it from your conscious mind but not your sub-conscious. I need to at least rule that possibility out, if nothing else."

Nariko thought about the implications, feeling her stomach tighten. "You think I'm just going to keep having these dreams?" she said uneasily. It was odd that she'd woken feeling as if the whole problem had been solved, crazy really. She'd dreamed the whole thing! How could she have allowed herself to believe her problem had been solved?

She had, though. She'd been behaving, and thinking, like all she had to do any time that thing got after her was summon Xalen and she'd be all right.

How crazy was that?

"So … you're going to the orphanage?"

"We are going to the orphanage."

Chapter Four

"May I help you?"

Nariko glanced at Dr. Savage. It was odd the way people could use words that sounded perfectly polite and still make it come out as more of a challenge. If the receptionist had only looked bored, she wouldn't seemed nearly as rude. Her entire attitude, however, was that they'd interrupted her.

"I'm Dr. Shayne Savage. I'd like to speak with the director, if I could."

"Do you have an appointment?"

His eyes narrowed momentarily at her abrupt tone. Finally, he smiled faintly. "If I did, I wouldn't have asked."

The woman seemed to lighten up a bit at that smile, but his comment made her stiffen once more. Without a word, she flipped through the appointment book. Nariko couldn't read what was written there, but she could see there was very little.

The receptionist slammed the book shut and looked up at them again. "If you'll have a seat, I'll see if Ms. Townsend can see you today."

Nariko felt an unpleasant jolt go through her at the name. She supposed it had been too much to hope the old bat had died since she'd left the orphanage. Or retired. She must be a hundred, and still she clung to her position with the tenacity of a pit bull. Without a word, she turned away from the desk, glanced around at the handful of chairs in the tiny waiting room and finally picked one and sat. Dr. Savage stood, although he moved across the room to stare out of the window.

Nariko kept glancing at the ugly round clock on the wall. Five minutes passed, then ten. They were rapidly approaching the twenty minute mark and Dr. Savage had begun to pace when the receptionist finally returned. Without a word, she sat down and began to peck at her keyboard.

Nariko glanced at Dr. Savage and saw that he was giving the woman a narrow eyed look.

She supposed he wasn't accustomed to people treating him as if he was a non-entity.

She supposed she should have warned him that that was the way everyone was treated at the orphanage, but then she hadn't expected them to be as rude to him. He was a doctor, after all. They generally commanded respect.

It wasn't as if the old bat knew he was a sleep therapist, but then Nariko could well imagine how much old dragon lady Townsend was enjoying the idea of keeping a doctor pacing about her waiting room.

Dr. Savage strode to the desk. "Well?"

"She can't see you today."

Nariko could see he was fighting a round with his temper. After a moment, he stopped grinding his teeth and forced a grim smile. "Perhaps you can help me then?"

The woman looked up at him, her expression surprised-- as if she couldn't believe he had the gall to ask her to help him.

"I need the records of one of the patients I'm treating."

"Name?"

"Nariko Suzaku."

The receptionist's gaze flickered toward Nariko. "I'm not sure we still have medical records on her. She was released almost seven years ago."

Dr. Savage gave her a look. "I need to see all of her records--from the time she was brought to the orphanage."

The woman studied him in tightlipped silence for several moments and finally got up and left the office once more, muttering, as she left, "You might have asked that while I was up before."

Dr. Savage turned and exchanged a look with Nariko, and she bit back a smile. "You didn't mention that this was such a warm place."

Nariko chuckled but shrugged. "It's the only one I was ever in. I thought they were all like this."

Dr. Savage frowned, but he didn't comment.

He got tired of leaning over the counter that separated the receptionist's desk from the waiting area and began to pace again. This time only fifteen minutes passed before the woman returned--empty handed. She sat down at her desk once more and resumed pecking at her keyboard. When Dr. Savage leaned over the counter again, she threw him a smug smile. "Ms. Townsend says they can't be released without a court order."

Dr. Savage fought another round with his temper. "Why?"

The woman shrugged. "They're sealed."

"Why?"

She gave him a withering look. "I don't know. That's what I was told."

"Did you tell Ms. Townsend that I was Nariko's physician?"

"You didn't tell me you were," the receptionist said coldly.

Dr. Savage lost his temper. "I hate like hell to drag you away from whatever you're doing to do your job, but do you think you could ask again?"

The receptionist glared at him. "I'll have to have some identification."

Dr. Savage dragged his wallet out and tossed his ID on the woman's desk.

She studied it skeptically. "This says you're a sleep therapist."

He ground his teeth. "Exactly. Doctor Shayne Savage, specialty, sleep therapy."

The receptionist stalked from the room, slamming the door behind her that time. She was back within ten minutes, tossing Dr. Shayne's ID on the counter. "Ms. Townsend says you'll need a court order."

Dr. Savage palmed his ID and stood away from the counter. After a moment, he turned and motioned to Nariko. When they'd left the building, she glanced at him. "What now?"

He didn't answer at once. Instead, he escorted her to his car and held the door until she got in. When he'd climbed behind the steering wheel, he sat staring out the windshield for several minutes, as if he was studying the building.

"Do you think it would be worth it to get a court order?" she finally asked.

"I think there's something damned strange going on here," he responded tightly.

Nariko waited a few moments, but when he said no more, she prodded him again. "What are we going to do now?"

"Break in."

* * * *

"Excuse me?" Nariko asked.

Dr. Savage's face was grim when he glanced at her. "I need the information in those files if I'm going to help you. And I have no intention of allowing anyone to stop me."

Nariko blinked at him several times, deciding she must have heard him wrong. "But--so you're going to try to get a court order?"

He studied her thoughtfully for several moments. "That could take a year or more. I don't think you can wait that long. Do you?"

A year. Nariko didn't think she could stand what she'd been going through another week. What would happen if that evil thing caught her and finally managed to do whatever he'd been trying to do? That was what she feared--especially after she'd woken with the bite mark. "But--breaking in? What if you were caught? You'd be in all sorts of trouble. I can't let you do it. I appreciate it more than I can say, but I'd be responsible if it went badly and you were arrested … or anything."

He looked amused. "I wasn't asking your permission. You asked me what I was going to do ... but you don't have to take the risk. I can handle it. In fact, it'll be better if I go in alone."

She stared at him for several moments while her shock and surprise turned to irritation. "So--what you're saying is that I would get us caught? If you're going to do it, you need me. I lived here practically my whole life. I know it like the back of my hand. It would be better if you just let me do it. That way, if I get caught, you won't be in any trouble and I won't have anything to feel guilty about."

"Do you know anything about breaking and entering?"

She gave him a look. "Probably as much as you do."

"We'll do it together," he said firmly.

* * * *

Nariko gave Dr. Savage an "I told you so" look when the light finally went out in Ms. Townsend's office. Unfortunately, it was dark and he missed it.

She'd told him the old bat always went back after dinner to do her paperwork and never left her office--which adjoined her apartment--before ten in the evenings. They'd been waiting for a good hour and now they would have to wait longer still.

Hopefully, the old battle ax was deaf, because she'd always slept like a watch dog and Nariko doubted if that had changed any. One sound and she'd come boiling out of her apartment snarling and slavering at the mouth.

It had only taken Nariko one such nasty encounter to decide that she wasn't doing anything else that might get her into trouble.

When another hour had passed and virtually every light in the orphanage had been switched off or dimmed, they finally left the shrubs and moved stealthily toward the building.

They'd fed the watch dogs meat laden with something to make them sleep. She sincerely hoped they could get in and out before the damned dogs woke up. One thing she didn't need to top her evening was a Rottweiler chewing up her ass.

When they'd reached the kitchen door, which, in Nariko's time was often left unlocked because the mechanism was so old it was hard to turn, they discovered a bright, shiny new one had been installed.

Nariko stared at it in dismay, but Dr. Savage merely pulled something from his pants pocket and began working on it. In a few minutes, he had the door open. She looked at him with a mixture of surprise, doubt, and … respect. "How did you do that?" she whispered.

"An old trick I learned in my misspent youth."

When they were inside, they closed the door quietly and locked it behind them. The orphanage only had a couple of security guards that patrolled the interior of the building, but they didn't want to take the chance that the unlocked door would be discovered and alert them to an intruder.

Waiting until their eyes adjusted, they set off through the kitchen to the corridor. After peering both ways, they left the kitchen and moved quickly down to the stairs at the end, staying close to the wall as they ascended. The stairs creaked anyway. Every time one let out a noise, both of them paused, holding their breath.

One of the security guards passed the stairwell as they reached the second floor. They waited, listening as his steps came closer and closer and then began to diminish once more as he passed the stairwell and disappeared down the hallway. "Midnight rounds," Nariko whispered when he'd passed beyond hearing. "He's supposed to come every half hour, but he probably won't be back before one."

Savage glanced at her. "Probably?"

"When I was here, their rounds took forty-five minutes … because he'd usually stop for a smoke or a cup of coffee. I don't know if it's the same guys … or even the same schedule … but it is midnight and he just passed."

Savage studied her a moment. "If we should happen to run up on the guards, just do as I say."

Nariko stared at him wide-eyed a moment, wondering what she'd gotten herself in to, but finally nodded.

Opening the stairwell, he glanced in both directions. When he saw it was clear, he motioned for Nariko to show him the way and they moved quickly but quietly to the door to the main office. Again, Savage picked the lock. Moving across the office, Nariko headed toward the records room and went in. Savage pulled a small flashlight from his pocket and flicked the light over the filing cabinets.

Ten minutes later, they'd located Nariko's file. To Nariko's horror, Savage pulled the contents out, replaced the papers with part of several other files and stuffed the contents of her file into his shirt.

"You're taking it?" she said on a breath of sound.

He put his fingers to his lips, shut the drawer and turned off the flashlight.

Nariko had already grabbed the doorknob when they heard the office door slam open and heels clicking briskly across the floor. She turned to Savage wide-eyed with horror. Grabbing her arm, he hauled her to the back of the tiny room, pushed her up against the wall and pressed up against her. "Not a sound," he whispered, his lips against her ear.

A shiver skated through her as the heat of his breath touched her ear.

Nariko heard the doorknob creak as it was turned. "Sh--"

Savage grabbed her upper arms, pressing her tightly against the wall with his body, covered her lips with his and thrust his tongue into her mouth. The jolt that went through her was fifty percent pure physical reaction to Savage's rough caress and fifty percent sheer terror when the light abruptly came on.

He was totally mad! She should have known he was crazy when he suggested they break into a state run facility to steal her records.

Why had she allowed him to talk her in to this?

She stiffened when the light came on, expecting any moment to hear Mrs. Townsend's screech. Instead, after a few moments, the light was turned off again and she heard the retreat of the heels across the office floor.

It wasn't until total silence reigned once more that Nariko realized Savage was in no great hurry to pull away from her and break the kiss. Her lips throbbed from the pressure of his mouth, sending inappropriate signals to places that had no business getting calls in this sort of situation. Finally, however, he lifted his lips from hers and stepped back.

Nariko was too stunned to fully appreciate the kiss they'd just shared. In fact, she couldn't remember doing anything but standing there with her mouth hanging open as he plundered it. Vaguely, she could taste him on her tongue--sweet with a bite, like sugared mint. She looked up at him in the dimness, gasping for air, not quite believing what just happened. "She didn't see us. How could she not have seen us?"

A faint smile curled his lips. "They'll hear us if you aren't quiet."

Nariko's jaw dropped when she realized what he was suggesting--thought he was suggesting, that she wanted to him to use his 'trick' again. Glaring at him, she led the way from the office and down the stairs. She didn't know whether she was more relieved or disappointed when they emerged from the building without further incident.

"All right," she demanded as soon as they'd gotten in the car and Savage laid the papers from her file on the seat between them, "how did you do that?"

Savage started the car. "I opened my mouth and stuck my tongue in yours," he said coolly.

She blushed furiously. "That's not what I meant!"

"She didn't see us. That's all that really matters, isn't it?"

"I just don't understand how she could've failed to see us, that's all! We were in plain sight."

"You weren't. I was between you and her. I was very still. I blended with the background."

Nariko gave him a look. It was true that he was wearing dark clothing, but she wasn't buying it. On the other hand, she couldn't think of an explanation that actually made any sense and puzzled over it most of the way back to her place until her focus shifted to the file.

When they'd parked in front of her apartment, they both got out and headed for the door without a word, but Nariko, at least, felt a strange sense of unreality settle over her.

In one sense, she felt surprisingly comfortable around Dr. Savage, considering the fact that she hardly knew him. She did hardly know him, however, which was why it made reality seem just a little skewed that Dr. Savage presumed his welcome in her home like a long time acquaintance.

And then there was that kiss and grope thing. She didn't know how he'd felt about it, but her knees still felt like they were filled with jelly instead of bone and cartilage. She supposed he thought that had been a good way to get her quiet fast and keep her that way until the threat had passed, but had he done it purely out of necessity? Or had it made him feel all hot and bothered like it had her?

If it had, she had to admit he hid it very well.

Once she'd unlocked the door to the apartment, he headed for her couch, dropped the file on the coffee table, opened it and began studying the pages inside. More than a little disconcerted, Nariko watched him for a few moments and finally followed him, settling next to him on the couch and picking up each page and studying it as he discarded it.

Most of it was pretty boring, even to her. There were notes, however, about behavioral problems beginning around puberty. Mentally, Nariko shrugged. She supposed the problems outlined did correspond to the beginning of her nightmares. On the other hand, it seemed to her that pretty much everyone went through a change in behavior when they hit that period of raging hormonal unbalance that corresponded to the transition from child to adult.

Savage cursed under his breath, drawing Nariko's attention. She leaned closer, reading over his shoulder. Her heart seemed to jolt to a halt in her chest when she saw it mentioned her mother. Grabbing the edge of the paper, she gave it a tug. After a moment, Savage released it.

Her mother had been sent to an asylum for the insane!

Nariko read it through twice and looked up at Dr. Savage with a mixture of chaotic emotions. "She thought ... she believed she'd been impregnated by a demon?"

Chapter Five

There was something about the look on Dr. Savage's face that penetrated Nariko's turmoil, although she couldn't quite pin it down. He didn't look particularly surprised. It was almost as if he'd been expecting the information he'd found. In fact, there seemed almost an underlying sense of purposefulness or maybe even excitement about him.

"She named him."

Nariko blinked. He'd said it as if her mother had identified an assailant by name, someone real--someone he'd heard of.

"You know that name."

He shrugged, looking away from her as he got up and began to pace the floor. Nariko watched him, trying to figure out what might be going through his mind, but she couldn't seem to get her own mind around the fact that her mother had been insane enough they'd locked her away.

Some forms of insanity were hereditary.

Was that it? Was she crazy like her mother had been? How bizarre was it that her mother thought she'd gotten knocked up by a demon and now she was having dreams about a demon that seemed pretty damned determined to fuck her stupid if he got his hands on her?

She could've almost felt better about being abandoned-- knowing she actually hadn't been thrown away--except that her mother had been a nut case and now she had to worry that she might have inherited something awful.

"You think I'm crazy?"

Dr. Savage stopped pacing and glanced at her absently. "What?"

Nariko licked her lips. "My mother obviously was, and now I'm having dreams about demons, too. But how could something like that be inherited? I didn't know her. I've never seen the records. How could I have dreams about being chased by a demon when I didn't know anything about my mother's psychosis?"

He shook his head. "I don't think you're crazy. I'm not convinced she was either--at least not at first, anyway. Being locked away with the insane is enough to drive a sane person over the edge."

Nariko felt her jaw go slack. Was he saying he believed her mother actually had been impregnated by a demon?

This was worse than the blind leading the blind! The insane leading the nut case!

"We need to try to talk to your mother," he said suddenly.

A mixture of excitement and revulsion filled Nariko instantly. It had never occurred to her that she might even get the chance to meet her mother--but in a mental institute? Visions of a drooling, wild haired woman in a straight jacket filled her mind. She felt sick.

"I … uh … I'm not sure I'm up to this one."

He studied her a long moment. "You don't have to go."

The only thing she could think of that would be worse than seeing the vision she'd pictured, was Dr. Savage seeing the vision she'd pictured in her mind. "I don't see what good you think it would do to talk to her," Nariko snapped angrily. "If she's still there after all this time, what mind could she possibly have? I mean, they medicate them, right? Between her insanity and the drugs, she wouldn't be able to answer questions even if they let you in to see her."

His lips thinned. "I have to try. She might be the only one with the answers we need."

* * * *

Depression settled over Nariko like a thick black cloud as they left the sanitarium where her mother had spent the last years of her life.

Her mother was dead! As vacillating as her feelings were about seeing her mother, and in such a state, she had felt a terrible sense of loss the moment she was told that her mother had died, that she'd lost the chance to get to know her even a little.

Despite everything, she'd been hopeful when they'd left her apartment to drive to the asylum. She'd allowed herself to believe that Savage was right. Her mother wasn't really and truly insane … certainly not to the extent that she'd envisioned.

After a few moments, she shook her dark thoughts off. It was absurd, really, to grieve over a woman she'd never even known.

She glanced at Dr. Savage as they reached the car. "Was that weird, or what?"

He stopped, turning to look at the building they'd just left speculatively.

Nariko didn't particularly like the look in his eyes.

"If I didn't know better, I'd think someone had gone to a lot of trouble to make sure you, nor anyone else, ever found out anything about yourself."

"I thought I was just being paranoid … I mean, I can't actually prove that I'm her next of kin."

Shrugging slightly, he got into the car. "Maybe," he said when Nariko had settled beside him. "And maybe not."

Nariko frowned. "You think all of my problems are somehow connected to my father?"

Savage glanced at her sharply. "It would explain a lot of things," he said after a moment.

Nariko waited for him to continue. He didn't. "What things?"

"The possibilities are too endless to speculate on without more information."

Nariko fell silent as he started the car and negotiated his way off the grounds of the sanitarium. Instead of asking him to elaborate, since she knew he wouldn't, she considered what he'd said, speculating on what he'd left unsaid.

She supposed it was possible that things had happened to her that she just didn't remember and that that might be the underlying problem that was causing the dreams. The 'demon' thing was just absurd, but maybe her mother had only meant he'd seemed demonic? Or maybe he had been crazy and thought he was one?

But she hadn't even been a year old when they'd put her mother away and put her in the orphanage. Even supposing there was something to the 'father was nuts' theory, how could he have made any sort of impression on her while she was so young? And why would it come back to haunt her now?

And, more importantly, how could the dreams be so vivid that they affected her physically?

She discovered when she emerged from her abstraction that they'd arrived at her apartment once more. This time Savage made no attempt to get out of the car, however.

"You're going in after the records, aren't you?"

"Yes."

"I'm really starting to get uneasy about all this."

"All what?"

She turned to study his profile. "I just didn't expect you to get so deeply involved in my situation as to risk … the things you're risking."

To her surprise, he smiled, albeit somewhat grimly. "As much as I'd like you to think I'm going way beyond the call, the truth is the risks are minimal … and, in your case, even if they weren't, I'd still consider it worth doing."

Nariko frowned, trying to decide if there was an underlying meaning in what he'd said. "I think I could understand it a little better if I'd been your patient for years

... or if there was something ... uh ... personal between us, but I'm practically a stranger."

He slid a glance her way. He was frowning faintly. "I seem like a stranger to you?"

It was Nariko's turn to frown. "Actually, it's really odd--because you should--but you don't."

To her surprise, he chuckled. "Good. It would have been a real blow to my ego if you'd said yes. Mostly, I figure once I've had my tongue in a woman's mouth, we've moved beyond considering ourselves strangers."

Nariko blushed to the roots of her hair. "But that was a ... distraction, wasn't it?"

"It sure as hell distracted me."

She hadn't thought it was possible to blush any harder but she managed it. "That's not what I meant."

To her surprise, he reached across the seat, grasped her hand and dragged her toward him. She fell against his chest, looking up at him with a mixture of surprise and burgeoning anticipation. He was aroused. She could feel it beneath her bottom. The knowledge made a peculiar warmth spread through her limbs.

"What did you mean?" he asked, a faint smile playing about his lips. There was an intensity in his gaze that Nari found both unnerving and electrifying.

"Uh ... I thought you were trying to keep me quiet because you thought I'd give us away."

"Hmmm," he murmured, his eyes dropping to her lips.

"Was I wrong?" It was a mere breath.

"Completely." His head dipped toward her. Nari felt her own head start to whirl. She parted her lips on a harsh breath that stopped completely when his lips finally touched hers. Every nerve ending in her body focused on him, on the softness of his lips, the pounding of his heart against her chest and her own echoing heartbeat.

The kiss they'd shared before was nothing like this, merely an appetizer that hadn't done nearly enough to satisfy her appetite.

Heat shot through her body, so intense she seemed to liquefy. Her bones turned to jelly. His tongue probed the seam of her lips, his hand tightened at the back of her neck, holding her steady, allowing her no retreat. Even had she been able, she couldn't stop this. She craved it ... had been craving a connection to him since she'd first set eyes on him.

Her lips parted on a ragged breath. His tongue thrust its way inside, staking bold possession, stroking the roof of her mouth, her teeth, her tongue.

She whimpered, unable to control the mewling sounds she made as he invaded her mouth.

He moved an arm around her back to support her, freeing his right hand to rest at her waist, fingering the hem of her shirt a brief moment before he was pushing beneath and upward, striving for her breasts. The skate of his fingers over her never-before-touched skin cause shivers to course over her.

Just looking at him made her pulse quicken. To have him touch her was nearly more than she could bear. And when his hand closed around her breasts, pinching her nipple between his fingers, she cried out in his mouth, clutching at his arm, afraid he'd pull away and stop what he was doing to her.

Pleasure radiated from her nipple, converging in an arrowed line straight to her cleft. She was melting again. Her blood turned to lava in her veins. Her clit throbbed with the rapidity of her pulse. Frenetic heat tore at her as he broke from her mouth and slid his tongue along her jaw and down the cord of her neck. Everything he did to her was new, yet not. She felt comfortable with him, eager to have him lay claim to every inch of her body. She wasn't scared or reluctant as she should have been.

She reveled to have him.

He explored her ear, nipping, tasting, sucking the lobe into his mouth. All the while, his fingers plucking at first one nipple then the other, drawing them into hard knots of pleasure.

She knew what she wanted. She wanted his mouth there. Everywhere. But the car was too confined. It was like a trap. She could couldn't quite reach her goal.

Frustrated, Nari pushed his hand aside, reaching down to push the lever to make the seat recline. It went back with a pop that startled them both, making her flatten against his chest.

Panting with arousal and exertion, she shifted until she sat astride him, leaning low to keep from bumping her head.

Shayne looked at her, his eyes heavy lidded with lust. He sat up, pushing her top up until he could lay his lips on her, nuzzle her breasts, taste her. She strangled a gasp as his teeth scraped over her flesh, gently biting, teasing her nipples to hard points. "Oh, God, Shayne...."

He circled her back, cupping her against him as he sucked her breasts to piercing points of arousal.

She bit her lip, rocking her hips until her cleft reached his encased cock. He groaned and lay back, arching, thrusting his hips upwards. The huge bulge rammed against her, hard as a rock. Even muted through the fabric, she felt his heat, his strength. Her cunt had soaked her panties, seeping into her lightweight pants. She rubbed herself against him, the smell of light sweat and lust arousing her more than she'd dreamed possible.

Shayne grit his teeth, dropping his hands to her hips until he could control her movement and his own. He thrust again, rubbing hard against her clit, fiercely plunging her into a swirl of pleasure that heightened with each passing second.

Nari gasped, flattening her palms against the roof of the car, riding him as waves of bliss crested inside her. A wild excitement engulfed her. She was straining toward fulfillment, her muscles tightening, her throat hoarse and achy with the effort of controlling her screams.

He groaned loudly, his hands near bruising her hips, and then he was driving against her like mad, roughly rubbing, hands cupping and massaging her ass, bringing her hard against him. She felt his cock shudder, her own arousal peak, culminate in a rapture that zipped through her erogenous zones with the speed and lingering effects of lightning.

Nari fell against his chest, gasping, goose bumps shivering across her skin.

It took her many moments until she could find her voice. When she was able to speak, she said, breathlessly, "You're not leaving without me."

He shifted beneath her, and she looked up at him. He was grinning crookedly, looking sexy and mussed, with strands of hair clinging to his damp forehead. "Okay. But I think we're both going to need a change of clothing."

* * * *

Nari stared at the darkened sanitarium with a sense of deja vu. This time, however, she'd been ordered to wait in the car. She didn't like it, but she could hardly argue that she knew the lay of the land as she had at the orphanage. Savage had insisted that he was safer to try it alone and she didn't feel comfortable about arguing with that assessment. It was bad enough that he was determined to risk yet another excursion for information despite all of her attempts to reason with him that getting her mother's files just wasn't worth the possibility of getting caught and the consequences attached to it.

She sighed as she watched Shayne disappear into the shadows of the sanitarium grounds, wondering if she'd really tried as hard to convince him not to make the attempt as she should have.

The truth was that the nightmares had been becoming more frequent, and getting worse all the time despite Shayne's efforts to help her, and she was too scared to think of much beyond stopping it. In some ways, she supposed it wasn't as bad as it had been since she'd first sought Shayne Savage out. At least now she dreamed of having someone to help her, someone she could turn to when the demon who called himself Onyx invaded her dreams.

She didn't doubt that it was the fact that Shayne monitored her when she slept that she'd gained that much of a sense of security, but realistically, she knew it couldn't continue as it had indefinitely. Sooner or later Shayne would throw up his hands in defeat and leave her to her own devises--or maybe even just give up and try to have her committed.

She desperately needed a solution to the problem or she really was going to go nuts.

It had occurred to her, more than once, that it might already be too late. She'd begun to feel as if she was being followed whenever she went out. She never actually saw anyone, but the feeling of being watched persisted. She'd considered mentioning it to Shayne several times, but each time she'd been on the verge of mentioning it, she had dismissed the temptation.

It had all the earmarks of paranoia.

He didn't seem to think she was crazy and she rather thought she would prefer to keep it that way.

She didn't want to end up like her mother had.

After she'd checked her watch about a dozen times in thirty minutes, she got out of the car and paced for a while, trying to focus on her problem rather than her anxiety about whether Shayne would manage to pull off his break in. When she'd walked off some of her excess nervous energy, she settled on the hood of the car and stared up at the night sky.

The dreams, she realized, had become more solidly threatening since she'd begun seeing Shayne for sleep therapy--more real and less dreamlike. She wondered if there was a connection or if it would have happened regardless. It seemed to her that she'd already been heading in that direction–which was why she'd sought his help to start with but she couldn't help but wonder about the way it seemed to have accelerated just within the last few weeks.

She'd been dreaming for years. Up until recently they had only been disturbing, but almost as soon as she'd started seeing Shayne about the problem, the dreams had become to manifest physical after effects. Was there a connection? Or was it only coincidence?

Or was it connected to something else that had happened in her life?

What if she wasn't being paranoid about being followed?

She hadn't considered that before, but she realized that that sense of being watched and followed had begun after they'd visited the orphanage. Was it only a guilty conscience that made her feel it, or had she triggered something by going back--something in the real world.

The hostility she'd felt when she'd tried to get the records wasn't something she'd imagined, not the determination to keep her from learning what was in the file. It was about her, after all. Apart from pure meanness, why might old Townsend want to keep the information from her? Particularly when there didn't seem to be anything especially important in the file.

Except the information about her origins.

And, now that she thought about it, Shayne was strangely focused on her origins.

She'd thought he was just downplaying her mother's claims of having been impregnated by a demon, but surely he'd taken that information in stride surprisingly easily … and become more determined than ever to find out what he could about her birth parents.

If she set aside her fear that she was losing her mind, what did that leave her with?

Her mother was telling the truth and either hadn't been able to handle it and had been locked away, or she'd been locked away for another reason entirely … to keep her quiet? To make certain she couldn't influence, or protect, her child?

The scrape of gravel snapped Nari from her thoughts. Whirling toward the sound, she saw that Shayne had returned and relief flooded her. Slipping off the car, she met him. To her surprise, he wasn't carrying anything.

"You didn't get in?"

Instead of answering her, he motioned for her to get into the car. He didn't speak until they'd headed back to town.

"I looked through the file. I didn't think it would be a good idea to remove it."

Nari glanced toward him in surprise, but it was dark in the car and she couldn't read his expression. "Why?"

"Somebody went to a lot of trouble to bury your origins."

Surprise and uneasiness went through Nari at the same time. "You think so too?"

He shrugged. "You never know the way they guard records these days--and it's possible the director of the orphanage is just a bitch who enjoys wielding what little power she has, but I definitely got that feeling when we met with the same resistance to seeing your mother's records."

Nari digested that a while, relieved that someone seemed to share her paranoia and at the same time further unnerved. "What could it mean, do you think?"

He shook his head. "Your mother was killed in a freak accident--at least that was the way it was described. According to the story, they thought she was trying to escape. She had gone up to the roof of the building and was attempting to climb down when the fire ladder came loose and she fell to her death."

"But you're not buying it?"

48

"It would take a freak accident to kill somebody falling no more two stories. The building just isn't that high. Broken bones, I could accept, but plenty of people have fallen even further and lived. The thing is, she was cut to ribbons and there just isn't any logical explanation for that in a fall."

Sickness welled inside of Nari as a vision of her mother's broken, bleeding body rose in her mind. "She was attacked."

Chapter Six

Shayne had left Nari with her own morbid thoughts after that, refusing to discuss the matter further until they'd reached her apartment. Nariko hadn't really prodded him, embroiled as she was in her own thoughts. She had doubts that he could really shed any light on the mystery in any case. It only seemed to deepen the more she learned, not to become more clear.

She was accepting a lot on faith, of course. The truth was, no matter how companionable she felt about Shayne, she really didn't know him that well and she didn't know how much trust she could place in her own instincts considering the distress she was under.

In her heart, she felt like she could trust him, but how much of that was dependence? How much was based solely on her attraction to him?

He knew her. She suspected he knew a lot more about her than he'd revealed. But she knew almost nothing about him.

She found by the time they'd reached her apartment once more than she really didn't want to deal with anything else at the moment. She was weary to her soul, not just physically. As ridiculous as it might seem to anyone else, she mourned the loss of her mother and that sense of loss was magnified by the horrible way her mother had died.

All she really wanted to do was to escape to her room to mourn in private and think things through for herself.

Shayne, however, insisted that the matter was something that needed to be discussed then, not put off until later.

She settled on the couch, feeling resentment slowly overtaking her confusion and sorrow as she watched Shayne pace her living room.

"I don't see why this can't wait until tomorrow," she said finally when he showed no indication of being forthcoming anytime soon.

Shayne ceased pacing and turned to study her speculatively for several moments. "I don't think it's something that can, or should, be put off. I think you're in danger."

Nari's heart skipped a beat, remembering that pervasive feeling of being followed ... hunted. "Why? How? From whom?"

He frowned, seemed to wrestle with his thoughts for several moments. "Have you considered the possibility that your mother actually was impregnated by a demon?"

"That's insane!" Nariko snapped, jumping to her feet. In a moment of weakness, she had toyed with the possibility, but she knew damned well there was no such thing and to consider it was to slide a little deeper toward the madness that had consumed her mother.

"You're that certain?"

Nariko stared at him, wondering yet again if he was entirely sane himself. He seemed perfectly lucid, and yet he'd done a lot of things that were certainly rash for a man in his position. "I don't believe in ghosts, or goblins, or things that go bump in the night!" she said irritably.

He looked away from her and began pacing once more. "Humor me, then. Let's, just for a moment, consider it as a possibility.

"According to the records, your mother wasn't committed. She went into the sanitarium voluntarily, and I believe she did it because she was hiding ... or hoping to hide. I think she placed you in the orphanage to keep you safe and then committed herself, hoping they wouldn't find her."

"Hoping who wouldn't find her?"

"The demons looking for the child ... you. But they did find her. Maybe they killed her trying to find out where you were.

"Maybe they managed to get the information out of her before she died."

Nari glared at him angrily. "You're saying I haven't been dreaming? That the demons have found me? And they want me, why? Why would they have any interest in me at all?"

"Because you're half demon."

Nariko's anger boiled over. "Get out! You're as crazy as she was!"

He stopped, his lips tightening angrily. "Be reasonable. You could be in danger."

"I think I am. I think you're crazy and I want you out of my house! Leave now, or I'll call the cops!"

He took a step toward her and Nariko skipped aside, putting the coffee table between them--insubstantial as it was as a barrier. He stopped.

"I have to go if you're determined to send me away, but I'm asking you to reconsider. You need protection. You haven't found your powers."

"I'm not a demon!" Nariko shouted at him. "Half or otherwise! I'm not evil!"

"I didn't say you were," Shayne said tightly. "Your father wasn't. Everything in nature has a balance, a dark side and a light side. Not all demons are evil."

Nariko gaped at him. "You're trying to say you knew my father?"

"I did."

Nariko leapt toward her phone. Grabbing it up, she punched the numbers with a shaking finger.

"911. What's your emergency?" said a feminine voice on the other end of the line.

Nariko glanced at Shayne. "There's a man in my house."

He glared at her furiously for several moments and finally strode out, slamming the door behind him. Nariko depressed the button on the phone, threw it down and ran to bolt her door.

She might be confused, but she damned well wasn't so nuts that she was going to take advice from somebody that was crazier than she was!

* * * *

Nariko hadn't expected to sleep. She had hoped she would be able to compose herself for rest. She had tried a hot, soothing bath. She had read for a while in bed. She had finally gotten up, put on an exercise video and worked out until she'd begun to feel like she would drop in her tracks, but physical exhaustion wasn't enough to overcome her distress, her anger, or her uneasiness once she was alone in the apartment.

She had finally decided that she would lie down anyway and close her eyes. Even if she couldn't sleep, surely doing that much would rest her at least a little so that she could face the next day.

Despite her angry dismissal, however, Shayne's words assaulted her. Every time she closed her eyes her mind went round and round with the argument. It was going on three AM when her mind finally began to wind down. Bits and pieces of nightmares began to batter at her almost the moment she drifted away, however, and she found herself starting into wakefulness each time she sank toward slumber.

She thought when first she sensed the presence at the foot of her bed that she was still sleeping. The nightmares had become so real to her that she'd begun to have difficulty sorting dream from reality at times.

The moment Onyx grabbed her and hauled her from her bed, however, she knew absolutely that this was no dream. Before she could scream, or even put up much of a fight, he'd captured her so tightly against his hulking frame that she could barely even squirm. She struggled anyway, trying to wiggle free of his grip.

"The time has come," he said in his deep, rumbling voice.

Nariko definitely didn't like the sound of that. "What time?"

"Tonight you will help me open the doorway so that I can achieve my full powers," he said in the same growling voice.

"Like hell I will!" Nariko snapped angrily.

"You will. And you will enjoy it as much as I," he promised.

He lifted her free of the floor then, launching the two of them upward with such force Nariko cringed, expecting momentarily to collide with the ceiling. Instead, she discovered when she opened her eyes that the Earth was far below them. Her heart slammed into her chest wall like a caged bird trying to beat its way out of a trap.

This could not be real. It had to be one of the nightmares!

She was afraid to struggle now, however, and realized she wasn't so convinced that it was a dream that she was willing to risk breaking free and falling to her death. Instead, she drew in a deep breath to scream for Xalen to come to her.

Onyx silenced her before she'd managed to emit more than a squeaking syllable. She wasn't certain how he'd silenced her when he held her firmly gripped in both arms, but she felt as if her mouth were covered tightly. She couldn't open her mouth. She couldn't breathe.

The fear of suffocation very quickly ousted every other thought from her mind, even her fear of falling to her death. She fought frantically to free herself, to drag air into her lungs, but absolute blackness began to swim around her within moments. The stars dimmed and one by one winked out.

Cold was the first sensation that filtered through her mind when she swam upward toward consciousness once more. Light flickered through the thin skin of her eye lids and she stirred. Realizing she couldn't move, Nariko opened her eyes at last and found that she was staring up into the darkness of a cavernous ceiling.

The light she'd seen, she discovered, was the flickering fire of torches set into sconces on the dark stone walls that surrounded her.

It looked rough hewn, crude--she was in a cavern, she realized finally.

She couldn't move because she was pinned by the manacles around her wrists and ankles.

With cold terror washing over her, she lifted her head.

Almost as if they'd been waiting for her to do so, as if it was a signal to them to commence, shadowy figures clothed in dark, hooded cloaks stepped from the darkness and surrounded the stone altar where she lay.

Low, so low it was more like muttering than chants at first, they began to speak words she'd never heard before. Gradually, their voices became louder, the words falling faster from their lips.

She sensed Onyx's presence before she felt his touch on her leg.

He meant to take her and this time there would be no escaping him.

She screamed then, as loudly as she could, summoning Xalen to her aid. No one was more surprised than she was that she actually managed to break the hold that had sealed her lips before, but the chanting was so loud by that time that she despaired that she had made herself heard above it.

And she was in a cavern, far below the Earth. How could he hear her? she thought despairingly.

The thought had no sooner occurred to her than she realized how totally irrational it was. If Xalen was "real" then he was a demon. It shouldn't matter where she was ... unless this cavern shielded the cult from the other demons, the good demons?

The skate of Onyx's hand along her thigh jerked Nari abruptly back to her situation. Straining, she lifted her head to look down at him just as he curled his fingers into her mound. She jerked as she felt his finger parting the flesh, probing her.

His gaze moved up her body and locked with hers. He was frowning. Slowly, he climbed onto the altar, licking a path all the way up her belly as he moved. Nari squeezed her eyes shut, trying to ignore the leap of her flesh beneath that damp, heated caress. To her relief, he withdrew the tortuous tongue from her. When she opened her eyes, she saw that he was studying her almost curiously.

"I can give you pleasure," he said in his deep, rumbling voice.

Nari gritted her teeth. "Only in your conceited mind!" she snapped.

He frowned, but more thoughtfully than angrily. "I am so repulsive to you?"

"You disgust me!" she spat out angrily.

He closed his eyes. As she stared at him in surprise, his features began to shift and change. She blinked. When she opened her eyes once more, she saw that it was Savage who hovered above her.

She swallowed. Onyx was playing with her mind.

Or was he?

Was it possible there had never been a Dr. Savage at all? Had this demon appeared to her in a form he thought would please her more? Tried to gain her trust by appearing to her as an attractive human being?

Almost as if he had read her mind, he asked, "Is this form more pleasing to you?"

Instead of answering, Nari looked away from him, feeling ill at the thought that she'd kissed Savage with such pleasure when he might only have been Onyx all along.

"Perhaps this, then?"

Despite her unwillingness to be drawn into his game, whatever it was, Nari found she couldn't resist looking at him when he spoke again. To her horror, she saw Xalen above her--Onyx looking like Xalen--or maybe there'd never been a Xalen either? Maybe there'd never been anyone but Onyx.

He growled angrily when she merely stared at him. "There is no pleasing you."

"You can not please me," Nari retorted.

His eyes narrowed cunningly. "I can wring pleasure from your body whether it is your will to feel it or not. You responded to me before. I smelled the sweet scent of your desire, felt the heat of your body."

Nari swallowed with an effort. She could lie and deny it, but he would know.

She steeled herself as he lowered his head, turning her face away. He sucked the flesh of her neck, almost to the point of pain, but heat flooded her despite that. She felt her nipples pucker and stand erect.

Onyx felt it, too. The hard little tips drew his attention and he moved down her body. Nari gritted her teeth as his mouth covered one tip, trying her best to ignore the rampant, pleasurable sensations that shot through her. Despite her efforts, her body sang to life, began to tremble as he continued to suckle her determinedly, flicking his tongue over the sensitive tip. She was struggling to catch her breath by the time he turned his attention to its mate.

There was no bracing herself for the onslaught. As repulsed as she was by the evil in Onyx, her body had no conscience. It sang beneath his touch, soared. Moisture gathered in her vaginal passage, welcoming his possession and when he reached his hand down to probe her once more, he grunted in satisfaction.

Shifting, he pressed his hard cock along her cleft, searching, finding the passage that quivered with need in spite of all Nari could do.

Pain shot through her as he lunged, plunging deeply inside of her in one powerful thrust and rupturing her hymen as he claimed her. She screamed, the euphoria he'd created vanishing instantly. He looked down at her with Onyx's eyes in Xalen's face, his gaze calculating, impatient, filled with lust.

Slowly the pain subsided, became a dull throbbing. Twisting, he began to tease her flesh with his mouth and tongue once more. Gradually, beneath his persistence, her body responded until she was gasping with need once more, squirming beneath him. He began to move then, thrusting his cock deeply inside of her, withdrawing slowly and thrusting once more. Euphoria intoxicated her, building inside of her in an ever tightening band until she felt her body could not continue to withstand the ever mounting pleasure, until she felt her body trembling, reaching for appeasement.

Without warning, the bubble that had been building inside of her toward explosion, erupted. She screamed with the force of it, feeling as if it would rend her body into tiny fragments, feeling such white hot fire and power explode forth from her that she feared for many moments that when it ceased to flow outward from her that there would be nothing left but an empty shell.

Around her, she heard the shock waves spreading outward, heard the terrified screams of the cult members who had gathered to watch, heard Onyx roar in pain.

It continued rippling outward, jerking from within her. Her flesh heated, a sheen of sweat coated her skin in response, and still the ruptures of ecstasy rolled from within. Something had happened, different from her orgasms before, as if having demon flesh inside her had awakened an innermost part she hadn't known existed.

She felt that part now, called it forth, but there was no controlling it. A crack of thunder shook the cavern walls, bouncing through the cavern in a deafening echo. Her eardrums spasmed.

Her mind whirled dizzily, and she blacked out. For how long, she couldn't know. When she opened her eyes at last, she discovered she had not imagined any of it. The room around her was decimated, burned, the bodies of the cult members crumpled.

Nari sat up in surprise, discovering the manacles were broken, twisted fragments now.

Disbelief filled her as she stared at Onyx, far across the room now, struggling to rise. She looked down at herself, but she didn't have so much as a scratch. What had happened?

She screamed when Xalen materialized beside the altar. He caught her arms, giving her a slight shake. "Nari! You summoned me!"

Nari swallowed with an effort. "Is it ... really you?"

He frowned, pulling her close as he surveyed the damage to the room; the dead and dying cult members, the blackened walls, the blasted stones. Seeing Onyx, he released Nari. She caught his arm. "No. Let him go."

His lips tightened. "He is weak now. If we allow him to go, he will grow strong again."

Nari's chin wobbled. "Please, just take me home."

After a moment, he nodded and scooped her into his arms. Grateful, Nari wrapped her arms around his shoulders, burying her face against his neck. A sensation of movement filtered through her beleaguered senses. Slowly, Xalen's warmth began to chase the chill of fear and shock from her and then she felt herself being lowered and looked around to discover she was in her own bedroom once more.

She clung to Xalen when he would have released her. He settled next to her on her bed, holding her close.

"What happened?" he asked softly.

"I don't really know," she responded, the words muffled against his neck. "Onyx ... raped me. And then I felt this powerful force building inside of me."

Xalen was silent for a time, rubbing her back soothingly. "He wanted you to unlock his own powers. Instead, he unlocked yours and it nearly destroyed him. I have to confess you are far more powerful than I had imagined possible. I have never seen anything even approaching the powers that you have. I have heard tell of such things in legend, but I hadn't believed they were anything but tales."

Nari leaned away from him, studying him in confusion. "I don't understand."

"You do. You just don't want to accept. You are half demon, Nari. The demon who was your father was well known to me."

Nari pulled away from him. "He raped my mother."

"He loved your mother ... in as much as a demon is capable of loving a human being. He was destroyed trying to protect the two of you from harm."

An uncomfortable knot of sorrow rose in her throat. With an effort, she swallowed against it. "How do you know this? And, if you knew, why didn't you come to me sooner?"

He frowned. "When Daxen was destroyed, your mother took you and disappeared. We believed that you had both been killed when he died. Until you came to me and we found the records, I had no way of knowing you still lived."

Nari stared at him. "Wait a minute! I didn't...."

Even as her voice trailed off to nothingness, Xalen transformed, became Savage right before her eyes. Nari sucked in a frightened breath. "You! Onyx appeared as you, transformed himself into Xalen."

His hand closed around her arm when she would have leapt from the bed. "You know me! No matter what form I take, you know me, Nari."

Her fear began to subside almost at once, for she realized it was true. She sensed that he was Xalen, and she realized that she had always felt that she could trust him, as Savage, and when he appeared to her as Xalen. No wonder she had been confused about her feelings for both of them.

When she ceased to resist, he pulled her close to him, fitting her against his length. The soothing skate of his hand along her flesh calmed the last of her fears and, as she relaxed, kindled a spark of warmth. When he lowered his head and brushed his lips along her cheek, she lifted her own lips to meet his. Warmth flooded her as his mouth moved over hers, as his tongue slid sinuously along hers in an intimate caress, then became heat as longing began to build inside of her.

Reluctantly, she broke the kiss. "We can't," she protested weakly.

"As much as I wish to argue the matter, I agree," he responded. "Now that your power is awakened, it must be controlled before we can ... do more."

Nari blinked at him in surprise. "You're not serious."

There wasn't a touch of humor in his eyes. "I am. You are awakened now, however, though I am certain this was not in Onyx's plan. He cannot harm you in your dreams without retaliation."

For that, she was thankful, but what it entailed scared her. What if she dreamed of sex and something happened? She could hurt anyone without even knowing it. Nari swallowed fearfully, thinking about what could've happened if she'd decided to have sex with him before she'd known. "I almost destroyed Onyx." I could have killed you, she left unspoken. They both knew it.

He smiled faintly. "In time, I will teach you how to control, and use, your powers. You will need them, Blazearc. There are others out there, like you, with powers. We must find them. We will need their help to fight the demon horde, to destroy them, or send them back beyond the gateway and then we will need to destroy the gateway."

The End … or just the beginning…?

WITH GREAT POWER

Brenna Lyons

DEDICATION

When Jaide put out the call for this anthology, it fired my imagination. Between hearing my son "invent" one superhero after another, having a younger brother with a degree in graphic arts and reading comic books when I was growing up, I've always had a fondness for the genre. Right away, I decided I didn't want to create a world of superheroes in the normal sense of the word. The thought that immediately lodged in my head was simple. What if superheroes evolved ala X-Men and were forced to live in service to society with no choice in the matter?

I have to thank Stan Lee and Marvel Comics for my fascination with the subject and for the concepts that I have come to associate with superheroes in general. My major sources of inspiration were the X-Men, Superman, Batman, The Justice League, and most especially ... The Amazing Spiderman and Professor Xavier.

I hope you enjoy "With Great Power." I had a great time writing it.

Brenna Lyons

Prologue

Memo

To: Mindteacher, Dean of Discipline, Head Trustee, Calante Academy, Central City

From: Visionchaser, spokesman for the trustees, Calante Academy, Central City

Date: June 15, 2052

We heartily agree with your analysis of the situation. The trustees are unanimous in their decision. Soulchaser is to be brought to the academy to begin his training tonight. We cannot risk a repeat of Empathen's loss. Use whatever means you find necessary to secure the boy before the Grellan can strike again.

End trans.

* * * *

Julien startled awake as his mother cried out in fury and frustration.

"You can't," she protested. "I have two more years. The law says--"

"You know he can't stay here, Patrice," a strange man insisted. "How will you protect him? He has Empathen's powers and more. They know that."

"Then take me, too."

"You know I can't do that. If you were an operative--I can't let a human live inside the main complex. That's why your quarters are outside the wall."

"You won't break that rule, but you'll take him early?" she asked sarcastically.

The man sighed. "You would have to leave the main complex in two years. How would we explain it to him then? How would we explain you being there to the other cadets now? The jokes would start tonight. The mighty Empathen's son needs his Mommy to come with him? Children can be very cruel, Patrice."

Julien snuck to the bedroom door, daring to peek at the man from the academy--the operative they sent to try to take him from his mother. His heart pounded at the sight of the grim-faced old man. Julien looked to his mother's tortured expression in dismay. She was considering it. Patrice was actually considering handing him over early.

Please, don't agree. Don't let him take me. Julien bit back a sob as he felt her wavering.

"He's my son," she managed through trembling lips. "He's my only child."

The old man took her hands. "You will lose him either way, Patrice. This way, you know he's safe. If he stays here--" He let the threat hang between them.

She nodded. "You'll bring Julien to see me? Promise me that much."

He took her shoulders in his hands, nodding. "A guard detail will bring him once a month and accompany you where you wish to take him. You have my vow."

"What--What is my son's name?" she asked solemnly.

Julien shook his head in disbelief. His name--The name chosen for him when he was tested at the age of three would be spoken for the first time tonight, two years ahead of schedule.

"Soulchaser."

Julien shivered. If they were really taking him to the academy, he'd heard his true name for the last time until he found a confidant. No one dared speak a power's true name unless he or she was invited to do so, and his parents never would. That was the law.

The old man chuckled. "Come, Soulchaser. It is time to go."

"That is not my name," he replied stubbornly. "It will not be my name until I turn ten. That is the law."

The door opened, and the man stared down at him, amusement curving his lips into a cruel smile. "Are you inviting me to use your true name?" he asked pointedly.

Julien felt his cheeks burn. He glared at the old man. "No. I don't trust you."

"That's good. People should earn your trust."

"That's not what my father says," Julien groused. "He says to trust your gut instincts about people." I don't trust you. But, Empathen was dead. Word had come to them that afternoon that his father had fallen in the line of duty.

The man's smile disappeared. "Your father trusted the wrong person. That is how he died. You should remember that."

Julien didn't answer that. How could he argue that a power like Empathen should never have let a Grellan get close enough to kill him? Why would Empathen let down his guard?

"On your feet, Cadet Soulchaser."

He cringed as he rose. I am not Soulchaser. I am Julien Cross. No matter what name I answer to, I will never forget who I am. He met the old man's eyes. "What is your name--sir?"

"My name is Mindteacher, but almost no one calls me that, as you will soon learn."

"They use your true name?" Julien asked dubiously. Surely not. There was too much power in knowing an operative's true name. The law said--

"No. They call me 'the old man.' People have always called me 'the old man,' even when I wasn't one."

Julien scowled, unsurprised by that discovery.

"Say goodbye to your mother, Soulchaser. You will see her next month." Mindteacher laid a hand on Julien's shoulder.

Julien stilled, meeting the old man's eyes as Mindteacher's thoughts coursed into him like a waterfall. In the moment before he yanked his hand away, Julien learned a lot about Mindteacher.

The old man blamed Jake for his own death. Mindteacher thought of Empathen as Jake, though he didn't trust Jake any more than Jake trusted Mindteacher. The old man knew everyone's secrets. He was the academy Dean of Discipline and the Head Trustee. Julien laughed aloud as Mindteacher's true name settled in his mind. Then the connection was gone.

Mindteacher motioned to the doorway. He waited for Julien to turn to it before he nodded to Patrice. "Next month," he assured her.

A chill coursed along Julien's nerves and he grasped his mother in a fierce hug, abruptly certain that he would never be permitted to see her again.

* * * *

Memo
To: Visionchaser, spokesman for the trustees, Calante Academy, Central City
From: Mindteacher, Dean of Discipline, Head Trustee, Calante Academy, Central City
Date: December 20, 2055

No account can be made for the sudden cessation of hostilities. One can only assume that the Grellan are plotting our end, but what new means they have discovered remains to be seen. Our operatives report less and less signs of the Grellan in and around all cities over Suraden.

Training has been stepped up. Be ever vigilant, my friend. Millennia of fighting will not end so easily.

End trans.

Chapter One

Assignment Status
To: Soulchaser, Unit Leader, Unit 1255, Central City
From: Fire Mother, Communications Center, Calante Academy, Central City
Date: March 12, 2064

Report to Tower 1022, quarters 13 N 17. Use extreme caution. Reports of Grellan activity in abandoned quarters.

The old man says he thinks it's your group again. Take care, Soulchaser. Serve well.

End Trans.

* * * *

Julien stared at the woman before him. She was his own age with auburn curls that cascaded over her shoulders. She was also naked. She was always naked.

She was so familiar that Julien could note every curve with his eyes closed, the pink scar above her left breast, and even the tattoo of the Siberian tiger on the back of her right shoulder. Julien recognized her scent, something of musk and Jasmine, and the touch of her mind. The one thing he could not do was name her.

She strode toward him, her hips swaying in invitation. Her hand stroked Julien's rising cock through the gray cotton of his over-cover. "I knew you would come," she purred.

"Why me?" he asked.

"Only you will see the truth," she whispered, her fingers tracing the head straining against his clothing.

Julien took a calming breath. He should stop her, but he needed information. As maddening as her touch was, he had to know why she was here, and that wouldn't happen if he put her on the defensive.

"Come to me without your unit," she requested again. She'd made that request the last three times he'd encountered her.

"Why?" Why would she want to talk to him alone? What purpose could there be in getting him isolated and unprotected?

Her blue eyes sparkled under dusty red lashes. She pulled his hand to her breast, laying it over the hard nipple.

Julien bit back a groan, fully aware that the other members of his unit could see everything his physical body did and hear every sound he made aloud. "What is your name?"

"Promise you'll come to me alone."

The softness of her breast teased his palm. She shifted, brushing the point of her nipple against his sensitized skin.

"If you promise to come to me alone, I will tell you my name.."

"Next time. I will arrange it next time," he promised, already working out how he would make that happen.

She leaned toward him, laying a kiss on Julien's lower lip. "They call me Starseeker. My name is Angel."

"Angel?" She trusted Julien with her true name. Was that intended to prove that she wanted his trust, that she trusted him? Did the Grellan think there was anything special in a true name? Was it a trick? Julien wished he knew for sure. "When will I see you again?" It had been almost three weeks since he had seen her last.

The hand on his cock stroked harder. "Soon." Her essence faded away, leaving only her haunting scent to tease him.

Julien took a shuddering breath and forced his eyes open. The glass of the mirror, only slightly warmed to his touch, made a mockery of the memory of Angel's skin beneath his fingers.

He took another deep breath, separating phantom strands of Angel's scent from those of her unit, one so close to hers that the man must be a relative. A brother, perhaps? His essence spoke of youth--but of infirmity of some sort, a feeling of not being whole.

"And?" Firebrand asked impatiently. As always, his incendiary nature reached from his powers to his personality. "Come off it, Soulchaser. Give me information."

Julien shot him a quelling look, reminding Firebrand silently who the leader of their unit was. He nodded as the new operative blushed and looked away. It wasn't unusual for a power to forget that Julien was a unit leader. Operatives didn't typically graduate to the field until they were eighteen, and it generally took them five years in police service with human suspects until they moved on to a unit or to a position in research or administration. There, only the strongest and most capable were made leaders.

Julien had never been the typical power. Taken from his mother at the age of eight instead of ten, he finished his training at sixteen. He spent three years working the police beat before the old man let him move up to the units, but he was granted his own unit within two months. Julien was in complete control of his unit. He alone chose his unit members and gave them orders outside of the initial assignment order.

It would be all too easy for Julien to replace Firebrand with an older operative who showed more control, but Julien prided himself in having the best of the best in his unit. So, when Julien requested Firebrand after only a year of police service, the old man signed the order without question that the young man, only a little more than a year younger than Julien, belonged in the units where the real challenges existed.

"It was the same five," Julien informed them, removing his hand from the mirror.

Sky Master shook his head slowly. "Why would they continue to come here? Is there a traitor they are meeting?"

"No. There is no sign of any Calante here or at any of the sites. Or any human. Whatever is drawing them into the city is internal to their unit."

Sky Master stared at the deep green of the Suraden sunset through the streaked window. "Can you tell us more about the two new powers with them?" he asked quietly.

Julien ran his fingertips over the mirror, drinking in the last fibers of Angel's presence, taking them into his mind and body. He had identified Night Warrior, Sky Child, and Moon Current immediately, but Angel and her relative had evaded his usual tactician success rate for six encounters. It was unheard of, and it was a source of embarrassment for the whole unit.

"Starseeker," he breathed. "One of them is named Starseeker. The two are related. Siblings, I believe."

"Believe?" Water Demon rasped in her usual strained tones. "That is not a term you use often."

Julien took in her purple-clad body, covered in synth-cloth, as everyone in his unit was save Julien himself. Water Demon's cover was the purple of the deepest sea beds. Sky Master wore green the color of the sunset sky. Firebrand wore the blue of the powerful flames he controlled.

Their over-covers were designed for comfort and safety. Water Demon's suit was outfitted to withstand deep-sea pressures and to safeguard her from radical changes in pressure. In addition, it circulated water over her gill slits and aerated the water for her when she was operating on land. Firebrand's suit cooled his body, keeping his tissues from combusting when he used his powers.

Sky Master's suit was most impressive. The suit pressurized automatically when he reached altitudes that required it. At that point, the retractable faceplate would extend and provide him with oxygen to sustain him in flight. The suit monitored his physiological state and was designed to notify med-flight if he suffered suit failure. Unlike Water Demon, a failure in Sky Master's suit could be fatal within minutes. The trainers learned long ago that the ability to do something did not always come with the physical design to withstand the rigors of the act.

Julien had no synth-cloth cover. The material interfered with his powers. The trainers joked that a natural power like his required a natural environment. His cover was thick cotton fleece covered with a wool jacket that hid his lessening erection from his unit. His shoes were leather with cotton laces, and his suit fastened with a simple metal zipper.

He could wear no specialized protection, not even the Kevlar silk built into all the other operative's covers. Julien's team was his protection. They were also his keepers. Julien couldn't carry electronic surveillance gear as most operatives did. Even his team couldn't use comm units in an area he had to work. The comm circuits wrecked havoc with his powers, just as they had with his father.

"Believe?" Sky Master reminded him.

Julien nodded, an idea taking shape. He'd never lied to his team before, but he had to learn what Angel and her unit wanted in the city, what they wanted with him. "Starseeker's essence is much like my own." It was. Maybe that was why she was naked when she came to him. "It seems--your presence disrupts the unstable strands left behind."

Sky Master looked at him uncomfortably. "What are you suggesting? You want us to leave you here? Alone? The old man would have a fit."

That much was true. Julien immersed himself in the strands to the exclusion of all else when he was on a track. His unit was his protection. The old man was sure to balk at what Julien was suggesting.

"No. The damage is already done here. The next time we are called out, I want you to form a containment ring. I'll take in an emergency beacon, but I have to go in alone." Yes, the emergency beacon wouldn't send out a destructive signature unless he hit the button, but would Julien see danger coming before it was too late to push that button? That would be what the old man would consider.

"Are you crazy?" Firebrand exploded. "You will be completely unprotected at your most vulnerable moments."

"The old man will never allow it," Sky Master decided.

Julien sighed. "He will. If he wants to get more information about Starseeker, he will allow it." He pushed away an unwelcome thought. Despite what the old man wanted, Julien wanted to know more about Angel and not in any way the old man would appreciate.

* * * *

The old man's true name was Adrien Carter. Julien was one of the few who knew that, perhaps the only living person who did. Of course, Julien was the only one beside the trustees who knew everyone's true name at the Center City Academy. All it took was a touch on their person while they weren't clothed in synth-cloth, and he knew. Over the years, it became a game to learn them all.

Adrien regarded Julien over his steepled fingers, probing uselessly at the shield Julien learned to project when he was nine. "We cannot risk you," Adrien decided. "Permission denied."

Julien shrugged, locking down control on his desperation. "As you wish. When will my unit be reassigned?" he asked calmly.

Adrien furrowed his brow. "Reassigned? Why would you be reassigned?"

"You teach us to always play to our strengths. If I cannot progress, I would better serve elsewhere."

"And you feel you cannot progress with your unit close to the source strands?"

"What I am sensing indicates that," he lied smoothly. In truth, Julien wasn't sure how Angel controlled the information she left behind in the strands or how she connected to him when he was at the source. That uncertainty made him all the more determined to learn how she did it.

Adrien sent him a searching look. Julien met his eyes evenly, confident of his safety. No one else could lie to the old man. Only the fact that Julien was so useful saved him from some sort of artificial hobbling to place him solidly under Adrien's control.

It was a good thing the old man couldn't read Julien's mind. If Adrien knew he planned to connect to a Grellan, Julien would be shackled in a synth-cloth room--or worse. If Adrien knew what Julien hoped happen when he connected to Starseeker, 'or worse' was the best he could hope for.

"Permission--" Adrien scowled.

Julien arched an eyebrow at the old man's attempt to unbalance him. It was amusing that Adrien still tried. Julien willed his muscles loose. Showing tension would alert Adrien that there was a weakness to be exploited.

"Permission granted," Adrien growled.

Julien nodded once. He swallowed a sigh of relief--or perhaps a laugh of triumph. "One tower," he decided.

The old man sighed. "One tower containment zone," he agreed grudgingly, "and you carry a beacon."

Chapter Two

Julien smiled as he closed the door to the living quarters behind him. Adrien sought to test him, but it was about to backfire in the old man's face. He should know better than to play head games with Julien by now.

The scent filled his lungs, the musk and jasmine he associated with Angel. The strands crossed over each other, telling the tale of the Grellan's time in this place. They had only stayed a day before using power that would alert the Calante to their presence. They hadn't even spent the night this time.

All of them left imprints in the main room. "Strange," he mused. Angel's sibling was easier to read now. Had they planned that or had Julien inadvertently told the truth about the interference of his unit? It was a boy, a child too young to have ended academy training, maybe the age of a seventh or eighth-year cadet.

"Starfire," he whispered with a wide smile. The boy's name was--Anthony. His power was the ability to see living conditions on far-off star systems. That and--Julien growled as he lost the weave of that strand. It was almost as if they knew how to hide things from him. At any rate, Julien knew about one of Starfire's abilities. It was akin to astral projection, which explained his name, and it was a power that the Calante would prize highly.

Julien moved around the room slowly, touching one thing after another. They ate two meals here, food they carried in with them. Anthony had a telescope. He called Night Warrior and Moon Current 'uncle' and 'aunt.' He called Star Child--

"Names," he mused in awe. They all knew each other's names. Now Julien did, too. Night Warrior was Paul Andrews, and Moon Current was his wife, Debra. Sky Child was Sylvia Bryant. Angel and Anthony's family name was Taylor.

Julien sobered. It was a strange way to live. The ancient texts all agreed that only an operative's closest confidants were permitted to know his or her true name. The Calante was founded on those ideals, brought with them from Earth millennia ago.

He furrowed his brow. All of their essences were in the main room, but Angel's went further. Julien followed the strands deeper into the dwelling, drinking in the feeling of

Angel's soul. He shivered in anticipation as he pushed the door to the bedroom wide.

Julien closed his eyes and let Angel's strand lead him on, immersing himself fully now that he found the source strands that he needed to reach her. He laughed aloud as his knees connected with the bed. "I like the way you think, Angel."

Her laugh sent shivers down his spine. Julien opened his eyes, still deeply immersed in the connection. Angel lay on the bed, her auburn curls tossed over the sky green pillows, her arms laid under her full breasts, and her legs crossed at the ankles. Her deep blue eyes twinkled.

"Do you ever dress?" he asked.

"When I know you will come to me? What a waste of time," she teased.

Julien sank to the bed beside her, tracing a nipple slowly. The silk of her breast and pebbled softness of her nipple were flawless. Angel's smile disappeared, and a look of stark hunger took its place. Julien wondered how real this connection could become. He'd wondered that since she'd teased him back at Tower 1022.

Angel wrapped an arm behind his head and pulled his mouth to hers. Her lips parted, and Julien kissed her, ravenous for the connection he'd dreamed of. Every sensation was perfect; the heat, the taste of juice and toast in her mouth, the texture of her lips and tongue under his.

Julien dragged his mouth away, touching her swollen lips with shaking fingers. "I must be insane." For some reason, insanity sounded appealing if Angel was part of the package.

She smiled. "I've wanted to do that for months. I am real, Soulchaser."

He grimaced. Julien didn't want to be Soulchaser with Angel. Soulchaser was Calante. It was Soulchaser's duty to bring her to justice under the Grellan Act of 577. But, no one used his true name. No one had since his mother turned him over to the Academy for training at eight. According to the law, no one could use it--unless he offered it, but Angel was Grellan, and no Calante would offer a Grellan that power over him.

No one called him Julien. Even the old man and the three trustees called him Soulchaser. Those four held the terrifying power of knowing his true name, but they never used it for fear of punishment under the law. The trainers at the Academy were never trusted enough to know Julien's true name. Even his unit didn't know it.

But, Julien couldn't deny that he wanted Angel to know it. Did he want her to be his close confidant? Did Julien want her to be more than that? Operatives were free to marry human confidants or other operatives. Julien dreamed of marriage. He dreamed of long, slow nights of sex with someone who would call him by his true name.

Angel touched his cheek, nipping at his lower lip. "You can't do it. I understand. When you're ready, you'll tell me."

Julien darkened. "What do you want from me, Starseeker?" It would be inappropriate for him to use her true name now that he'd refused to give her his.

"No. I'm not Starseeker. Not with you. Call me Angel."

He closed his eyes, seeking her mouth urgently. "Angel," he breathed.

"I gave you my name, because I must confide in you.. You must know that I trust you."

"Tell me." Julien nuzzled his face in her hair. He'd wanted to do that since the first time he'd seen her walking toward him. "Tell me why you're doing this."

"Trust me. Trust me as I have trusted you."

A rational kernel in his mind argued that Angel was Grellan and was, by definition, not to be trusted. A larger portion wanted to trust her. Trust your gut instinct.

No. Empathen died, because he trusted the wrong person, a Grellan. "I will try," he promised. What more could he promise?

* * * *

Angel sighed inwardly. It wasn't enough. He had to trust her fully. She stroked him, searching his expression as he grew thick and heavy in her hand.

"Let me know when you trust me," she breathed.

Soulchaser groaned aloud to her touch. "How real can this be?" he whispered.

"I don't know," she admitted. Angel had never attempted what she was doing. Soulchaser was much stronger than any man she'd connected to in the past.

His fingers stroked her inner thigh. "Open for me."

Her heart pounded against her ribs. If the others knew about this, they would not approve. Angel spread her legs wide, bowing up as his cool fingers probed at her heat. "Yes," she hissed.

His mouth closed on her nipple, and Angel bit back a scream of pleasure, aware of her family in the next room. His hands were everywhere; stroking, squeezing, testing and teasing at her skin.

"Come for me." His voice surrounded her, the phantom touch of his breath on her ear.

Angel kissed him, using the sensation of his mouth on hers to remind her not to cry out as she was swept away. She sucked in gasping breaths as her body released for him.

Soulchaser nipped at her ear. "You smell so good." He moved down her body, laying teasing kisses on her stomach, her curls, her clit.

She bit her lip. "Soulchaser," she breathed. Angel would have begged if he'd asked her.

He didn't ask. Soulchaser's tongue caressed her inside and out--slowly, as if he read her need for that approach. He didn't back off, thrusting and stroking until she shattered again.

Angel ground her teeth against the scream building behind her lips, sinking to the bed beneath her and closing her eyes in exhaustion. "Will you come again?" she asked.

"Yes. Will you tell me what you want from me next time?"

"Come to me naked," she requested. Breaking his training would not be easy. She would have to make Soulchaser more vulnerable to accomplish her task. "Next time, come to me naked."

Angel faded from his mind, as Soulchaser groaned again. Yes. She would be able to break his training given time and the right incentives. She had to make him think and make him question. He was faltering in that respect already. But to win, she had to make him want something more than the life he had. Every Calante she'd contacted in the past had wanted out. Turning Soulchaser was much more difficult. He didn't realize that he wanted out yet, but Angel had to free him.

She pulled the quilt around her body, sinking into a twilight sleep. The connection was always wearing, but this time it was all the more so. Soulchaser had tired her body to match her overworked mind.

Angel smiled in her half-sleep, memories of Soulchaser making her warm and weak. Going to him in the nude had been a necessity of her power. The idea of teasing him sexually, of using her nudity to draw him in, stemmed from his interest in her. Soulchaser was adept at hiding his feelings from those around him, but that was impossible inside the connection.

It was never supposed to go this far. Angel never dreamed that it could go this far. She shivered in the memory of Soulchaser's insistent tongue and nimble fingers. Angel was looking forward to their next encounter, not to bring them closer to their ultimate goal but to experience more of their unique connection.

"Angel?" Debra called.

"Hmm," she yawned, forcing her eyes open.

"Any progress?" The older woman shifted nervously, winding a gray-streaked lock of black hair through her fingers.

"Yes. He's agreed to meet me again." Angel smiled. "Alone. His trust will come in time."

Debra nodded. "If you become uncomfortable--"

Angel waved her off. "Soulchaser is a good man." A man who thought only of my pleasure. A thrill raced over her nerves. He hadn't sought his own pleasure.

"Be careful, Angel. Good man or not, Soulchaser is Calante. He's been taught only his duty." Debra brushed Angel's curls away from her eyes. "I don't want you to get hurt again. You started playing this game far too early."

Angel sobered, nodding her agreement. She hadn't questioned her involvement with Soulchaser, rationalizing that anything that ultimately earned his trust would be worthwhile. She'd pursued her enjoyment as a reward for her service.

Soulchaser was Calante. The Calante enslaved her kind. The Calante had killed her parents. The Calante would take Anthony from her and kill the rest of their family--or worse. The Calante would use their family against them to force Angel and Anthony to work for them, if they knew what their true power was and how it worked.

Angel brushed her fingers over the scar on her chest, fighting back her anger. I was seven! I wasn't supposed to be fighting a war. No. No one else could have done what she and Anthony had that day.

She nodded. "I will Debra. I will never forget what the Calante are capable of." The next time she encountered Soulchaser, he would fall to her hands as she had fallen to his. Then he would remember what it meant to be alive. Before Angel was done with him, Soulchaser would want something she could offer, at least one of things she could offer.

Chapter Three

Julien stared at the ceiling, frustrated with himself and with his errant body. He wanted her. Angel's responsive nature was enough to drive Julien crazy, but he had to stay rooted in the reality of the situation. Angel was Grellan, and she had a reason--a hidden purpose for the things she did. Whatever her reason, could he trust her?

His mind warred on that subject. His training said he couldn't. The Grellan killed his father. It was a societal axiom that her kind were not to be trusted. Julien sighed. His powers told him something vastly different. Angel was honest and earnest in her dealings with him.

Or was she? Julien could lie to the old man, a perfect cover for his true purpose. Could Angel do the same? He grudgingly admitted that it was possible. He'd wondered whether she was capable of manipulating the strands she left behind, erasing bits she didn't want him to see. She might be able to hide her true intentions if her power allowed it, but a real-time strand could not be faked. A strand was a bit of the person's essence. A strand never lied.

Julien chuckled, drawing the smell and taste of Angel's climax into his body. That had been no act. For those few moments, Angel had been need unleashed in his hands and his mind.

He rolled off the bed, smiling. He would know what Angel's purpose was soon enough. Julien was highly trained. His body would obey his mind, while Angel could be made a traitor to herself.

Julien pasted on a stern face as he rode the stairpad down to the east exit. Firebrand stood, flicking a blue fireball from hand to hand like a third-year cadet.

"On report," Julien barked, making his displeasure clear.

Firebrand straightened, the fireball flying up into the air and disintegrating into a puff of smoke. He met Julien's eyes, nodding sheepishly. "I deserve it," he admitted.

"It's a week of extra duties this time, isn't it?"

The boy nodded.

"The old man isn't going to be happy," Julien noted.

"I know." Firebrand grimaced at the idea of incurring the old man's wrath.

Julien nodded. "Report to him. Now."

"But, you," he began uncertainly.

"The others will see me back."

Firebrand nodded and turned away, his face showing a good deal of the agony he was feeling at the order Julien gave him. It was a harsh lesson. Being sent back from assignment for a disciplinary was one of the worst things that could happen to a new operative. Rumors would be circulating that Soulchaser was looking to replace Firebrand by the time he hit the Academy.

Chances were that Firebrand feared that very thing. If Julien dismissed him, he would return to police duties, and Firebrand's duties had been high-temperature disposals, some of the most boring work a power could be assigned.

Julien felt for him. Like most Calante, Firebrand would not have chosen to serve, but the law was the law. Powers who did not serve as operatives of the Calante were renegades--Grellan. Their powers represented a sacred trust. The ancient texts stated, "With great power comes great responsibility." The ones born with powers were born to serve. Anyone who refused his or her responsibility to safeguard life and keep the peace broke with that sacred trust.

Firebrand's breach of faith had been a minor one, but minor infractions led to major ones. The humans they protected were unnerved by unnecessary displays of power.

Making the humans fear them defeated the Calante's purpose. Not to mention that Firebrand's actions denoted a lack of control.

Julien mused over his own actions as he took the walkway to Sky Master at the north exit. Was he doing the same things he'd penalized Firebrand for? Unarguably, Julien had been lying to the old man for most of his life, but his lies had been largely unrelated to his missions--until now. Julien sighed. That would change when he reached the Academy.

He was pursuing a sexual relationship with a Grellan suspect, connecting to her consciousness. The fact that he continued on his course had less to do with his duty than his libido, and that was flirting with treason.

* * * *

"Well?" the old man asked impatiently.

Julien scowled at him. "You sent in other operatives before I got there--Seabeast, Birdspeaker and Mindtouch."

Adrien paled, his eyes going wide in shock.

"Yes, old man. I felt their presence, and it interfered with the strands," he accused.

"How--"

"I felt them. I feel everyone to some extent. So, what did Mindtouch tell you?"

He darkened. "Nothing. Nothing that you haven't already told us."

Julien dropped into the chair closest to his desk, rubbing his neck. "You all but ruined my ability to read the strands and got nothing in return?" he asked acidly. "Why did you waste my time?"

"All but ruined it?" Adrien questioned. "Then you got something?"

"Despite your meddling." It wouldn't do to claim that he hadn't gotten anything. Adrien might decide to reassign him. "The fifth Grellan is named Starfire. He is a boy. I'd estimate him at roughly seventeen years old, but he's powerful. He also has an ailment that I haven't managed to nail down yet."

Adrien nodded. "Anything else?"

"Everything else was muddled, trampled. Sending in the others destroys the spin and weave of the strands. Not for the others but for Starfire and Starseeker."

"Very well. I will give you an untainted field next time. You have my word. In trade--" Adrien stroked his chin, seemingly deep in thought.

Julien raised an eyebrow. The old man knew better than to place pressure on an operative when he wanted something. "Yes?"

"Find out how they travel in and out of the city without being detected by the checkpoints and identi-card checks."

"I'll do my best. You know I can only read what is in the strands."

"I know. Get some sleep. You look worn."

Julien smiled weakly and left the office.

He ambled toward his quarters, taking time to watch the younger cadets training with their mentors. Most operatives were given classes to teach once they graduated from police service. Julien was only assigned to the most stubborn of the cadets. Anything else was deemed a waste of his time. At the moment, no one was considered enough of a problem to be sent his way. On some level, it bothered Julien that it was considered a punishment to be one of his students.

Sky Master had three fourth-year students in the smaller skydome, the one with mesh blocking the open sky-panels and a padded floor. Water Demon had her hands full with a reluctant first-year sea-mutant. Many students feared their powers and their trainers, at first. It wasn't unusual, but that didn't make ignoring their distress any easier.

Julien sighed and turned into the training room. The strands of fear from this one were especially strong. If Julien didn't step in now, the child would be sent to the old man, then most likely, assigned to Julien. If he acted now, he might be able to save her the embarrassment and terror of facing Adrien.

Water Demon nodded to him. "You need to speak to me, Soulchaser?" she rasped. As always, she sounded out of breath. The strain of forcing human speech past her uncooperative body style was not something he felt she should attempt.

The child looked at him, stark fear in her pretty lavender eyes.

Julien sank to his knees, ignoring the seawater soaking his pantlegs; the heavy liquid pungent in proteins, electrolytes, and minerals that even the purification system for drinking water couldn't completely remove. He shook his head, reaching to uncover the child's face. She wasn't a gilled mutant like Water Demon was, and her cover was equipped to let her breathe underwater.

"Her name is Sealife," Water Demon offered.

Sealife darkened, her eyes disappearing behind the frosted sea-lenses that most sea-mutants had. It was a protective response that they learned to overcome with time. Sealife forced the lenses back, going a deeper crimson in embarrassment that she had succumbed to that childlike response. Children can be very cruel, Patrice. Yes. If the other young cadets had seen that, they would have been cruel to her, though they might still do it themselves in the same situation.

"Am I in trouble?" she asked meekly.

He smiled. "No. Even if you were, I am not your trainer or one of the trustees. People don't get assigned to me until they have been sent to the trustees. I simply want you to be at ease with your training." And with me. I don't want the children to fear me.

Julien closed his eyes and stroked her bare cheek, letting Sealife's strands weave into his being. She was ten, typical for a first-year cadet. Her powers were primarily in communication with sea animals. The change was jarring, the loss of her life and identity. She was unhappy at the Academy as most first-years were, knowing that they would train for eight years and serve their lifetimes, always alone.

Sealife was more alone than most. She came to the Academy as an orphan. Julien felt for her. When he left his home, he tried to convince himself that he'd see his mother again. The law said he would. The old man said he would. But the old man and the law couldn't hold a candle to fate. Before his first visiting day arrived, Patrice was dead, the victim of a murder that was never solved. His trainers claimed that Julien had simply been a victim of circumstance. There was no chance that he was a precognitive. The tests never revealed that he was, and Julien was thankful for that. That was one power he had never wanted.

He leaned close to her ear, peeling the synth-cloth back over her deep brown hair without opening his eyes. "Do you trust me?" he whispered.

She sucked in her breath in surprise, latching onto his hidden meaning. "Yes." She did. She was desperate for someone she could trust.

"Then I will call you Jennifer--when no one else can hear." Julien opened his eyes as her joy assaulted him. "Would you like that?" he offered loud enough for Water Demon to overhear.

Jennifer threw her arms around his neck and hugged Julien to her damp body. "Yes. Thank you, Soulchaser."

He sobered. Julien could trust Jennifer enough to give her his name, but now was not the time to give the old man a hold over him. Julien had avoided that for half of his life. "For every deal, payment comes due," he warned her. "You promise to follow Water Demon's instructions?"

"I do." Jennifer scrambled to the edge of the seawater pool and straightened her synth-cloth cover over her head and face. She slid into the water with a wave at Julien.

Water Demon watched her go, her short, pointed teeth showing in her gaping mouth. "What did you promise her?"

Julien pushed to his feet. "A little normal conversation," he lied.

"Thank you for your assistance. I would have had to send her to the old man soon."

"Your unit is your family," he quoted the Academy teachings.

Julien left quickly, something nameless eating at his gut. No. His relationship with Water Demon wasn't a family. His new friendship with Jennifer was more of a family than his unit was to him. He'd never considered telling his unit his true name. It never hurt to hold it back from them. He wanted to tell Jennifer, and he wanted to tell Angel. What Angel had with her unit was a family. No one was afraid to use anyone else's true name.

He shook away that thought. Julien remembered family, though it was a family where he couldn't call his father by his true name. He also remembered how fragile that link was. Julien should have had two more years with his mother, but after the Grellan killed his father, the old man convinced his mother to turn him over early--for his protection.

Julien still wondered at that. The Grellan were seldom seen. They seldom killed Calante. Even if Empathen was one of the rare casualties, why would Julien be in danger? At the time, he had been nothing but an untrained child.

Chapter Four

Julien closed the door to the living quarters, cursing himself for his lack of patience. It had been ten days since he'd contacted Angel, but it felt like months. His dreams had been full of nothing but her, and Julien had woken hard and needing more nights than he cared to remember.

He kicked off his shoes, letting the carpet caress the soles of his feet. The strands surrounded him, making his senses swim in the flood of knowledge. He knew these people intimately--all but the two he needed to know. Julien laid his jacket on the back of a chair, stopping long enough to take in a clear memory of Angel. She hated blackberries with a passion.

Julien smiled as he unzipped his cover, sliding it off his shoulders. He tossed it over the jacket then pulled a packet from the pocket. Julien picked up the beacon, letting it lay heavily in his hand for a long moment. No. Angel wanted proof of his trust. If he was going to prove that, he had to go to her conspicuously empty-handed. He shoved the beacon back in the cover pocket and fingered the condom he still held. Well, not entirely empty-handed.

He took a deep breath and strode to the bedroom door. Her scent tantalized him. The feeling of her body surrounded him. Julien closed his eyes, giving himself up to the connection.

Angel's mouth was on his; tasting, teasing, demanding. Her hands traced over his chest and pushed, guiding him back to the door. Julien moaned as her mouth left his. She nipped at his jaw, rubbing the tips of her breasts over his male nipples. Julien's half-erect cock rose, matching his skyrocketing need. He bent his knees, capturing her mouth as he rubbed the head in the moisture gathering for him. Angel gasped as she rocked over him in invitation.

"You know what I want," Julien whispered. He reminded himself that he should remain in control, but something about Angel defied that concept.

"No. We can't. Not unless you trust me."

Julien cupped her buttocks, pulling Angel's body tight to his. The urge to ease inside her beat at his tenuous self-control. He wanted it too much, much more than was prudent. And, she'd refused. Julien couldn't take her, even this way, without permission.

He nipped at her ear. "What do you want from me? Why do you want me to come to you like this?" A sneaking suspicion that she was trying to drive him crazy settled in his mind.

"You have to trust me."

"I can't. You know that I can't."

"You're here with me. You're completely unguarded." Her smile widened. "You even left your beacon behind, yet I have made no move to injure you. Part of you wants to trust me."

Angel rocked against his length, coating him in the sensation of her fluids. "Or maybe you just want this," she mused.

Yes. Oh, gods alive, yes! "No. Trust me, and I will trust you."

"How?"

"Tell me how you travel. How do you get in and out of the city without being seen?"

"When you trust me completely, I will trust you with that." Angel bit at his lower lip. "Ask something else," she invited.

"How did you form your family?" The question was out before Julien analyzed why he would want to know it.

Angel looked at him in surprise. She kissed him, her tongue tangling with his. Julien gasped as memories of Angel and Anthony stumbling through the wilderness sifted into his mind. They were ragged, dirty, and bloodied. Debra found them and took them to the others.

Julien nodded. "And your parents?"

"Dead. Killed by the Calante." There was no animosity in that statement, just a deep sadness.

"Interesting," he noted. Julien found her breast more interesting, the nipple turning to a peak at his touch.

"Is it?" she asked, mirroring motions with the same results from his body.

Julien met her eyes. "It is.." He watched her for a response, carefully gauging her emotions in the strands that surrounded them. "Your parents were killed by Calante. My father was killed by Grellan."

Angel gasped, her eyes going wide. Strands of disbelief and confusion wound around her, almost but not completely masking a single strand of sadness and anger entwined.

"Very interesting, don't you think?" he asked.

She nodded. "You must hate us," she whispered.

Julien stroked her breast again. He should hate them, but with Angel in his arms, her consciousness touching his, hate was the last thing on his mind. "I want you," he admitted.

Angel eased down his body. "Trust me as I trusted you."

He barely had time to question what she meant when Angel's mouth closed around his cock and slid deep around him. His hands fisted against the door, fisted on a condom that Julien vaguely realized he should put on. There was no fear of infection or pregnancy. Rather, without a physical body encasing him, Julien would come into the air, a mess he would have to eradicate later.

He watched her taking him into the heat of her mouth, encasing him in a slice of paradise. This had always been his favorite way to come. Julien bit his lip. The condom be damned! He'd scrub at the stain before he'd make her stop what she was doing.

Julien panted, as she became more insistent. The suction of her mouth increased, inviting him to forget his careful control. Long red, ringlets of her hair teased his inner thigh, and one of her breasts brushed the skin above his knee. Angel's fingers traced the taut muscles of his legs, cupping the swollen sac beneath his cock. Her fingernails scraped lightly as she forced him deep inside.

His lungs ceased to function for a moment, and bright colors swam before his eyes. The instant of release crashed over him. Julien allowed a shuddering groan to pass his lips as he gave in to the need to surrender control to her. Her mouth continued to move, forcing his body past the peak and toward another.

Julien sank to his knees, and Angel went with him. He wound his hands in her hair, watching her take him ruthlessly. "Please," he begged. Anything. Almost anything, he corrected himself.

The second climax came faster. There was a vague sensation of heat--a realization of fluid on his hands. Julien's mind argued that she wasn't real, but that thought was washed away as aftershocks shook him. Angel was real. She was more real than any person Julien had met since he started his training. There were no masks, no fake names, no fake emotions or lack of them.

She released his length and pushed up his body, her breasts pressing to the wall of his chest and her breath hot on his mouth. Angel teased at his lips, sucking in first the top and then the bottom slowly. That simply, he wanted her again.

Her hand feathered over his cheek. "You are completely unguarded, at your weakest physically and emotionally," she reminded him. "I want nothing but your trust." Angel kissed him passionately, stroking at his body. "Trust me, Soulchaser."

"What must I do to prove that I trust you?" Almost anything...

"You know how a Calante shows trust. Prove you trust me, and you will have everything you desire most."

"What do I desire most?" he asked weakly.

/"Family. Freedom. The truth." She brushed her curls over his half-grown cock. "And me."

Julien nodded. She knew everything he wanted most, but he had a duty. Julien had taken vows. But, not of my own choice. If I didn't serve, I would have been hunted down. "I--" I want to. Gods, how I want to.

Angel nodded. "Come to me again."

He groaned. Julien wanted her desperately, but having her meant breaking the most sacred of laws, trusting a Grellan and telling her his true name. "I shouldn't," he replied miserably.

"You will," she replied confidently. "Even if you don't desire me that much, you want the other things I've offered. You want the truth."

Julien gathered her close to his body. "I want you," he assured her.

Angel faded from his arms then from his mind. "When you trust me." She was gone, the last of her strands disappearing with her.

He growled in frustration. Julien knelt in a dim room, his come on his hands and the carpet. He wanted her desperately. What kind of a damned fool was he that he wanted her this much?

Julien retrieved a cloth from the bathroom and started cleaning the evidence of his treason. He shouldn't go to her again, but he would. Angel represented everything Julien wanted, but taking it would make him Grellan like she was.

* * * *

Angel launched off of the bed, pulling on her robe. They damn well should have told me, she fumed. She stormed into the main room, taking in the hazy sunshine filtering through the vines over the windows in annoyance.

Debra looked at her in concern. "What is it?"

"They told him we killed his father," Angel exploded. "How am I supposed to get him to trust me this way?"

Paul sighed, pinching the bridge of his nose between two callused fingers. "What did you expect them to tell him? The truth?"

"Soulchaser--" Angel blushed. She wasn't talking to him now. "Sorry. I have to think of him as Soulchaser. If I don't, I may say something stupid."

Debra nodded. "He has to offer his name willingly. The shock of hearing it from you without that step could be catastrophic to him. Julien has not heard his name spoken aloud since the night Jake died."

"He is so fragile," Angel whispered.

Paul nodded. "It is what the Calante do to their kind, what the Academies and their service do."

Debra sighed. "We made a promise to Jake--The adults did, but you are not bound by it. If you would rather not do this--"

"No," Angel gasped. "No. I owe Jake that much. I--owe Jake everything." She retreated to her room, pressing a shaking hand to her stomach, glad that Anthony was off somewhere with Sylvia and not here to feel her reliving that horrible moment. Even if Angel didn't want Julien, she owed it to Jake to save his son. The moment Jake placed himself between her and death, Angel vowed as much.

Chapter Five

Julien smiled as Jennifer collapsed in a giggling fit. He motioned to the book in her hand. "It's true. There was a time on Earth when there were no powers. People depended solely on human police and weapons to keep themselves safe. There were wars and violence in the streets--not like we have now. I mean that there were murders every week in any large city you visited. It was a truly frightening way to live."

"Is that why our people came to Suraden?" she asked solemnly.

He nodded. "Earth had torn itself apart before the age of the powers. When Dr. Suraden discovered this world, those with the means to make the trip came here for a new life."

"But there were no powers among them?" she asked curiously.

"No. There were not. According to the early histories of our world, the powers stayed on Earth to protect those who needed them most."

"Then how did the powers get here? Did they settle the upheavals on Earth and come to help us?"

Julien sighed. He'd always thought that even pure humans should be taught the tales. As it was, the only cadets who came to the Academy with a firm grasp of history were those who were raised by parents who were both operatives, those few who chose to live inside the main complex.

"Every human has within them the potential to mutate to a power--to a higher form of being with the ability to protect. It only took a few dozen generations for the mutants to begin appearing among us, the blessed first few who formed the first Academy."

Jennifer nodded, taking up the stories she'd only recently learned. "Anicore, who was once known as Calan, Sky

Father, who was once known as Thomas, and Mind Mother, who was once known as Grelda."

He nodded his approval. "Go on."

"They disagreed. Anicore believed that the Academy should adopt the ideals set forth by the ancients on Earth. Mind Mother wanted to start fresh, to create a new system for a new world. In the end, they battled. Sky Father and the others who supported Anicore gathered in the inner cities and called themselves the Calante. Those who supported Mind Mother mobilized in the outer ring cities and called themselves the Grellan.

"The tales don't say why they disagreed. Why would Mind Mother reject a system that had worked so well on Earth? The massive wars before the time of the powers all but destroyed Earth, but humans were gaining peace and prosperity under the powers' protection."

"On a broken world that would take centuries to fix, if it could be fixed at all," Julien reminded her. "I don't know why Mind Mother balked at the system."

Then why am I questioning it so much lately? It was treason to question the laws that guided the Calante, but the more Julien looked at his existence--at the world he and those like him inhabited, the more seemingly unnecessary hardships he noticed. Was this what the Mind Mother foresaw? Perhaps the Academies on Earth hadn't been in place long enough to gauge long-term psychological effects.

Julien shook off that thought. No matter what her reasons, Mind Mother led a civil uprising against the Academy. The battles of the first few generations were bloody and brutal. What possible defense could there be for causing such unrest on a peaceful world?

"I don't know her reasons," he repeated. "The histories don't say why, but she started a war over it, the only war on Suraden."

The victors write the histories. His father told Julien that not long before he died. Empathen--Jake, his mind supplied his father's name, the name that it was illegal for him to say aloud--believed in that saying enough to teach Julien that it was true, but had Jake been wrong? After all, the Grellan killed Empathen. Were the old tales wrong? Or was Jake the one who had been wrong?

* * * *

Julien nodded to the old man grimly as he took his seat across the desk.

Adrien steepled his hands, a sure sign that he wasn't sure what to do with Julien. It was a pose that he had seen often since the old man lost the ability to read his mind eleven years earlier. "I wanted to speak to you about the last time you went to a scene."

He nodded, forcing down a mixture of panic and embarrassment behind a careful mask of indifference. It had been three days. Julien had felt he was safe from any backlash after two. He should have known not to allow himself to become complacent. "I've debriefed that account for you," he noted calmly.

"Everything?" he asked pointedly.

"Anything of use to us." That was a safe enough answer. "You always trained us to disregard extraneous knowledge."

"Then tell me everything."

Julien furrowed his brow, as if in confusion. "Why don't you tell me what has you confused," he countered, a bold challenge of the old man's authority. Why am I doing this? He can crush me. Only if he believes I am guilty of something. Yes. This tack might work.

Adrien darkened in fury. Strands of it escaped the old man's tactician control. "You masturbated there. Explain that, Soulchaser."

Julien smiled, shaking his head while he fervently searched for a lie that would save him from that synth-cloth-padded room. "Night Warrior and Moon Current are a couple, a married couple. They--engaged in some rather interesting sexual antics, and I encountered the strands. I have a man's needs. Play a memory of sex complete with wisps of sensation, and I respond. But, their antics were hardly important to the report."

"So, you are sitting there telling me that you beat off to their mental sex tape on assignment?" he demanded incredulously.

Julien allowed a blush to creep into his cheeks. That sure as hell beats admitting the truth. "It was less of a distraction than trying to sift around it. You know that letting strands play out is easier than ignoring them." He scowled. "Even

88

when strands are murders." He reminded Adrien of his early days on street crime. Julien had paid his dues in the nightmare images that would haunt him for the rest of his days.

"There is nothing else you have to tell me?" He was testing Julien's shield again, trying to gauge him for a lie.

"Nothing."

"Then go about your duties," he ordered.

Julien nodded and headed to the door, trailing his fingers over the surface of the old man's desk deliberately. Adrien seemed not to notice. Perhaps, he viewed the move in amusement. Julien wasn't sure what he intended even as he did it. The old man never left strands for Julien to read. Either he spent all day in synth-cloth to avoid a repeat of their first night together, or he used a comm unit of some sort to wipe his office clean before Julien came in.

No. He hadn't used a comm unit. There were strong strands in the room. Three first-years had been to the office that morning. One of them was Jennifer. Her terror made Julien ache for her.

He stilled as Visionchaser's essence assaulted his mind. The trustee had always been high-strung, and his panic was not unusual, but the panic wasn't what stopped Julien.

The memory was crisp. Visionchaser--Larry Meyer--sat forward with his fingertips pressed to the desktop. "What if he's become a traitor like his father?"

"We will handle it as we did the last time," Adrien answered calmly.

The vision was gone as quickly as it had come. Julien lifted his hand and ambled toward the door.

"Something interesting, Soulchaser?" Adrien drawled in that same suspicious, challenging tone.

"Sealife was in to see you, and she was very upset. I should check on her."

"You spend quite a bit of time with her," he noted.

"She's a smart little girl, and she's very powerful. Sealife will be a handsome asset to a unit someday, better than Water Demon, by far."

"Ah. I see. You're recruiting from the cadets again."

Julien forced a predatory smile onto his face. "A good leader never rests."

Adrien chuckled, but there was something uneasy in his manner. "No. He doesn't."

Julien headed for his quarters, barely taking note of the cadets at their training, waving distractedly as Firebrand instructed third-year cadets in fireball control.

Traitor? If there was any question in his mind that Visionchaser meant himself and Jake, Julien might not be so affected, but there was no question. The strand left no doubt. Julien couldn't argue that he was acting the part of a traitor, but had Jake done the same? Perhaps, not a sexual encounter. That was unlikely. By all accounts, Jake doted on Patrice. Still, there were other forms of treason.

Julien closed the door to his quarters slowly. His eyes locked on the shelf lined with his father's mementos and medals. Pieces of Jake's life and not a single strand of his father's essence to lead Julien, not a single memory to tell the truth.

I have to think logically. What do I have of him to guide me? The answer came, but Julien resisted it. Jake taught him. He left pieces of his wisdom behind for his son to learn from. The problem was that Julien always argued what Jake taught him versus what his training said. Maybe he needed to take every comment as a truth and see where it led him. What did he teach me?

The victors write the histories. The histories of Suraden were written by the Calante. That was suspect. If the histories were suspect, the axioms and accepted truths were suspect. The Grellan might not be what he had been taught they were.

For every rule, there is an exception. Julien was brought into service two years early. No cadet was brought into service early unless his or her powers posed a danger to child or society--except Julien. Perhaps, there were other exceptions. Was every Grellan a traitor? Should even the laws that governed the Calante be absolute? But, what were the acceptable reasons for an exception?

Julien shrugged off that maddening idea. Until a few moments earlier, he hadn't acknowledged the possibility that the rules might not be absolute. Defining it further was too much for his mind to process.

Always trust your gut instinct about people. Who did Julien trust? Jake and Patrice topped the list, but that was a dead end. He groaned at his own pun. Jennifer? Yes. Julien trusted Jennifer, but it wasn't wise to show that openly. Using her name showed less vulnerability than allowing her to use his. Did he trust Angel?

Julien shifted nervously. Don't use your mind, he reminded himself. Don't think what you were trained to think. From the gut. Do you trust Angel? Logic was the wrong course. Logic said that he should trust the old man, but Julien never had. He took a deep breath. It was time for another of Jake's teachings.

Have faith that your heart will lead you. When you meet a true confidant, you will ache to bare your soul to her. Julien nodded, biting back a laugh. He trusted Angel. He'd always wanted to trust her on some instinctive level.

Chapter Six

Angel took a deep breath, stretching out on the bed and following the draw of Soulchaser's mind. He looked up as she approached, nervous. He was fully dressed. Angel sighed. She'd pushed too far the last time. His loss of control must have shaken him.

She smiled. "I've made you uncomfortable. I'm sorry."

He shook his head, pulling Angel into his arms and covering her mouth with his. His movements were urgent, a pressing need that made her ache for him. A week had been too long.

Angel groaned, reminding herself that it was only his mind she was touching, only a simulation she felt--the interaction of thoughts and desires.

"I want you," he breathed into her ear.

She shivered. Angel wanted it, too. She'd dreamed of allowing him free rein, but she'd set a rule for him, a level of trust he had to prove to her. "Not until--"

"I trust you."

Angel blinked. She pulled back to meet his eyes. "You--" She had to have misheard him. It was too much to hope that she had been successful so quickly.

"My name is Julien," he whispered. His eyes darted about as if he would be punished for saying it aloud.

She gasped in surprise, nodding. "Julien." Angel was dumbstruck. He'd actually said it. For weeks, she'd wondered what she would do if he gave her a fake name to try and trick her, and he told her the truth.

He blushed. "Yes.."

Angel touched his face. "Welcome back to the land of the living, Julien Cross."

His eyes widened. "You've always known?"

She nodded. "You had to offer me that trust. Thank you." Her mind whirled, and her body heated. She drew his hand to her breast. "I made you a promise," she reminded him. Angel should be securing his safety, but rewarding his trust had to come first.

Julien stared at his hand, swallowing hard. "Not here. They suspect too much. I need--I need to give them something, something significant to throw them off my trail." He met her eyes hopefully. "Or will you tell me how to get past the checkpoints? If I leave now--You promised."

"I can't show you now. You'll have to come to me one more time."

Julien tried to rein in his disappointment, but Angel felt it clearly across the connection. He nodded, biting back a grimace that he had to go back to them. For a mad moment, Angel considered finding a way to free him immediately, but there was no way she and Anthony could arrange that on such short notice.

Angel shook her head. "I will take you safely out, but you have to come to me at a pre-arranged time, and you must trust me."

He nodded, a shaky nod. "Where and when?"

"Six days from now at sunset. Come to the place where you first touched me. Julien--" She bit her lip.

"Yes?"

"You do trust me, don't you? You would leave with me now, if you could?"

He took a calming breath. "Yes. I trust you implicitly." Julien wound his hand in her hair.

Angel sighed in relief. "Good. Then I promise that you'll leave with me that night."

He grimaced. "I still need something to tell them. What can I tell them?"

She smiled. "Tell them we are operating out of the armory outside the north gate of the city. Tell them now, as soon as you get downstairs."

His eyes widened. "If I do--"

"Hurry. Use your comm unit if you want to. I guarantee you will miss us by minutes, no matter what you do."

"They will track you down. My unit is the best."

"Impossible. Run, Julien. I'll race you. Do you remember that game?"

He nodded and turned toward the door.

"Run, Julien. Make a good show for them."

Angel returned to her body, as he bolted for the door, pulling his comm unit from his jacket pocket and switching it on. The race was on.

She launched into the main room, smiling widely. Julien trusted her. He'd come with them.

Debra looked up in surprise. "Angel," she admonished. "You're--"

Angel waved her off. She would have to be naked to make the jump. It was simply her appearance this way that caught Debra off guard. "We're leaving. Take anything of importance."

Sylvia gaped at her. "He's turned us in," she managed weakly.

Angel laughed aloud. "No. He hasn't. But, to save him, we have to let it seem he's almost caught us. Hurry. They are on their way."

The others scattered. They carried little with them, so collecting their belongings took only a moment. The helos were already approaching when Anthony grasped her hand. Sylvia looked at them nervously. This would be a close one but not their closest. She and Anthony wrapped the others in their shared power. They were long gone before the door burst open.

* * * *

Julien kept his expression studiously neutral. She'd done it. Angel had escaped without a trace. He moved through the room, touching items at random. "They've been here fairly steadily for more than two months." *The whole time they have been playing cat and mouse with me.* "The strands are strong. They've only been gone for a few minutes."

"How?" Firebrand demanded.

Julien shook his head. He stopped as a particularly strong mix of power, nervousness, and giddy happiness coursed through his body. Julien sank to the floor, closing his eyes as he opened himself fully to the sensations.

"What is it?" Sky Master asked.

Julien raised a hand to silence him then returned it to the floor. The pulse coursed through him again, an elusive strand. He drew it into himself and turned his face up.

Angel smiled as Anthony took her hand. Light surrounded them. It was beautiful but bright. Julien winced. Too bright! The sensation started at his toes and rushed up his body, a sense of loosing himself, of being sucked down a vortex of light and sound.

Julien threw himself out of the circle with a vicious curse. His eyes snapped open, but the colors remained, blinding colors that sent shards of pain through his mind. For a moment, the sensation of mind and body disassociating persisted. Julien fought back his panic, taking a wild swing at Sky Master when the older man reached for him. He didn't know what this was. If Sky Master touched Julien, it might well kill him.

He cried out as the sensation eased. His strangled breathing smoothed, and Julien relaxed to the floor. Everything seemed to dim. Colors were muted and dull.

Sky Master checked his pulse. "Medical, now," he ordered.

"What the hell was that?" Firebrand roared.

"Med-flight. STAT," Water Demon rasped into the comm unit. "It's Soulchaser."

"No," Julien managed weakly. "The strands." He grasped at Sky Master's cover, his muscles leaden and uncertain. Julien stared at his shaking hand in dismay. "No. The strands." The electronics would destroy the weave.

"Easy," Sky Master soothed him. "We lost this round. Whatever that was is better destroyed, Soulchaser."

Julien's protest was lost in the sound of a helo's turbines. Medical red filled his vision as his eyes slid shut.

* * * *

"He's coming up, sir."

Julien couldn't place that voice. It was female, not a woman he knew.

"Good," Adrien growled.

Julien licked his lips. His mouth was dry and his body ached.

"Soulchaser," the first voice called again. "I know you can hear me, Soulchaser. Give me a sign."

Julien forced his eyes open. The sea lavender walls swam before him. He cursed softly. They stuck him in medical. No operative wanted to end up in medical. For some reason, the med-techs always believed in putting the powers through hell when they were in, as if they were fragile.

"He knows where he is," Adrien chuckled.

Julien swung his eyes back to Adrien, moving tenderly. He took in the doctor in surprise, scanning his eyes over the white identi-card on her red work cover. "Human?" he asked.

She nodded. "We do have some talents," she teased.

"I'm sorry. I just thought--"

"Quite all right. We were closer."

"What the hell happened?" Julien demanded weakly, trying to raise an arm to rub his neck, and finding the task nearly impossible.

"Medically? Shock complicated by an electrical imbalance--roughly the same thing that would happen if you got hit by a sonic wave unit blast coupled with a lightening strike," she answered dryly.

"Lovely," he growled. "That's about what it felt like."

She winced. "You're stuck here overnight," she informed him. "After that, your own people will handle you--beside the ones they have camped in the hall protecting you now."

"How long have I been out?"

"Overnight." She headed to the door, nodding to Adrien. "He's stable, sir. I'll leave you alone now."

Adrien smiled warmly. "My thanks, doctor, and the Calante's thanks as well." The old man waited until the door closed behind her. When he turned back to Julien, the smile was gone. "What the hell did you think you were doing, Soulchaser?"

"My job. How was I supposed to know it would bite back?"

"You're trained to know."

"You didn't train me for that," Julien groused.

"What precisely was that?"

"If I knew what it was, I would have been trained for it."

Adrien glared at him.

Julien sighed. He was too damn tired to spar with the old man today. "I don't know. Light. Pain. A feeling that I wasn't--there."

Adrien nodded. "Understood. Who did it?"

"Did?" he asked in confusion.

"Which of the Grellan tried to kill you?" Adrien asked impatiently.

"Kill me? You think that was a trap?"

"Of course. It's the same way they killed your father. Luckily, you have faster reflexes than Empathen did."

Julien let his anger have free rein, though he hid his mind carefully. He was angry, and Adrien would accept that, but Julien wouldn't let the old man know why he was angry. Julien had no doubts that Adrien was lying to him.

We will handle it as we did last time.

Julien pasted on a weak smile. "Yes. I watch my back much better than Empathen did."

Chapter Seven

Julien took a deep breath, scanning his eyes over his quarters, hopefully for the last time. He couldn't take anything with him. It would look suspicious if he did. He straightened his mandarin collar and smoothed the shirtfront over his dress slacks. Julien took another deep breath. It was show time.

He ambled through the corridors, waving to other powers as he went, assuring those who asked that he was fit and ready to return to duty when his ten-day restriction from duty was lifted. Julien smiled and handed his identi-card to the guard at the door.

"Afternoon, Soulchaser," Ice Warden greeted him. "Have to check the database."

Julien raised an eyebrow. "For?"

"Have to make sure you're cleared for this."

He nodded. That wasn't surprising. Julien had spent the day after his release from the civilian medical center in the Academy medical wing. The following two days, Julien had been confined to his quarters then the Academy. He had begun to worry that he would still be on lockdown when Angel came for him.

Ice Warden grinned, his pale blue eyes crinkling over his snow-white cheeks. He handed Julien's identi-card back. "All clear, Soulchaser. Have a nice day."

"I will. I haven't had a full day out for a long time."

"With great power comes great responsibility," he quoted.

Julien nodded. "Yes. It does."

* * * *

It didn't take Julien long to realize that he was being followed. The three operatives were good, but they weren't good enough.

With more than five hundred operatives and cadets in the city, it was a given that other operatives had the day off. They were all dressed in civilian clothes as Julien was. Any power capable of blending into the populace did so to avoid the usual power-chasers, humans who wanted to bed powers for the thrill or for bragging rights. Of course, their identi-cards would identify them when they paid, but most operatives frequented establishments that were discreet about what they were.

The identi-cards told even the most casual observer all they needed to know. If the standard white card was edged in green, the bearer was a cadet through fourth year. Blue denoted an older cadet. Yellow marked an operative, and red marked a unit leader like Julien. Only metallic gold outranked him. Gold marked a trustee.

No. They might have been operatives out for R and R, but they weren't. After Julien noted two of the three in each of his first two stops, a coffee shop and a bookstore, he purposely led them all over the city. As he expected, two of the given three appeared at the music shop and clotherie he chose to visit.

Then came the acid test. Julien chose a restaurant near the tower he needed that was typically overrun with power-chasers, not the type of place that most operatives would frequent. Even cadets tired of power-chasers quickly, once the novelty wore off.

Julien sipped his coffee, glancing at the two who followed him in through his lashes. What now? If he went to Angel, he'd lead these three bozos in. If he didn't go, he'd blow his chance at everything she offered.

He went to the restroom, considering slipping out a window or a back door, but one of the operatives followed him in. Julien went about a normal bathroom routine, checking his watch critically. It was less than an hour until sunset. Whatever he did, Julien would have to do it soon.

Julien nodded to the operative at the sink on his way past, resisting the urge to brush past him to gain momentary access to the man's thoughts. There was no need for it. Julien knew who sent them, and he knew their aim. What else did he need to know?

He needed somewhere the operatives couldn't follow him, but where was that? Their clearance would have been expanded to match his own. There was nowhere Julien could access that they couldn't. He was still considering his predicament as he paid his bill.

The hand that touched his as Julien accepted his identi-card back shouldn't have surprised him. Julien had chosen this restaurant for its reputation for power-chasers, after all. The strands of her blatant invitation settled in his groin, and Julien shivered in response.

She leaned close to his ear, her full breasts brushing over his arm. "Interested?" she purred.

Julien took her hand, searching the connection. "Depends," he answered. An idea took shape. If this one wasn't optimum to his purpose, perhaps another would be. If it meant getting to Angel, Julien would dust off his wild days of bedding power-chasers. He knew how to make it clear he was available, and a red card was a ticket to any woman he wanted--if he used it right. Few unit leaders played the game.

The information came in no certain order, as usual. She was twenty-five, an only child. Her name was Elaine. She had her own apartment. Stunning! Elaine was a major player. Soulchaser would be her seventeenth power. Her quarters were close. Good sign. They were in the same tower as the quarters Julien had to reach, second floor, outside access.

Julien grinned and kissed her knuckles. "Ever been with a psychic operative, Elaine?" She hadn't. He knew that, and he knew the challenge of a new conquest--a unit leader, no less--would convince her to jump at almost anything he suggested.

"My place is--"

"Tower 1022," he teased, kissing her hand again. "Shall we go?"

Julien smiled the whole way to her quarters. This would work. The operatives didn't dare follow him into Elaine's quarters. Better, their spread would be by the book: in the hall, at the back stairpad, and in the lobby. It would be a full twenty minutes before they'd cover the other exits. They wouldn't call in backup until they were sure that Julien intended to take his time about the liaison.

Elaine wasted no time, turning into his arms as soon as the door shut behind them. Julien allowed himself a single moment of reveling in her urgency. It had been more than three years since Julien had gone home with a power-chaser. He'd forgotten how wild sex could get when it was one who enjoyed the game.

Thirty-seven minutes, he reminded himself. Julien broke off the kiss. "Undress for me."

Elaine smiled. She stepped back, pulling off her form-fitting mini-dress and kicking off her shoes. There was nothing else to her outfit. Elaine had gone trolling for a power, and she was ready for the natural conclusion. She reached for his clothes.

Julien pulled her hands away, shaking his head at her look of confusion. "If that's what you want, why did you choose me?" he teased.

Her eyes widened. "What did you have in mind?"

He advanced on her. "Would you rather the bed or the lounge?"

She hesitated. "The bed."

Julien motioned his head toward the bedroom, adding a hungry look that was not entirely for show. He followed Elaine in, trying to ignore the sway of her hips.

Elaine sat on the edge of the bed, striking a sultry pose with her shoulders thrown back and her breasts offered up.

"What are you going to do, Soulchaser?" Her breathing was quick, already heavy in excitement.

"Promise me anything, and I will give you the ultimate rush."

Her cheeks darkened. "Which is?"

"I'll make you come without touching you--at all." The challenge was made. He knew from experience that the answer wouldn't take long. Either Elaine would jump at the chance, or she would ask him to define what she would be giving in return. With the level she played at, chances were that she would accept outright.

"What should I do?"

"Lie back. Close your eyes. Let go for me."

She did the first two. The third wasn't happening. Julien sat at the edge of the bed. He leaned over Elaine and kissed her. She relaxed into the more familiar idea of his hands on her. Julien eased back, sending the appropriate sensations to her mind.

Elaine bowed her chest up to the sensation of his mouth. Her arousal washed over him, and Julien stroked his aching cock in response. He closed his eyes, using Elaine's mind to drive the encounter.

She groaned as he supplied fingers stroking at her clit. "I thought you said you wouldn't touch," she taunted.

Julien snapped his eyes open, checking his watch. Twenty-two minutes. He eased off the bed and strode to the open door, lounging against the frame with a grin. "I'm not," he assured her.

Elaine looked at him in surprise, and Julien mentally eased his fingers inside her. She shifted her legs wider to accommodate him as if the hand were a physical body.

"Soulchaser," she gasped. He'd heard that voice before.

"Close your eyes, Elaine. Imagine what you want me to do." That step wasn't necessary for him to do this. Julien had used this trick many times before. Women got off on watching the hands and mouth that weren't really there, but Julien couldn't let Elaine watch him. It was better to let her think he needed her eyes closed.

She nodded, closing her eyes. Julien rewarded her with a slow lick over her clit that had her arching off of the bed. Julien nodded and slid from the room silently. He crossed the main room, placing his forehead against the glass door and willing his arousal back. If Julien wasn't careful, he would climax with Elaine.

That was how this particular game started. In Julien's earliest days with the power-chasers, he would make this offer. He'd stand close beside his partner, unclothed and ready, feeding his arousal off of hers until just before her climax. When Julien suggested the repayment he wanted, none of the women ever balked. He made a habit of delaying his release just long enough for the woman's crest to dim to a glow before he brought the head of his cock to her lips--

Julien forced his eyes open. Not this time. Angel is waiting. He checked his watch. Nineteen minutes. Julien forced his mind to two levels, his thinking mind handling his strategy while his semi-conscious layer handled Elaine. It was no different than following strands when you didn't allow yourself to become immersed in the flow, he reminded himself.

He opened the door and eased through. Julien raced up the outside emergency stairs. At three floors up, he started checking the corner doors. It was six floors before he found one that was both unoccupied and unlocked.

Julien closed himself inside and checked his watch. Fourteen minutes. He laughed aloud at the sound of an Academy helo. "Just in time," he mused.

He hurried through the corridors to the north corner and took the stairs further up. It was another five floors up, and Julien was winded by the time he reached the thirteenth floor. He shook in a mixture of exhaustion and sexual tension, but Julien couldn't risk using the lifts, as he couldn't risk using his identi-card to unlock doors.

Julien was keeping Elaine at the edges of release, holding off the moment when she would discover his absence as long as he could. Once that happened, the operatives would search for him, and a search of the tower wouldn't take nearly long enough for Julien's comfort. He checked his watch, groaning.

"Five minutes," he groused.

Julien checked the corridor carefully and strode to the quarters as if he belonged there. He grumbled a complaint as he kept Elaine from going over yet again. I wonder if I could screw her into unconsciousness, he thought bitterly.

Julien sighed. There was little chance of that, though it would solve his current problem. If Elaine were unconscious, she couldn't alert his shadows that Julien had ducked them.

He pushed at the door to the quarters he needed, praying for miracles and smiling at his luck--or Angel's planning. The door was unlocked. Julien slid inside and locked it behind him. Two minutes.

It was becoming more difficult to hold Elaine off--and to order her not to seek him out with her eyes. She was begging for release, desperate for it. *Two minutes*, he begged. *Just two minutes, and I will give you the orgasm of a lifetime.*

Julien pressed his back to the door, waiting for a tap behind him announcing Angel's arrival. He shook his head in disbelief as the blaze of white light filled the center of the near-empty room. His eyes watered, but Julien couldn't look away. Angel and Anthony stepped out of the light, and it faded away. Julien started swearing fluently.

Chapter Eight

Angel smiled at the sight of Julien. He was really here. It was over. Her smile disappeared as he started pacing, running a shaking hand through his hair.

"You are fucking crazy if you think I'm doing that again," he growled. Julien rubbed his forehead, groaning. "Dammit! I am completely and utterly screwed."

"What is it?" she asked, confused and frightened by his explosion.

"I got distracted and let her come," he informed her miserably. "Now she knows I'm gone, and--" He stilled, paling. Julien shook his head, his jaw tight in fury. "Oh, yeah. Just perfect. They know. I can't go back now. I am so screwed."

"You want to go back?" Angel asked indignantly. *What the hell am I risking myself for?*

Anthony gestured frantically.

Angel waved him off. "I am well aware that we have ten minutes or less if they are searching the tower," she snapped. She planted her hands on her hips. "I asked you a question, Julien."

Julien laughed harshly. "Well, I don't want to travel that way again. It damn near killed me the last time. Thank you very much for that warning, by the way. I suppose I'm facing a choice of death or a synth-cloth padded cell. Lovely choice, but what do I have to lose?"

Angel groaned. "So like your father. You tapped into the power and almost got sucked along?" she asked urgently. Angel knew it was a possibility, but when Julien hadn't appeared on the other side, she assumed he hadn't chanced investigating a power level so high.

His eyes widened. "He did die that way," Julien accused.

"Not at all. Jake was smart enough not to fight it. Thankfully, fighting it didn't kill you. It could have. That was why I needed your absolute trust." She smiled weakly. "If you hadn't fought it, the jump site would have brought you straight to us, and this would all be unnecessary."

"You could have told me that," he groused. Julien stilled. "You knew my father?"

Angel went to him and took his hands, leading Julien further into the room. They were running out of time. "Yes. I did." She vaguely noted Anthony returning to the jump point.

"How did he die? The Grellan didn't kill him, did they?"

"No. We didn't. I will give you the whole truth when we are safe. Please trust me."

He nodded slowly, seemingly lost in the revelation that Angel was so intimately tied to him. Angel sighed. Stunned was nearly as good as accepting. It would have to be enough.

Anthony took one of her hands, casting nervous looks at Julien.

She nodded, tugging Julien's body to hers and holding his gaze locked with hers. "Trust me," she whispered.

The energy wrapped around them. Anthony raised the level gradually, letting Julien accept it in gradients.

Julien cupped her cheek in one hand. "Promise me."

"I promise." Angel would promise him anything. It didn't matter if he was asking for assurances that he wouldn't be injured again, assurances that he wouldn't regret leaving his life behind, or assurances that she would honor her promises to give him the whole truth and to make love to him once they were safe.

He stiffened as the portal formed around them.

Angel rose on tiptoe and brushed her lips over his. "Trust me," she reminded him.

Julien nodded, meeting her lips urgently. Angel gasped as his power joined the feed, coursing through her like a wave.

He raised his head, looking past her as the door swung wide. A devilish smile not unlike his father's curved Julien's lips. "Speed it up, Anthony," he requested. He stepped around Angel, blocking her body with his own.

Angel grasped at Julien's clothing, memories of the night they both lost their parents searing her. She looked past him, stifling a scream of dismay as the old man raised his weapon.

Julien waved. "Goodbye, Adrien."

The old man faltered, his eyes widening. Julien laughed aloud as the room melted away outside the circle of light.

Angel closed her eyes as she felt her body make the jump--lengthening, thinning, disassociating her mind from her body. She came back to herself in the workroom, collapsing under the force of Julien's body.

* * * *

Julien groaned. His limbs felt leaden much like they had in the hospital. The startling colors faded away, and he blinked his eyes, taking in the beige walls and banks of electronics curiously. The panels were strange, like nothing Julien had ever seen before.

Angel eased from under him, touching Julien's face in concern. "Relax. The first time is always the hardest. You'll be weak for several minutes. The dizziness will last longer--a few hours." She accepted a bright-colored robe from Anthony and pulled it on, cinching it at the waist.

Anthony motioned to Julien, his hands a flurry that made Julien's head spin.

She nodded. "We will be fine," Angel assured her brother. "Go rest. Long distances always tire you, but we'll be able to relax for a few days here."

The boy smiled at Julien and made more hand motions. He waved and strode from the room.

"What did he say?" Julien asked weakly.

Angel blushed. "I'll tell you later," she promised.

"Where are we?"

She reached above her and pulled a strange red container from the countertop. "Drink this, and I will explain everything to you--slowly."

Julien sucked in a mouthful of the sweet liquid. He swallowed in surprise, coughing a bit as it fizzed against his tongue. The flavor was new but appealing. "Where?" he asked again, staring into the metal container.

"This is called the workroom. The free powers use this as one of our communications centers."

"How--Why have the Calante never found this?"

"That is a little difficult to explain. Let's start slowly." She motioned for him to drink again.

"My father--"

Angel tipped the container to his mouth with a look that brooked no argument. She nodded as Julien took another drink. Whatever it was, it was good.

"Drink all of that. You'll need your mental fortitude to read me. What I have to tell you--You aren't likely to believe me, unless you read it from my mind."

Julien drank down several mouthfuls. As if the elixir were some sort of magic, his extremities started to strengthen a bit, and his head cleared. "He followed you into that--transport circle."

She smiled, touching his face. "He was terrified."

"I think I know why," Julien grumbled.

"Jake was transported to our headquarters in what was once Glenvale City, unable to move and surrounded by people he perceived as enemies. It didn't take Jake long to understand that we were not what the Calante painted us as."

Julien finished the drink and offered it back to Angel. His limbs were tingling, sensation returning much faster now. "How did you convince him?"

"Anthony touched his mind. After that, Jake wanted to know everyone. I think, he believed we were deceiving him--at first."

He pushed to sitting, leaning heavily against the console at his back. "He changed sides. I know that much."

Angel sucked in a ragged breath. "You really know?" She reached down another of the strange containers and drank deeply from it before turning it over to Julien.

He nodded, taking a drink. If the contents of the containers were what was healing him, the Grellan had medical knowledge far beyond the Calante ability to heal him.

"How?" She took the container back again and drank then passed it into his hand.

Julien chuckled. "I've made a habit of picking the old man's mind. A thought here and there. Adrien certainly didn't expect me to know his true name." He sobered, the moment he learned that true name bringing him back to more important issues. "Tell me about the night my father died."

Angel nodded. "Jake devoured information, every record we had of the war between the Calante and Grellan. We knew why our originator, Grelda, opposed the Academy, but even we didn't know the whole tale."

"What was her reason?"

"Calan and Thomas lied. The ancient texts did not demand the system they implemented. The powers were not born with a duty to live as slaves."

Julien drank another mouthful, trying to internalize that concept. "But, we were born special," he protested weakly. What other reason would we have these powers for if not to use them for the good of mankind?

"An accident of nature. We knew that much, but we needed Jake's help to locate the ancient texts. We arranged a rather dramatic scene to put the old man off guard. To all appearances, Jake escaped back to the Calante with knowledge of a few old bases that we left new trails in to make the story more convincing."

Julien motioned for her to continue. The tingling in his arms was subsiding, though his limbs still felt weak, drained.

"Jake agreed on one condition. When we had our proof, we were to take you and your mother from the city to safety. Your mother--We weren't in time. I am sorry for that. That is why we came for you. We had a duty. We owed Jake that much."

"I was a duty?" he asked in disbelief.

Angel ran her fingertips up his chest, shooting him a look of invitation that he wished he could take her up on.

"Well, not just a duty," she commented coyly.

"Good. My father found the texts?"

She nodded. "He went with us. My parents had the electrical and telekinetic abilities to retrieve the texts. Anthony and I--"

"Had to get the group in and out."

"Yes. Jake went in as a witness."

"What happened?"

Angel offered her hand. "We knew my parents' outlay of power would bring the Calante. It did."

Julien set the drink aside, taking her hand. He opened himself to her thoughts, letting them wash over him. Julien closed his eyes as the memory solidified around him.

* * * *

"Hurry," Jake urged, looking toward the doors nervously.

The woman--Anna reached into a small vault and removed a metal case, handing it to her husband, Sam.

"Take the charts, too," Sam instructed. "We'll need them."

She nodded, grasping a handful of micro discs and storing them in the case he held.

"Good. Let's go," Jake commanded in a tense voice, taking the case from Sam. He stalked to Angel's position, looming over the children. Jake managed a stiff smile. "Time to go."

Angel screeched as the doors exploded in. A laser pulse lit the air, and the smell of seared flesh burned her nose.

"Sam," Anna pleaded in a voice choked with tears.

Jake pushed the case at Angel, as Anna fell to the next volley. "Leave," he ordered, turning away. "Go home."

Anthony grabbed her hand, starting the reaction and enticing Angel to join him despite her shocked tears.

"Stop," Jake demanded, trying to wave off the operatives. "There are children here."

"Stop the children," Adrien instructed coldly. "Shoot them if you have to."

Jake looked to Angel and Anthony in desperation, throwing himself into the circle on his knees and using his body as a shield.

The laser fire was eclipsed by the discharge of a conventional weapon. Angel collapsed under Jake, screaming in a combination of pain and terror as the room faded away. Adrien threw the handgun at them with a howl of pure fury.

Angel's eyes closed as the world spun around her and lights flashed. She groaned as Jake's body landed over her more forcefully. Angel pushed at him, her shoulder protesting her efforts.

"Jake," she whispered, pleading for a sign of life that she instinctively knew he wouldn't provide for her. Angel sobbed in the realization that they were truly alone.

Anthony looked at her with frantic eyes, pressing at the pain in her chest.

Angel surveyed their surroundings. At five, Anthony's control was questionable when he was pressured. He'd short-circuited again. Angel had no clue where they were, but she prayed they were close to headquarters where Sky Child could locate them quickly.

* * * *

Julien opened his eyes, touching the scar on her chest lightly. "The bullet."

Angel nodded. "It would have killed me. Jake saved us both. The laser fire killed him. He didn't--I don't think he felt the bullet."

Julien pulled her to his chest. "Thank you for that."

"For letting you know that he didn't suffer?"

"No. For showing me that he died with honor, that he was a hero, as I've always believed he was."

She nodded. "Are you ready to hear the rest?"

"Yes. I think I am."

Angel pushed back then to her feet. She went to a glass cabinet and pulled out a half dozen pieces of faded artwork. Angel brought them to Julien and placed them reverently in his hands.

"What are these?" Julien asked.

"The ancient texts."

He looked at the plastic-wrapped drawings in confusion. "I don't understand."

Angel drew the thin books out one at a time, opening them to marked pages.

Julien read them in growing understanding. "These are--" He pressed a hand to his heart, barely breathing in glee.

"Children's books. Fantasy," she assured him. "They were entertainment."

"Myths about famous Earth heroes," he mused. "The best of their time. Human children read these, didn't they? I've always said that human children should know--"

"They're not real," Angel whispered. "These people never existed."

"But the histories--"

"Were written by the victors, Julien."

"But--" He held a book out to her uncertainly. "Here is the first academy run by Dr. Xavier." He set the book aside carefully and picked up another. "Heroes in disguise serving the public under assumed names." Julien rifled through them for the one that touched him the most. He pointed to the quote excitedly. "With great power comes great responsibility," he crowed.

Angel cupped his face between her hands. "There were never heroes on Earth, Julien. These stories were inventions of writers and artists."

He shook his head. "It can't be. How can you know for sure?" he challenged. "You can't, can you?"

She rose and helped Julien to his feet, steadying him as she guided him to a door. Angel opened it and led him onto a wide balcony.

Julien looked out over a blue-green sea in awe. A bright blue sky was littered with fluffy white clouds unlike the pale yellow clouds he was accustomed to. Manicured gardens surrounded the mansion, full of plants he could not recognize.

"I know all of Suraden," he breathed. "Where are we?"

Angel took his hands. "We took a chance that all the stories Grelda told were true. We used the charts to find our way home."

"Home?" Julien asked, watching the waves crest and crash up on the rocky shoreline.

"Anthony's sign language--" She smiled. "He said, 'Welcome to Earth,' Julien."

He reached for the stone railing, collapsing to his knees. Julien gasped for breath, the dizziness intensifying.

Angel eased him to his back. "Calm down, Julien. You need to sleep this off. I know it's a shock."

He grasped her hand, trying to find the words to ask her to stay with him.

She nodded, holding his hand tight. "I'm not going anywhere."

Julien nodded, closing his eyes.

Chapter Nine

Angel stroked her fingertips over Julien's chest. It hardly seemed possible that he was really here. She kissed his shoulder, smiling as he draped a hand over her waist.

Julien buried his face in her hair, and his hand traced her hip. "I'm dreaming," he grumbled.

"I hope not," she teased.

"Tell me this isn't a dream," he begged. "Tell me I'm in bed with you--on Earth. Tell me I'm not crazy."

Angel circled his cock and stroked him. "Does that feel like a dream?"

His hand tightened on her hip. "Too early to tell," he groaned. "I have a lot of vivid dreams about you."

"Do you?"

"Mmm." Julien trailed his lips down her cheek. "So real."

Angel nuzzled his lips. "Would you like it to be real?" she whispered.

"Yes." Julien nipped at her lips.

"You are on Earth. You are free. You are in bed with me." She drew his hand to her breast. "Naked."

"Please tell me this isn't something you've done before."

Angel furrowed her brow. "Slept with a man?"

He shook his head, looking sheepish.

"Oh. No. Sleeping with me isn't part of the service." Angel bit back a laugh at that.

Julien pulled her to his body. "What about me?"

She guided him to her core, tugging Julien over her. "This is not a dream."

"I hope not." Julien hesitated. "I've wanted you for so long."

"I know."

Julien's mouth covered hers, his hands exploring her body. Angel pushed her pelvis to his in invitation, and his fingers eased inside her. His mouth became more urgent and his fingers more insistent, driving her toward the edge.

"Now, Julien," she pleaded.

His hand retreated, and he seated his cock in her, meeting her eyes and filling Angel in a single thrust. Julien shivered as Angel cried out. She grasped his buttocks, guiding him deeper as she wrapped her legs around his hips.

"Oh gods," he breathed. "I should--"

Angel shook her head. "No. You shouldn't. It's taken care of. Do you trust me?"

He took her hard and fast in lieu of a verbal answer. Julien clasped her hips to his own as his movements all but lifted her from the bed, capturing her nipple in his mouth.

She wound her hands in his hair, her body exploding in pleasure. Ripples of awareness radiated from her breasts downward, echoing and intensifying as they reached the length of him thrusting into her.

Julien pulled lightly at the first nipple and moved to the other, his suckling as slow and thorough as his pistoning hips were fevered. The ripples spread until her entire body pulsed in time with his ministrations, matching his thrusts then slowing to keep time with his mouth. The sensations swung back and forth wildly in a maddening cycle. Her muscles tensed as Angel fought back the inevitable. He sucked hard as she lost the battle.

The ripples ignited into a flame-thrower jet of searing heat as Angel molded every inch of her body to him. She threw her head back and screamed out his name, every muscle relaxing at once. It was like the jump, the intense sensation coupled with a disconcerting disassociation at the height of her pleasure.

Julien released her breast, capturing her mouth as he tensed. Wave after wave of his heat filled her, and Julien's mouth left hers, his eyes closed and his breathing ragged as his climax wore on. "Angel," he pleaded.

"Yes," she urged him.

He shouted her name, his cock pulsing inside her. Julien pressed his forehead to hers, shivering, while his fingers stroking a nipple. "Tell me this is real," he whispered.

"How much more real can I make it?"

"Marry me. Let me tell you about my life. Let me give you my innermost self."

Angel stroked his cheek, wanting to laugh in the joy bubbling up. "We have discussions we have to have first," she soothed him.

He met her eyes, his face serious, earnest, pleading with her. "I want as many children as you'll give me," he assured her. "I don't like these escapades to Suraden, but I won't try to stop you or talk you out of them. What you are doing is important," he rushed on.

She put a hand over his mouth, stilling his flow of words. Angel cocked her head, scowling at the sound of the Earth-style jet helos. "No. We have to attend to the formalities. Get dressed. We have company."

* * * *

Julien watched the people streaming into the conference room in unease. There were so many--a council of men and women. He shifted nervously, suddenly worried that he was on trial. Were these his jailers for war crimes on Suraden?

Angel took his hand. "It isn't an inquiry," she assured him. "You were raised by the wrong side on Suraden. You are not a criminal for doing your duty."

He nodded slowly, blushing. Julien reminded himself that he trusted Angel and squeezed her hand.

A dark-haired human with a sprinkling of gray at the temples reached a hand out to Julien over the table.

Julien hesitated, looking at the offered hand curiously. "You realize what I am?" he asked.

Angel laughed heartily. "Tyler has met powers before, even psychics. He is our liaison."

Julien shook the man's hand, letting a myriad of information wash over him. He smiled at the man's honest, open nature. "What kind of liaison, Mr. Meadows?"

The man chuckled as he took his seat. "Tyler will be fine. Would you like me to call you Mr. Cross?"

Julien shuddered. "To tell the truth, I'm still trying to get used to someone using my true name. I haven't been called--" He took a calming breath, trying to still the panic rising in him. "You--You all know my true name, don't you?"

Tyler poured a glass of the sweet water they drank on Earth, clear-colored and without the heavy mineral taste of Suraden water. He passed it to Julien.

"Yes. We know all about you. I realize this is hard on you. Most superheroes that come through know the truth before they agree. They come to terms with the idea of themselves as a part of society before they make the jump. Do you prefer to be called Soulchaser until you adjust?" he offered.

Julien swallowed a sour lump, shaking his head. He took a drink of the water. Julien could drink nothing but Earth water for the rest of his life--unless Cola was available. "No. Not that. Julien--will be fine. Thank you." He furrowed his brow. "Superheroes?"

Angel touched his cheek. "The fantasy powers were known as superheroes. It is a hard idea for the Earth-born humans to shed."

Tyler darkened. "I apologize."

Julien laughed weakly. "Don't. I have to learn these things if Earth will be my home. Now, what sort of liaison are you, Tyler?"

He nodded. "I am the liaison between the Suraden-born powers and the United Federation of Peoples. We arrange your move into society."

"Arrange? Am I--Am I in service to your political hierarchy?" he asked nervously.

"Only if you wish to be. We may ask your help, but you are never required to take an assignment." Tyler rustled a stack of papers in front of him, pulling out a yellow one and scanning his eyes down it. "I see that you worked murder tracking."

Julien nodded once, curtly, forcing his muscles to ease. Not that, he begged silently. How many years would they want him to serve in that capacity?

"Three years in hell," Tyler spat in disgust, throwing the paper back on the pile. "That was one of the reasons the Federation granted immediate shelter to the refugees from Suraden. Forcing sensitives to live that."

"Tyler," Angel soothed him.

He nodded then met Julien's eyes. "It is my pleasure to tell you that you are free to refuse any case we ask your help on. We won't ask unless we have a serial killer that may strike again or there is a strong possibility of recovering the victim alive, but we understand what we are asking. If you cannot face it again, you cannot."

Julien fought for a decent breath. "If I don't track, what am I expected to do?"

Tyler smiled. "What would you like to do? What would you choose to do?" He waved a hand as if to still a flood of words that were not forthcoming. "Don't limit yourself to your powers. There are programs providing job education and degree programs. You can pursue any job you wish, and we can help you decide on a job."

Julien looked to Angel, dizzy and lost in the concept. He'd dreamed for years about the things he would do if he were free to do them, but they all seemed frivolous when the choice was a reality.

Angel nodded. "You don't have to choose today," she assured him. "You have all the time you need."

Julien nodded, wishing Jennifer had this choice--now, before she forgot what she really hoped for. He sucked in his breath as an idea assaulted him, the only thing beside Angel that had made him happy in years.

"What is it?" Angel asked.

"Children," he whispered. "I want to help troubled children, children who have problems."

She nodded, smiling. "You're thinking of Sealife," she guessed.

"Jennifer. How--"

Angel handed him a small pouch. "This is yours."

Julien opened it, dumping his father's medals and the micro discs of family photos into his hand.

"You had to leave everything behind," she explained.

"You have someone inside the Academy." But, who?

Angel nodded. "We agreed to bring him through once we had you. He ransacked your quarters for your most prized possessions after you left the Academy. He had hours to store them in the tower quarters before we came for you."

"Who is it? Who do I have to thank for this?"

She laughed. "Your old buddy Jason," she teased.

"Firebrand? I knew he was going to get himself in trouble." Julien grinned. "For once, I'm glad I was right about him. When are we getting him out?"

114

"Anthony and I are getting him out in a few months," she assured him.

"Months?"

"He wants to be sure no one suspects him before he runs."

Julien sighed. "I want to go back."

"What?" She paled.

"Not permanently," he soothed her. "There's someone--I trust Jennifer. She trusts me, and I can get her out, if we do it now."

"Soon. Give us time. For now, we have decisions to make."

Julien nodded sadly. He would get Jennifer out as soon as he could arrange it.

Tyler motioned for Julien's attention. He handed over an identi-card. "This is yours. You may travel where you wish with it."

"Any city?" he asked, stunned that no one was listing his allowed zone.

"Any city."

Julien searched the card.

As if he understood Julien's concern from years of dealing with new Suraden-born powers, Tyler removed his own card and passed it across the table. "They are the same. It doesn't mark you as a power in any way. You have to choose many things--and learn a few things."

Tyler motioned the people with him in turn. "Mary will tutor you in history, customs and laws. Neil will help you choose where you will live."

Julien looked to Angel. "Where do you live?" he asked solemnly.

She laughed heartily. "The Greek isles, but I've considered relocating to Eire."

He waited patiently for her answer.

"Eire," she decided.

Julien nodded and looked to Neil. "Eire--if you please."

Tyler looked from Julien to Angel in confusion. "If you'd like Neil to show you the choices you have," he began.

Julien nodded. "For travel," he assured them. "I would like to know this world."

Tyler shrugged and moved on. "Sarah will help you choose clothing and belongings with your initial stipend. Since you are uncomfortable with your situation, we will do as much as we can via electronic purchases. Last but not least, Evelyn will arrange for your job certifications, education, and other paperwork."

Julien darkened. "What paperwork does one need to marry on this world?" he asked.

Angel choked. "I haven't said yes," she managed in a harsh whisper.

Tyler stifled a laugh and hid a smile behind his hand.

Julien smiled and stroked her cheek. "Aloud? No. You haven't--yet."

She blushed and shot a sheepish look at the end of the table. "Evelyn, if you don't mind," she hinted.

Julien drew her face back to his. "Tell me."

Angel smiled. "Yes. I will marry you."

The End

HEROES INCORPORATED

Joy Nash

Chapter One

Wednesday, 10:47 p.m.
Three days, one hour, thirteen minutes, and counting…

Oh, man. It was his lucky day. An original 1951 Action Comics #158, The Kid from Krypton, shimmered before his eyes, thirteen minutes from closing on eBay.

Yes! Clark Kendall raised both arms in a two-fisted salute to the superhero gods. He'd lusted after this particular Superman comic book for ages. Now it was as good as his.

He typed in his bid the old-fashioned way. On his laptop keyboard. It launched into cyberspace just as the telephone shrilled.

He snagged the receiver. "Heroes Incorporated. Yeah, we deliver. Go ahead."

He shifted the phone to one shoulder as he watched the eBay screen refresh. "One roast beef hero sandwich, no onions. One Italian hero, hold the mayo. Drinks with that? Two Cokes. Your address? Right. Got it. Twenty minutes."

He cut the connection, wondering how long it would be before the hungry customers figured out their dinner wasn't coming. Amazing. Even with absolutely no advertising, the fake New York-style sub shop four levels above his head still managed to attract business. Almost made him want to open a strip mall take-out restaurant in Newark, New Jersey for real.

Almost, but not quite.

He pushed his glasses up the bridge of his nose and squinted at the laptop screen. Damn. Someone had topped his bid. He typed in a counteroffer and sent it scurrying across the broadband connection.

"Hey, Clark."

He swiveled his desk chair toward the door, swallowing hard. Diana Price had come looking for him? More luck. That only happened in his dreams.

He watched as the shapely Amazonian princess sashayed into the Heroes Incorporated control room, forty-four-and-a-half double D's all but exploding out of her skimpy costume. When she leaned over the back of his chair and brushed her chest against his shoulders, he nearly passed out.

"What are you doing?" she asked, peering at the computer screen.

Trying desperately to breathe, Clark thought, but masculine pride prevented him from cluing Diana in on that little bit of information.

"I'm on eBay," he told her. "I put in a bid on a Superman comic book."

"Think you'll get it?"

He craned his neck to get a better look at her boobs without being too obvious. Did he think he'd get it? God, he hoped so.

"Clark? You okay?"

He gave himself a mental shake. "Yeah, fine. Listen," he said, forcing a casual tone. "My shift's almost done. You want to go out for a drink afterward?"

Diana's red lips quirked knowingly at him. Too knowingly. He knew he was toast even before she started laughing.

"I can't." She presented him a smile reserved for children, puppies, and guys who were about to get the shaft. "I've got a date with Bruce."

Clark's fist closed on his mouse so tightly it was a wonder the thing didn't let out a squeal. Bruce Wynn, superhero. Scratch that. Superjerk.

"He's just using you for the sex, you know."

Diana only laughed. "That's what makes it fun." She gave him a little hug. "Aw, Clark, are you jealous? That's so sweet."

He felt his cheeks heat. Sweet. Yeah, that's what every superhero aspired to be.

As if on cue, Bruce appeared at the door, arms crossed over his steroid-enhanced chest. Muscles bulged under his gray spandex shirt and black tights. He wasn't wearing his cape, but Clark could almost see the shiny black fabric flapping in an imaginary breeze.

Bruce nodded toward Diana. "Babe." His moody gaze shifted the tiniest bit to the right. "Clark."

Diana gushed a reply, making Clark slightly nauseous. Sure, Bruce was something to look at--and if you believed half the rumors, a veritable god in bed--but was that all a woman wanted in a guy? You'd think the ripped physique, perfect profile, and gloomy angst would get old after a while.

Bruce and Diana melded into a liplock. Clark pushed his glasses up the bridge of his nose and turned back to eBay. Only two minutes left, and he'd been knocked off the top again. Hell. He upped his bid into four figures and sent it flying. No way was he going to let this one go.

The phone rang again.

"Heroes Incorporated," Clark droned, then snapped to attention when Captain Marvelous' radio-announcer voice crackled across the line.

"Clark, round up the troops. We've got a situation."

"A situation, Captain?"

From the corner of his eye, he saw Bruce and Diana disengage.

"Can't say any more on an unsecured line, son, but I can tell you it's not good. Tell every hero we've got on the books to report to my ready room in one hour."

Damn. Clark couldn't remember the last time the Captain had ordered a full HI assembly. This was major. Another threat to life as they all knew it, most likely.

His gaze drifted back to eBay. His mysterious opponent had posted a winning bid two seconds before the countdown expired.

It looked like Clark's luck had run out.

* * * *

Wednesday, 11:00 p.m.
Three days, one hour, and counting...

Yes!

Blossom Breeze sprang to her feet and did a little victory dance around her chair. That last minute bidder had come out of nowhere. She'd practically broken out in a cold sweat, but somehow she managed to squeak in under the wire to win the eBay bid for Action Comics #158, The Kid from Krypton. She'd only been looking for that particular issue forever. After it was framed, she'd hang it on her wall right between her signed portraits of Christopher Reeve and Dean Cain.

She collapsed in her chair and beamed at the screen. Life was perfect.

A nanosecond later, an Instant Message from Bernie popped up on her screen.

<Hey, Blossom>

Okay, well maybe not so perfect.

<Hey, Bernie> she typed back. If there were an emoticon for rolling eyes, she would have added it. Bernie was sitting on the other side of the cubicle partition on her left, less than five feet away.

Another geek occupied the cubicle to her right. Oh, sure, she could put a positive spin on things and say she spent every night surrounded by single men under thirty, but where would that get her? She'd still be right here in the computer lab at Megalopolis Polytechnic Institute.

She sighed as a series of numbers materialized in her IM window. Another one of Bernie's freaking mathematical cryptograms. A second later, his head popped up over the partition, all bright eyes and big ears.

"Well, what do you say?"

Blossom squinted at Bernie's coded message, but late as it was, the numbers could have spelled out "Do you want to get naked?" and she wouldn't have even known it.

She blinked at the screen.

Hey. Wait a minute.

Do you want to... A sudden vision of a naked Bernie appeared in her brain, nearly shorting out the major synapses. Oh, please. No. Anything but that. Bernie weighed all of one hundred and thirty pounds, soaking wet. Naked or clothed, he wasn't a feast for the eyes.

She steeled herself to decipher the rest of the coded sentence. ...go to the Star Trek convention tomorrow?

Her breath left in a rush. Thank you, God.

"So? Do you?" Bernie's goofy grin stretched from ear to ear, his tongue lolling out of his mouth, puppy-dog style. No doubt he thought encrypted IM propositioning a very clever way to procure female companionship.

"James Doohan's going to be there," he said in a wheedling tone.

Blossom gave him a thin smile. "I'd love to, Bernie. I really would. But tomorrow's not good for me." I have to feed my goldfish. And wash my hair. And visit my gynecologist. "Maybe some other time."

"Geez, that's too bad. A bunch of us are going to my place afterwards for a TOS marathon." TOS, Blossom knew only too well, was Geekspeak for Star Trek, The Original Series. As in Captain Kirk and Mr. Spock.

"Sorry. I'll have to pass."

"Your loss," Bernie said, and ducked back into his cell.

Sighing, Blossom logged off and shut down. Bernie wasn't a bad guy, really. You could even make the case that his brain made up for what he lacked in physique. Of course, that was pretty much true of all the guys lurking in the bowels of the MPI computer department.

Call her shallow, but Blossom just couldn't seem to get past appearances when it came to men. She liked them with muscles. Lots of muscles, bulging out all over. She drooled over sculpted pecs and corded biceps. She spun elaborate fantasies starring men who looked like the superheroes on her apartment walls.

Which could only be termed an ironic twist of fate, since Blossom's off-the-charts IQ had dumped her squarely into geekdom. In her world, men who fit the superhero mold were very few and far between.

Life was a bitch sometimes.

Chapter Two

Thursday, 12:13 a.m.
Two days, twenty-three hours, forty-seven minutes, and counting...

Clark couldn't remember the last time he'd seen Captain Marvelous looking so grim.

In his long and illustrious career as CEO of Heroes Incorporated, the Captain had faced down more no-win situations than a marriage counselor. He excelled at snatching victory from the jaws of defeat. His keen mind and unerring instinct invariably chose just the right superhero to neutralize each dire threat that came across the hotline.

Clark shifted in his seat, trying to catch the faint breeze wafting from the overhead vent. When you crammed twenty-seven muscle-bound superheroes--and a few superheroines--into a small conference room, you tended to overload the air conditioning system. Too bad the ready room was three levels underground. Clark would have emptied his bank account for an open window. A little air freshener wouldn't come amiss, either.

Bruce Wynn sat right up front, of course, shooting the room's testosterone level right off the scale. As far as Clark was concerned, the guy didn't even belong in HI. Bruce didn't have any real superpowers. He was all cash, flash, and gadgets. Without his fortune and his technology, he'd be just another pretty face in the unemployment line.

Clark unzipped his laptop case and eased open his computer. He was HI's official secretary, partly because he was the only superhero in the organization capable of stringing words into coherent sentences, and partly because his specialized psychic superpowers made it easy for him to take notes. He sent a burst of mental energy into the computer, causing the hard disk to whir in response. Bruce looked over, as if the sound irritated him.

Captain Marvelous took his position at the podium. Clark sat up straighter in his seat and gave HI's fearless leader his full attention.

"Thank you all for arriving at such short notice," the Captain said. "I won't beat around the bush, because frankly, we haven't much time. Our operatives in the field have just uncovered a DP of massive proportions."

Clark and the entire assembly of superheroes gave a collective gasp. DP was superhero slang for "Diabolical Plot." DP's were perpetrated by EMG's, or "Evil Maniacal

Geniuses." Clark shook his head. You just never knew when an EMG would snap. When one did, it wasn't pretty.

Captain Marvelous cleared his throat. "According to my sources, Lex Loser's tenuous hold on sanity has finally crumbled. He's retreated to a secret underground lair to detonate a computerized neutron bomb. He intends to kill the entire population of Earth--without damaging its resources. After the explosion, he'll live in luxury, attended by an army of robotic servants." The Captain exhaled heavily. "The bomb is set to go off Saturday at midnight."

A buzz of horror zapped back and forth across the room. Lex Loser was an EMG capable of perpetrating the worst atrocities, but this DP far surpassed any evil he'd previously conceived. Clark concentrated on thought-streaming his notes onto the computer even as his blood turned to ice in his veins.

Back in the last row, young Peter Parkington jumped up so quickly he almost dropped his camera. "I volunteer to take Lex down, Captain!"

Captain Marvelous shook his head at the kid. "I'm sorry, Peter. Superhuman speed and arachnid reflexes are not going to help with this one."

Dr. Banning stood up next, already looking a little green around the edges. "I'll rip him limb from limb," he growled. His chest expanded, snapping the buttons off his shirt.

"Uh, I surely do appreciate the offer, Doctor," the Captain said. "But I'm afraid superhuman anger's not the answer, either." He held up one hand to stop the verbal onslaught coming at him from every corner of the room. "In fact, no physical superpower will solve this dilemma. According to our latest intelligence, the computerized detonation device is so sensitive the slightest touch will set it off. We need someone with psychic skills to defuse it."

Clark looked up from his laptop to find every eye in the room on him. Psychic skills? Hot damn! That was his department. Finally, he'd get a chance to prove brains beat brawn any day of the week.

He pushed his glasses up the bridge of his nose. "I'll be happy to take on the assignment, Captain."

"That's good of you, Clark, but not quite good enough, I'm afraid."

"But sir--I can psychically defuse any computerized bomb. All I have to do is get within ten feet of it."

"Yes, well, that's just our problem. Lex Loser's lair is three hundred feet underground, and it's impenetrable."

Bruce Wynn stood. "Nothing's impenetrable. I'll blast my way in."

"Oh right," Clark said, not even trying to hide his sarcasm. "Blow up the bomb. That'll work."

A collective twitter swept through the room. Bruce's face turned scarlet. Luckily, looks couldn't kill, or Clark would be writhing on the floor, gasping for air.

The rich playboy turned on him. "What do you suggest, Geek Man? That we just beam over? Like on Star Trek?"

Captain Marvelous cleared his throat. "Now, now, boys. Petty rivalry won't save the day. I'm not exaggerating when I say the situation is bleak and getting worse by the second. The bomb is set to detonate in two days, twenty-three hours..." He checked his watch. "...and sixteen minutes."

That quieted everyone down in a hurry.

"Unless we can come up with a plan of action," the Captain said, "life as we know it..."

will ... cease ... to ... exist, Clark mentally typed into the meeting minutes. Bingo. The superhero buzz phrase set off a renewed wave of furious whispers.

Clark frowned as he considered the various superpowers currently claimed by HI personnel. There were the mundane powers of strength, speed, and flight, and the rarer ones of x-ray vision, magnetic levitation, and setting oneself on fire with no untoward consequences.

And then there was teleportation...

Clark blinked. That's it. If he could beam into Lex Loser's hideout, he could defuse the bomb. Well, what do you know? For once in his life, Bruce the feeble-brained superjerk had said something intelligent.

Teleportation wasn't a common superhero skill. In fact, it was the rarest. Currently, no one in HI claimed it. The last teleporting superhero, The Disappearing Man, had died twenty-four years ago while trying to teleport onto a stolen nuclear submarine. He'd accidentally materialized underwater and drowned.

That embarrassing incident was rarely spoken of. But recently Clark had uncovered an interesting addendum to the story.

Using his laptop for a launching pad, he shot his mind through the wireless link to the HI mainframe, racing along a complex web of pathways. He ricocheted into the database, plunging deep until he'd found the snippet of information he sought.

When he had it, he stood and waved one arm at The Captain.

"Yes, Clark?"

Clark pushed his glasses up the bridge of his nose. "Sir, I believe I have our answer."

* * * *

Thursday, 1:02 a.m.
Two days, twenty-two hours, fifty-eight minutes, and counting...

When it's too late for dinner and too early for breakfast, the only possible meal is ice cream.

Blossom snagged a quart of mint chocolate chip from the freezer. Tucking her feet beneath her on the couch, she hit the play button on the remote and settled in. The familiar intro music crooned. She dug her spoon into the cold, sweet cream and sighed with pleasure.

Faster than a speeding bullet... More powerful than a locomotive...

She looked over at the aquarium. Lois and Jimmy, the twin goldfish she'd won at the MPI Spring Fair, waved their fins at her. As if to say "Get a life."

Able to leap tall buildings in a single bound...

Okay, maybe it was pathetic to spend the wee hours of the morning curled up on the couch watching 1950s Superman TV episodes, but hey, everyone had to have a hobby, right?

Look, there in the sky... It's a bird... It's a plane...

Blossom spooned the ice cream into her mouth and let it melt on her tongue. Aaaah.

It's Superman!

The episode was one of her favorites--#24, Crime Wave, in which Superman fights a mysterious rash of crime sweeping Metropolis, only to be nearly done in by atomic rays. So, okay, it was a bit corny, but satisfying nonetheless. Superman rocked.

He graced her walls in endless poses, both animated and via the actors lucky enough to portray the Man of Steel in TV and film. Superman's chiseled jaw, bulging biceps, and cute forehead curl greeted her at every turn. She'd spent literally thousands of dollars on Superman collectibles.

She refused to apologize for what some people might term an obsession. So what if she had to eat spaghetti every night for a month to afford her latest purchase?

When you spent your life surrounded by wimpy geeks, you did what you could to survive.

* * * *

Thursday, 1:32 a.m.
Two days, twenty-two hours, twenty-eight minutes, and counting...

"She's what?" Captain Marvelous asked.

"Half-human, half-superheroine," Clark explained patiently.

"Then why don't we know about her?" Bruce demanded. "Every superhero offspring is supposed to be evaluated for superpowers at puberty."

"Well, usually that's true, but this is a special case," Clark said. "Blossom Breeze was born after The Disappearing Man's fatal accident. With all the confusion and embarrassment following that event, she was never registered in the HI database. I only stumbled across her birth records last month, when I hacked into Megalopolis General during the Dr. Squid incident. I made a note to check it out, but we've been so busy lately, I forgot."

"You forgot," Bruce sneered. "Isn't that special. What if I'd forgotten to stop city bus #64 from plowing into that Girl Scout troop last week?"

The Captain shot Bruce a quelling look. "Are you sure The Disappearing Man is Blossom's father?" he asked Clark.

"Positive," Clark said. "His name is on her birth certificate. If she's inherited his teleportation powers, it would be a snap for her to get me into Lex's lair in time to defuse the bomb."

He called up a picture of Blossom on his computer. Bruce, Diana, and the Captain all crowded around the laptop for a better look.

"Nice," said Bruce, letting a low whistle escape between his perfect teeth. "Very nice."

Diana elbowed him in the side.

"But not my type," he added hastily. "Too girl next door."

Clark looked at the picture. "Girl next door" described Blossom perfectly. No one would call her beautiful--not by a long shot. She was cute, with short red hair and lots of freckles dancing across her nose. Her lips quirked, as if smiling at some secret joke. He found himself wondering if she was as fun to be with as she looked.

Diana flipped a strand of long, bouncy hair over one bare shoulder. "She's twenty-four years old. Superpowers appear at puberty. If she could teleport, we would know."

"Not necessarily," Clark said. "Not if she kept the talent to herself. Remember, she knows nothing about us. She's a Ph.D. candidate at Megalopolis Polytech."

"We must investigate at once," said Captain Marvelous. "The fate of the world depends upon it." He scanned the room. "I'll need one HI operative to travel to Megalopolis to assess the situation."

Of course, Bruce volunteered first. "I'll do it."

Like hell he would. Clark had been itching for an excuse to get out of Newark for months. He sent another glance toward Blossom's picture. No way was he going to let Bruce muscle in on this assignment.

"This one's mine," he said quietly. "After all, Lex Loser is my nemesis."

Bruce started to protest, but The Captain held up one hand. "I agree Clark's the hero for the job, Bruce, and not only because of Lex. Blossom Breeze, despite her parentage, is living an average life as an average human woman. She could very well faint dead away if a magnificent, larger-than-life superhero showed up on her doorstep." He stroked the cleft in his chiseled chin.

"But Clark should do just fine."

Chapter Three

Thursday, 2:46 p.m.
Two days, nine hours, fourteen minutes, and counting...

"Mind if I sit here?"

Blossom looked up from her book, only to find that the geeks of Megalopolis were not confined to the boundaries of the MPI computer lab. Apparently, they frequented the library, too. Geez. Where did the guy get those black horn rimmed glasses--the family planning aisle of the drug store? She was pretty sure their effectiveness as birth control surpassed The Pill.

"Suit yourself," she said, and returned to her book, The Science of Superheroes.

The geek set his laptop case on the floor and took the seat across the table from her. He opened a large tome and started reading. Blossom turned her shoulder a little, in case he had any ideas about talking to her. It wasn't vanity on her part. His book, An Annotated History of Welding, was upside down.

Unfortunately, her subtle hint didn't work. Subtle never worked with geeks.

"That looks like an interesting book," he said.

"Hmm." She turned a little more, taking The Science of Superheroes with her.

"Is there any special reason why you're reading it?"

She looked over at him. "I like superheroes."

For some reason, that seemed to encourage him. "Do you believe they're real?" His dark eyes regarded her seriously from behind Coke bottle lenses. He probably wouldn't look too bad if he got contacts, she decided.

"Do you?" he said again.

"Do I what?"

"Think superheroes are real?"

"Yeah, right," she said, and went back to reading.

The geek slipped off his chair, rounded the table, and took the seat to her right. Someone should really tell this guy that the top button on a button-down shirt was meant to be left open. Not her, though.

128

"I mean it," he said, drawing her attention back to him with a low, rich voice that seemed totally at odds with his persona. She closed her eyes and let it wash over her.

"Did you ever imagine what it would be like if superheroes really existed?" he asked.

Did she ever. She thought about it every night in bed. But those kinds of thoughts weren't something a girl shared with a cute, geeky stranger. Or even a best girlfriend, for that matter.

"I guess there'd be less crime," she said.

"Maybe there is less crime."

"What's that supposed to mean?"

He took a deep breath. A springy lock of dark hair fell onto his forehead.

Cute, she thought. Then she remembered the laptop. Geeky.

"Maybe there would be more crime if there weren't superheroes," he said.

Say again? "Yeah," she said. "Maybe." Not.

"I know you've always felt different," he said.

She gave him her best frown. What was this guy talking about? He looked harmless enough, but... She scooted her chair a couple inches back from the table, just in case she had to make a run for it.

"It can be frightening to discover you have a superpower. Especially if you're just a teenager, and there's no one around to guide you."

Yep. Certifiable. Did she know how to attract them, or what? She closed The Science of Superheroes with a thud.

"Oh, would you look at the time," she said. "I've got to go."

His hand settled on her arm. "You don't have to pretend with me."

She jumped back, nearly knocking her chair over in her haste. The librarian sent her a disapproving glare.

"Look," she whispered to the geek. "I don't know who you are or what you think you know about me, but I'm warning you. Stay away from me or next time I'll call the cops."

* * * *

Thursday, 2:55 p.m.
Two days, nine hours, five minutes, and counting...

Well, that didn't go over quite the way he'd planned.

Clark stared morosely at the door through which Blossom Breeze had fled. Smooth one, Geek Man. He gave a heavy sigh. Either Blossom was hiding her superpower, or her human genes had proved dominant and she was just your everyday, average, appealing-as-all-hell woman.

He let his mind wander a bit on that one. Blossom didn't have Diana's curves or cup size, but when she'd blinked up at him with those big blue eyes he'd felt it like a sucker punch to the gut. He'd experienced a sudden urge to sift his fingers through her sassy red hair and plant a kiss on her lush pink lips.

She said she liked superheroes, right?

Well, he was a superhero, wasn't he?

Of course, she'd never guess it. Which was exactly why the Captain had sent him on this mission. A mission he might have already blown with his bungling attempt at contact. Clark gave an inward groan. Bruce would have come up with a suave opening line. Bruce would have been on his way home with Blossom right now.

He stared at her vacated chair. Something caught his eye, and he leaned forward. A single strand of red hair clung to the chair's upholstered back. He lifted it carefully.

Just what he needed to determine whether this trip to Megalopolis was humanity's best hope for survival or a complete waste of time.

Returning to his original seat, he shoved An Annotated History of Welding to one side and hefted his laptop case onto the desk. In a few moments, he'd powered up his computer and enabled the genetic testing program. He attached the sensor wand to the USB port. Then he ran the tip over Blossom's fiery strand of hair.

He watched as the string of genetic code scrolled up the screen faster than the human eye could read. Clark, thanks to his psychic computer superpowers, had no trouble following the analysis. As the lines of coded numbers streamed by, his excitement built. Blossom's super genes were no match for her human mother's contribution to her DNA.

She was most definitely a superheroine.

Yes!

"Young man, keep it down!" The librarian looked ready to kill.

Clark gave her a guilty glance. Had he shouted out loud? "Yes, ma'am." He took a calming breath and sank his mind into the readout.

Wait one minute. Something wasn't quite right. Yes, Blossom carried the gene for teleportation, but for some reason it didn't seem active. Currently, she couldn't change locations with a thought, taking whomever she touched with her.

Stomach churning, Clark launched another sequence of programs, further refining the genetic investigation.

Two-point-seven minutes later, he broke out in a cold sweat. According to his analysis, Blossom carried a rare genetic mutation that had prevented her superpower from manifesting with the first influx of puberty hormones, as was typical with super offspring. In her case, a more specialized hormone surge was needed to trigger the transformation.

Clark looked at his watch. Noon. Two days, twelve hours, and counting. Time to check in with HI headquarters. He opened a Velcro pocket on his laptop case and pulled out his cell. He punched in the Captain's private number.

"What's the word, Clark? Can humanity be saved?"

Briefly, Clark summarized his unexpected discovery. "All we have to do is initiate the specialized hormone flux and Blossom's superpower will manifest."

"How do we do that?"

Was it getting hot in here? Clark inserted his index finger into the collar of his shirt and tugged. "Well, Captain, the only way the precise combination of hormones can be released is..." He paused to take a deep breath.

"Go on."

"The only way to trigger the transformation is for Blossom ... uh, I mean Ms. Breeze, to..." Clark swallowed hard.

"Spit it out, boy. I don't have all day."

"Yes, sir." He felt his face flame. "The only way for Blossom to become a superheroine is for her to have a..." He glanced toward the librarian and lowered his voice. "...a sexual encounter. But not just any sexual encounter. It has to be off the charts. She has to experience toe-curling, mind-blowing, deep-muscle-contracting ecstasy."

For about ten seconds, dead silence poured across the cellular phone waves.

Then Captain Marvelous cleared his throat. "Well, Clark, what are you waiting for? The fate of humanity is at stake. Get right on it."

Chapter Four

Friday, 5:29 a.m.
One day, eighteen hours, thirty-one minutes, and counting...

Blossom shielded her eyes from the rising sun as she scurried from the MPI Math Center to her beat-up Volkswagen Jetta. Another all-nighter--one that hadn't included a single alcoholic beverage or grope in the dark with a muscle-bound stranger, unfortunately. She slung her backpack off her shoulder and fished around in it for her car keys.

Lois and Jimmy were right. She was pathetic.

"Hey," a deep voice said, right in her ear.

She nearly jumped a mile.

"Sorry. I didn't mean to startle you."

It was the crazy geek from the library, dressed in another short sleeve button-up-to-the-neck shirt--plaid, no less. His black flood pants were at least two inches too short. To complete the picture of pure geekiness, he held an enormous laptop case in one hand.

"No problem," she told him. "I love being scared out of my wits. The adrenaline rush will help get me home without falling asleep."

He smiled. "Up all night?"

"Yes. Had a bug it took a while to find."

"I get like that, too," he said. "Time flies when you're writing code." He plucked the keys from her hand. Before Blossom realized what was happening, he'd guided her around to the passenger's side, unlocked the door, and helped her in.

"Wait a minute," she said. "What do you think you're doing?"

"You're dead on your feet," he said. "I can't let you drive home."

"That's the worst pick up line I've ever heard," she told him. She climbed out of the car. "Do you really think I'd let some stranger drive me home? You could be an ax murderer or something."

"Do I look dangerous enough?" the geek asked. His eyes seemed hopeful.

"Looks aren't everything," Blossom said.

"I agree," he said. "But in my case you have nothing to worry about. I would never hurt you." He smiled.

He was kind of cute when his dimples were showing. But... "I don't know," she said. "You have to admit, you were a little over the top at the library yesterday. All that talk of superheroes being real--"

"A joke," he said quickly. "I have a ... um ... unique sense of humor." He dangled the keys. "I'll just drive you home. No funny stuff. I promise."

"No. Give me back my keys."

"Forget it. If you won't let me drive, I'm calling a cab."

"You don't have to do that."

"I know." He un-Velcroed a pocket on his laptop case and dug out a cell phone.

Twenty minutes later, the cab still hadn't come. "Megalopolis cab service sucks," he grumbled.

"I could have told you that," Blossom said. "Now can I have my keys? I really need to get some sleep."

He sighed. "All right. But I'm going to follow you home. Just to make sure you get there okay."

Great. Just great.

"One-sixteen Oakland, right?" he asked, handing the keys over.

She froze. "How did you know that?"

"Your backpack," he said, pointing.

Yep, there it was. Right on the tag, under her name, for any and all potential perverts to see. Lovely. She might as well have recorded her bra size, too.

She glared at him. He grinned back.

"Who are you?" she asked irritably. "And why are you following me around?"

He held out his hand. "Dr. Clark Kendall. I'm ... new at MPI. I'm here for a special research project."

She stared at him for a beat, then started to laugh. "That's good," she said. "A bit corny, but good."

"What?" he said, looking genuinely puzzled.

"Your name. Clark Kendall. Almost like Superman."

"Yeah," he said. "Almost."

She got in the car and grabbed the inside door handle. He leaned in, one hand on the roof and the other on the window frame, keeping her from shutting the door. "Listen," he said. "After I tail you home and you catch some sleep, how about going to dinner with me?"

"You don't give up easy, do you?"

He smiled again, a lopsided grin that showed twin dimples, one in each cheek. A thick shank of dark hair fell across his forehead. She looked up, trying to see his eyes, but with the sun striking just so on his glasses, all she could see was her own reflection.

"Come on," he said. "I'll take you to the Italian restaurant over on Broad Street. What's it called?"

"Luigi's," she said. "But you're kidding, right? That place is five star. It'll cost you a fortune."

"You're worth it."

"Why?" she asked. "Why are you doing this? You don't even know me."

He shrugged and looked away.

"You're really a visiting prof?" she asked. "What's your research project about?"

"Genetics," he said. "Hormone triggers in dominant and recessive DNA combinations."

"Wow," she said. "Sounds wild."

"You have no idea. So what do you say? Have dinner with me tonight?"

She hesitated, then sighed. Truth was, she loved authentic Italian food. She'd been dying to go to Luigi's ever since it opened last semester. But with no significant other in sight, she hadn't quite managed to get there. She might as well go with Dr. Clark Kendall. He was a geek, but hey, it wasn't like Superman was showing up at her door to ask her out any time soon.

"All right," she said.

He looked stunned. "Really?"

Her gaze drifted to his buttoned-up shirt, then further south to his where's-the-flood pants. She began to have second thoughts. "On one condition."

He pushed his glasses up the bridge of his nose. "What's that?"

"Lose the geek clothes."

* * * *

Friday, 1:06 p.m.
One day, ten hours, fifty-four minutes, and counting...

Lose the geek clothes.

Right. No problem. He could do that.

Clark stared at the rack of MegaMart polyester dress suits and heaved a sigh. Give him an FBI mainframe to hack into, no problemmo. Tell him to dress up for a dinner date, and he was up shit creek without a toilet brush for a paddle.

What would Bruce wear? He winced. Now wouldn't that make a good bumper sticker.

"Need some help, hon?"

He turned to find a fifty-something, big-haired, gum-snapping saleslady hovering at his elbow. She outweighed him by a good seventy pounds. He squinted at her nametag. Lorna Jean.

He stepped back so quickly, he nearly fell over his laptop case. "I'm not sure."

"Well, then, honey, I'm your dream come true. I know all there is to know about dressing men."

"Do you, now?" Clark said faintly.

"Damn tootin' I do. Got seven boys of my own, you know."

"That's amazing," Clark said.

She cocked her head to one side. "What you getting all gussied up for?"

"A dinner date," he told her. "At Luigi's."

Lorna Jean pursed her alarmingly red lips and whistled. "Fancy shmancy. You'll need the works."

"What do you suggest?" Clark asked, not at all sure he wanted to know, but seeing no way to politely back off from the conversation.

"The Seventies look is right popular these days," Lorna Jean told him. She fished through the rack and reeled in a blindingly white suit, with lapels wider than Clark's hand. She flung the pants and jacket over one substantial shoulder, then grabbed Clark's upper arm and manhandled him over to the shirts, where she slithered a slippery black one off a hanger.

Clark guessed the material was supposed to look like silk, but a glance at the price tag told him the garment was made of pure petroleum by-products.

"I'm not sure I--"

"Sure you are," Lorna Jean said, shoving him into the dressing room. "Didn't you see Saturday Night Fever?"

"No, actually I--"

The louvered door slammed. "Don't make me come in there and dress you myself," she called.

The threat was enough to scare Clark right out of his boxers. With a sigh of resignation, he set down his laptop case and got to work. He emerged a few minutes later, shaking his head. "I don't know..." He looked into the full-length mirror. "Are bellbottoms really back in style?"

"Honey," Lorna Jean said, "if you don't know the answer to that, you ain't got a fashion bone in your body. Them pants are just the thing. Your gal's gonna love you." She draped a heavy gold chain around his neck and winked. "Trust me."

* * * *

Friday, 6:41 p.m.
One day, five hours, nineteen minutes, and counting...

Perhaps his trust had been a little misplaced, Clark thought as he tried to catch Blossom's gaze across the intimate table for two at Luigi's. His date didn't seem too taken with his new clothes. Her gaze kept roaming, as if it were painful to look at him.

She, on the other hand, looked great. She was wearing a sleek, rust-colored, off-the-shoulder dress. It dipped a bit in the front, showing the slightest bit of cleavage. Classy, but not flashy.

Clark tugged at the collar of his faux-silk shirt. Was it getting hot in here? He wished he had a few days to ease into this assignment--feel his way around, so to speak.

But he didn't. Lex Loser's bomb was set to go off--he glanced at his watch--in twenty-nine hours, seventeen minutes, six seconds, and counting. It was do or die, Geek Man.

Literally.

"How's your ossobucco?" he asked.

Blossom's gaze focused. "What? Oh, fine. Very good. How's your calamari?"

He gulped down some Pinot Grigio. "Interesting."

"You've never had it before?"

"No." And he'd ordered it before reading the fine print on the menu. Squid. Ugh.

Manfully, he forked another dangling, suction-cup covered tentacle into his mouth. He swallowed without chewing, then washed the whole disgusting mess down his throat with more wine. Damn if it wasn't getting hotter in here by the minute. And he had an itch on his ankle. Surreptitiously, he inched his foot to one side until it came into contact with his laptop case. He rubbed it up and down. The relief was fleeting.

"So how long are you in town for?" Blossom asked.

"Uh, not too long," Clark said.

"Where did you move from?"

"Newark."

"Oh."

If the conversation went downhill from there, at least it hadn't had far to fall, Clark thought as he walked Blossom home. Trouble was, he'd never in his life asked a woman out with the goal of getting her into bed. Well, not on the first night, at least. It just didn't seem respectful. He believed in the getting-to-know-you stage. Which led to the falling-in-love stage. Which led to the hot monkey sex stage.

Not that he'd ever had hot monkey sex personally, but he'd seen pictures of it on the Internet. And he'd be more than willing to give it a try with Blossom. He sidled a glance in her direction. She was walking a step in front of him, her head up, high heels clicking on the sidewalk. Her cute round bottom swayed back and forth enticingly.

Don't panic, he told himself. He could do it. He had to. After all, the fate of the world hung in the balance. He was going to have to make a move. Tonight.

They reached Blossom's apartment door. "Can I come in?" Clark asked, shifting his laptop case from his right hand to his left. "I'd like a glass of water." Ah, hell. Another smooth line. He was full of them tonight. He wasn't kidding about the water, though. He was parched. And damn if his back didn't itch like crazy. He shifted his shoulders, trying to get some relief without being too obvious.

Blossom hesitated. "Well, okay. For a minute."

She fished her house key from her purse. It dangled from a Superman key chain.

Cool, Clark thought. He rocked back on his heels as she unlocked the door, then followed her over the threshold. She flicked the light switch.

He blinked, sure his eyes were playing tricks on him. He put down the laptop, took off his glasses, checked them for smudges, and put them back on again. No, he wasn't hallucinating. The keychain was the least of it.

Blossom's apartment was a veritable shrine to Superman.

Every square millimeter of wall space was dedicated to the Man of Steel, in all his various comic, TV, and movie incarnations. Vintage comic books, professionally framed and mounted, hung above the sofa. Posters of George Reeve, Dean Cain, Christopher Reeves, and Tom Welling marched along the opposite wall. A Superman lunchbox perched on a shelf in the kitchen. A revolving Daily Planet desk lamp adorned the table near the door.

Incredible.

"You got a thing for Superman?" he asked.

"Yeah," she said, giving him a sheepish grin. "Pretty weird, huh?"

"Not at all," Clark said quickly. "I think it's great. I'm a Superman fan myself."

"You are?"

"Yeah. Because of my name." He resisted scratching a fierce itch on the inside of his elbow. "I collect Superman comic books, mostly. I have a complete set of Golden Age Action Comics from 1947 through 1956." He frowned. "Well, except for #158. I tried to buy that one on eBay Wednesday night, but someone snatched it right out from under my nose."

Blossom's blue eyes went round. "You ran up that bid? You jerk! You cost me five hundred dollars!"

She was the mystery bidder? "You didn't have to go so high," Clark told her. "You could have dropped out."

"No way was I going to wimp out. I've been looking for that issue for a year."

"So have I," Clark said, then laughed. "But if I had to lose, I'm glad it was to you."

Blossom smiled. "Really?"

"Yes," said Clark, resisting the urge to claw the niggling itch on his thigh. He moved close, daring to brush his fingers over the freckles on Blossom's cheek. She didn't move away. His heart tripped up a beat, then settled in double time.

He started to sweat. Should he try to kiss her now? God, it was hot in here. Didn't she have air conditioning? His gaze dropped to her lips. They were full and lush, a little pouty. An itch hit him on the neck. He ignored it and leaned closer, until their lips were only inches apart.

Her eyes closed.

Was it his imagination, or was she swaying toward him? Emboldened, he framed her face in his hands, threaded his fingers through her hair. His heart beat so loudly in his chest it sounded like a car alarm.

Their lips touched. Clark felt the contact all the way to his toes, and in a few strategic places in between. He angled his head a little, to get his glasses out of the way of the kiss. He really should have thought to take them off earlier.

Blossom trembled a bit. Her hands came to rest on his arms. His thigh itched again, distracting him. He shook off the intrusion and kissed her again, a little harder and longer this time.

Was it too early for tongues?

Maybe, but he really didn't have time to waste. He decided to go for it.

He wrapped Blossom in his arms, urging her closer as he stroked her lower lip with the tip of his tongue. She sighed, opening her mouth and going all soft in his arms. An invitation? He hoped so. His tongue slid inside. Stroked in and out.

Oh, yeah. This was it. His little Man of Steel was so ready to save the world.

But the back of his neck itched like hell.

He moved one hand around Blossom's torso, toward her breast. Easy... Easy... He didn't want to scare her. After all, he knew for a fact she'd never had a memorable sexual experience. She was probably shy about things like this.

His fingers found their goal. Closed on soft, quivering flesh...

Blossom swatted his hand away. He tried an evasive maneuver. She attempted a block. He circumvented it.

She knocked him on his ass.

He lay flat on his back on the carpet, staring up at her. "Wha...?"

"Self defense class," she said, looking startled, yet satisfied.

"Jeez." Who would have thought?

"You have some nerve," she continued, hands on hips. "Trying to cop a feel on a first date."

He sat up, rubbing the back of his head. "Sorry."

Blossom pointed toward the door. "Out."

"Hey," he said, jumping to his feet. "Don't you think that's a little hasty?"

"No," she said. "I mean, it's not like I'm going to see you again or anything."

"Not see me--" Hell, that didn't sound at all encouraging. He wriggled to evade a sudden itch on his hip. "Why not? I thought we were getting along great."

"We were," Blossom said, "but that's not the point."

Even if he lived out the average superhero lifespan of two hundred and three, Clark would never, ever get the hang of female logic. "All right. I'll bite. What is the point?"

"The point is you look like John Travolta's scrawnier brother," she said. "I couldn't possibly go out with you again."

"I don't even like this outfit," Clark said, ignoring the negative comment about his physique. "A saleslady picked it out."

"And you let her," Blossom muttered. "That's even worse. Look, I spend all day and most nights surrounded by geeks like you. No offense, but I don't think I can go twenty-four seven with it. It's too hard on the eyes."

Clark eyed the collage of superhero muscle on her walls, his heart sinking. He had a pretty good idea what Blossom was looking for in a lover. No matter how you sliced and diced it, he didn't have it.

Still, he couldn't give up. Not with Lex's bomb set to blow.

He tried to reason with her. "Looks aren't everything. Didn't you say that yesterday?"

"Did I?" Blossom said. "I must have been out of my mind. Looks are huge. Ninety percent of the information humans receive from their environment is visual. For me it's probably more like a hundred and one percent." She sighed. "Look, I'm sorry, Clark. I just can't help how I am. You're a great guy and all, but--"

But. Clark hated when a woman said that word. In his experience it was usually followed by...

"--can't we just be friends?"

"Of course," he said, going for his standard reply.

The itch on his neck grew unbearable. Weighted down by Blossom's rejection, he finally cracked. He gave in and scratched.

The itch darted to his solar plexus. His fingers followed it. After that, it split, attacking both shoulders at once. Then it reached flashpoint, racing across his chest, down his arms and legs, up over his face...

"Are you okay?" Blossom asked. "Because, you know, you don't look so good."

Clark dropped to his knees, knocking over his laptop case on the way down. He tried desperately to reach a spot right in the middle of his back. But the itching was the least of his problems. It was getting hard to breathe. Little red spots swirled into his vision.

"Call 911," he gasped, just before he blacked out.

Chapter Five

Friday, 11:22 p.m.
One day, thirty-eight minutes, and counting...

"Hives and anaphylaxis," Clark told Blossom when he emerged from the emergency room cubicle, looking beat. "The doctor thinks it was the calamari."

She jumped to her feet. "You scared me half to death. I'm still shaking. You could have died."

"Look on the bright side," Clark said. "If I get bored tonight, I can play dot to dot on my chest."

She giggled. Then sobered as her gaze dropped. The top two buttons on Clark's shirt were, for once, unbuttoned. Angry red welts covered his skin, looking horribly uncomfortable.

"Does it itch bad?" she asked.

He grimaced. "Bad enough."

She clucked in sympathy, and looked at his chest some more. It might not be superhero material, but it wasn't really that scrawny. Suddenly, she felt a little ashamed at how she had treated him during their date.

"I'm sorry about what I said earlier," she told him.

"Which time?" he asked. But he was smiling when he said it. He had a nice smile. And he was so at ease poking fun at himself. There was something very appealing about that.

"When I said you were scrawny," she said.

"Oh, that." He glanced down at his chest. "No apology needed for the truth." He caught her gaze and held it. "I'm the one who should be apologizing. My behavior was less than gentlemanly."

"Forget about it," Blossom said, coloring. "No offense taken." The truth was, she'd enjoyed kissing Clark. Too much. That, more than anything else, had caused her to back off. She just couldn't bear the thought of a geek boyfriend.

"The doctor gave me a shot," Clark was saying. "It'll take a few hours to work." He gave a half laugh. "I don't think I'll get much sleep tonight."

"I'm a night owl myself," Blossom said. "You know..." She stopped herself, suddenly uncertain.

Just friends, she reminded herself.

"What?" he asked.

Why did it seem so hard to breathe all of a sudden? "As long as we're both going to be up," she said, "I was thinking maybe you'd like to come back to my place. We could..." She hesitated. No guy she'd ever dated had wanted to do what she was about to propose. Would Clark be shocked? Dismayed? Worse, would he laugh?

She drew a deep breath. There was only one way to find out.

"...watch some 1950s Superman TV episodes. I have a pretty big collection on video."

"Cool," said Clark without hesitating a beat. "Do you have the one where an asteroid gives Superman amnesia?"

Blossom's heart gave a funny little jump. "Episode #38. Panic in the Sky. Yep, I have it."

"Great," said Clark. "That's my favorite."

* * * *

Saturday, 5:59 a.m.
Eighteen hours, one minute, and counting...

Clark woke up slowly, every muscle protesting. Somehow he'd twisted himself into a pretzel on a couch that was way too soft to offer much support to his back. He blinked up at the wall and frowned at the four-color hammered tin image of a vintage Superman, chest muscles bulging as he tore apart a heavy chain with his bare hands.

Where the hell was he?

Oh yeah. Blossom's living room.

They'd had a great night, despite the residual itching from the calamari. They'd watched episode after episode of classic Superman, laughing over the cheesy special effects, but loving the stories all the same. Blossom had changed from her dress into a comfortable oversized T-shirt and men's boxers. She'd made popcorn and poured soda, and they stayed up until four a.m.

But he hadn't touched her once.

Groaning, Clark rolled over and eyed the door to her bedroom. The firmly closed door to her bedroom. Bruce would have been in there by now, he reflected bleakly. Bruce's physique would have blinded Blossom to his less-than-superheroic emotional traits, providing him quick and easy access to her bed. And once there, Bruce would have wasted no time in plying his legendary bedroom skills to give Blossom the sexual fulfillment she needed to trigger her own powers.

Still, things could be worse. At least he and Blossom shared the basics for a good friendship. They liked the same jokes, and she loved superheroes and everything about them. Plus, she seemed to be comfortable around him.

He grimaced. As long as she didn't look at him, that is. But he had spent the night at her apartment. She could have kicked him out, but she hadn't. That counted for something, right? Given enough time...

Except he didn't have enough time.

Shit.

He should have been expecting Captain Marvelous' wake-up call, but the cell phone chirp still took him by surprise.

He grabbed his glasses with one hand and his laptop case with the other. He tore open the Velcro and pulled out his cell. "Kendall here."

"What's the report, Clark? Are you in yet?"

Clark winced at the Captain's choice of words. "Uh, not exactly, sir."

"Not good enough, Clark, you know that. Time's running out."

Clark gave a surreptitious glance toward Blossom's door. "I'm working on it. I spent the night in her apartment."

The Captain perked up. "In her bedroom?"

"Uh, no," Clark said. "On the couch."

A brief silence ensued, then the Captain heaved a sigh. "Clark, much as I hate to admit it, I'm beginning to think I made a mistake sending you to Megalopolis."

Clark struggled to right himself on the understuffed couch cushion. "Not at all, Captain. I can do this. I just need a little more time."

"Unfortunately, that's something I don't have to give," the Captain said. "Lex's bomb is set to go off in..."

"...seventeen hours and fifty-eight minutes," Clark finished for him. "Believe me, I know."

"Then you understand I've got no choice, son. I'm sending in backup."

Clark's stomach abruptly knotted. "Who?"

"Why, Bruce Wynn, of course. Who else?"

* * * *

Saturday, 6:15 a.m.

Seventeen hours, forty-five minutes, and counting...

Blossom was dressing when she heard Clark's phone ring. Who would call him at this hour?

A girlfriend?

The thought made her stomach lurch, though she couldn't quite imagine why. It's not like she wanted him for herself or anything. Even though she'd had more fun last night in ... heck, she didn't know how long. Clark was really the nicest guy. She revised her theory about the girlfriend caller. It just didn't seem in Clark's character to cheat on an unsuspecting significant other. Not that any cheating had gone on, mind you. The whole night had been totally innocent.

Blossom zipped up her jeans and wriggled into a green and gold MPI tee shirt. She and Clark had watched TV for hours, but he hadn't tried to kiss her again. She felt a little conflicted about that. On one hand, he'd had plenty of opportunity. She should be insulted he hadn't taken advantage of it. On the other hand, who could blame him if he hadn't? When he'd tried it the first time, she'd decked him.

She eased open the door. "Clark? Are you up?" She wouldn't want him to think she was eavesdropping.

He snapped his phone closed and shoved it into his laptop case. "Yeah," he said, getting to his feet.

His white pants were a bit rumpled, but at least his black shirt was all the way unbuttoned now, and hanging loose. His feet were bare. Somehow, that seemed unsettling.

She made it halfway across the room before her legs refused to take her any further. "Your chest looks a lot better," she said. Inanely. "I mean, the hives and all."

"The itching's gone," he replied, not moving.

She changed direction, heading for the kitchen. "Want some coffee? I usually pick it up on my way to the lab, but I can--"

"No thanks," he said. "Let's go out to breakfast."

"Can't. I have a meeting with my Ph.D. advisor at seven."

"On a Saturday morning?"

"Yeah. Graduate students don't exactly keep corporate hours."

"Meet me after, then."

"I have a ton of work to do."

His tone turned desperate. "Lunch, then. You have to eat, right?"

"I guess. How 'bout the Burger Shack? It's a couple blocks down the street, on Main. At eleven forty-five?"

"It'll have to do," said Clark. "See you then."

* * * *

Saturday, 8:48 a.m.
Fifteen hours, twelve minutes, and counting...

Clark leaned on the stand up counter at the local coffeehouse and took a bracing gulp of his caramel latte. He had to do something about Blossom. The "just friends" thing was all very well and good, but with time ticking by like--well, like a neutron bomb ready to explode--he couldn't afford to kick back and wait for favorable developments. He had to come up with a viable plan for her seduction. One that would take Blossom's mind off her narrow visual focus and let her concentrate on her feelings. He knew she liked him a little. If she harbored even one one-hundredth of the attraction he felt for her, he would succeed.

After years of fantasizing about Diana Price, it was odd he should feel this way. Diana was every man's dream. The kind of woman you saw in a centerfold. Tall. Voluptuous. Gorgeous. Self-confident. Hot. And if Diana had a brain, it wasn't immediately apparent.

Blossom couldn't begin to compete. Sure, she was cute, especially with all those freckles on her upturned nose, but no one would have handed her first place in a beauty contest. Her breasts were barely a B cup, and her legs weren't long and shapely. Her hair frizzed a little. But she was smart. And fun, once you got past her I-hate-geeks façade. She had a great sense of humor, and to Clark, that counted for a lot.

She was a little unsure of herself, in an endearing kind of way. Maybe that was why she obsessed so much about Superman. Maybe subconsciously, she wanted to set her standard so high no man could reach it. So she wouldn't get hurt.

I wouldn't hurt her, Clark thought. If she wanted him, he'd be hers in three seconds flat. After he triggered

Blossom's superpowers and saved the world, they could hook up for good. He took a long sip of coffee, spinning that fantasy for a while. They could get married, buy a house in the suburbs not too far from HI headquarters, have two-point-three kids and a dog...

But he had to get her into bed first. Before Bruce arrived on the scene. When that happened, Blossom would take one look at Bruce's steroid-enhanced pectorals and melt into a gooey puddle on the sidewalk. All the women did.

A hot rush of anger surged through him. No way could he let Bruce Wynn, Superjerk, hurt Blossom. Clark would face down a whole freezer full of calamari before he'd let that happen.

If only he could get Blossom's mind off the visual...

He straightened abruptly. That was it. Get Blossom's mind off the visual.

Could he do it?

Chapter Six

Saturday, 12:15 p.m.
Eleven hours, forty-five minutes, and counting...

Blossom dumped three packs of sugar into her iced tea, all the while keeping one eye on the door. Clark was late. He wouldn't stand her up, would he? A little twitch of fear wiggled in her stomach. Maybe he'd decided she was too geeky for him. He wouldn't be the first guy to decide that.

"Hey, babe. Got a minute?"

The speaker was a man. A beautiful man. Blossom looked behind her, but she didn't see anyone he might have been speaking to.

She turned back. "You mean me?"

"Yeah, babe. You."

She drank him in. Over six feet tall, with dark hair, dark eyes, and chiseled features. And dressed all in delicious black. A T-shirt stretched so tight across his unbelievable chest it was in danger of coming apart at the seams. Leather pants hugged lean hips and long muscular legs with just the right amount of loving cling. Blossom's eyes widened. The incredible bulge between his thighs was definitely superhero material.

Her stomach executed an Olympic grade back flip. This guy outshone every last poster on her wall. God, he was hot. Scorching. Just touching him would probably give her third degree burns.

"Did you want me for something?" she asked.

"Oh, yeah." He let the words hang there in the air between them until she blushed. "Can I join you?"

"Me?" He had to be kidding. No man in his league had ever even blinked in her direction.

His gaze drifted over her, sending little tingles zapping all over her skin. "I saw you sitting here," he said. "And I thought, what a crime such a beautiful girl has to eat lunch alone. I'll buy you lunch, babe."

She stared at him for a good five seconds before she realized he was waiting for some kind of reply. "Sure," she said, waving toward the empty booth seat opposite.

Oh, wait. What about Clark? She gave another glance toward the door. Well, heck. He was late. It would serve him right to find her with another man. Not that it mattered. . After all, it wasn't as if she and Clark had anything going on.

She swallowed a little pang of guilt as the hottie's perfect butt slid across the vinyl bench seat.

She shoved a menu at him. "What would you like?"

He held her gaze. "I'm looking at it, babe."

"Oh," squeaked Blossom, her throat suddenly dry. She licked her lips. His incredible eyes darkened.

Oh, God.

"What did you say your name was?" she asked.

* * * *

Saturday, 12:31 p.m.
Eleven hours, twenty-nine minutes, and counting...

The key to success in any venture, Clark decided as he hurried to his lunch date with Blossom, lay in careful research and meticulous planning. Of course, promptness didn't hurt either. He checked his watch and winced. He was late, late, late. He hoped Blossom didn't think he'd stood her up.

He clutched his laptop case in one hand, thinking of the extra items it held. Items he'd purchased, then promptly hidden in the zippered and Velcroed pockets. The store he'd visited was the kind that didn't open until noon, and it had taken a little time--after he'd recovered from pure shock--to sort through its offerings. After all, the fate of the world depended on his choices.

He hurried the last few steps to the Burger Shack and shoved open the door.

And stopped dead in his tracks.

Shit.

Bruce Wynn was in town.

Clark plowed through the knot of customers at the door. He'd known Bruce was coming to hit on Blossom, but the fact hadn't registered until now. His stomach lurched as Bruce's manicured hand crept across the table to stroke Blossom's fingers. He said something. She laughed.

No way was this happening, Clark thought darkly. Blossom was much too nice a girl to get caught by a predator like Bruce. Clark pushed his glasses up the bridge of his nose and squared his shoulders. His grip tightened on the handle of his laptop case.

He marched to Blossom's rescue.

"Clark," Blossom said, not quite meeting his gaze.

"I thought we had a lunch date," Clark said tersely.

Bruce lounged back, draping one arm over the back of the booth seat, an amused smile playing on his lips.

Blossom's eyes sparked with annoyance. "You were late, Clark, but luckily I got another invitation for lunch." She waved a hand across the table. "This is Bruce."

"Pleased to meet you," Bruce said.

"Bruce thought it would be a shame if I had to eat alone," Blossom said.

"I'm sure," said Clark dryly.

"A word of advice," Bruce said, talking to Clark but keeping his gaze trained on Blossom. "Never leave a beautiful woman waiting."

Blossom giggled, soaking it up. Puh-lease, thought Clark. How could an intelligent girl like Blossom not see through Bruce's act? It was incomprehensible.

Clark shifted his laptop to his other hand. "I'm sorry I'm late," he said to Blossom. "But I really couldn't help it. Come on. Tell this joker to get lost."

"I can't," said Blossom. "We've already ordered. Maybe you and I could get together some other time."

"Fine," said Clark. "I'll wait until you're done lunch and walk you back to campus."

"Oh," said Blossom, looking nonplussed. "That won't work. Bruce said he'd drive me."

"Dinner, then?"

"I'm working late."

"I'll pick you up."

She shook her head. "No. Bruce and I--"

"Forget it," Clark cut in. "Just forget it."

He turned on his heel and strode off, seething.

"Clark..." Blossom called.

He paused, hopeful, not daring to turn.

"Let him go, babe," Bruce said. "He'll cool off."

"I guess you're right," he heard Blossom say.

Clark trudged on, toward the rear of the restaurant. He couldn't afford to leave the building, not with Bruce drooling over Blossom like a condemned man over his last slice of cheesecake. He banged into the men's room, deep in thought. He needed help, and fast. But who...

That's it. He tore open a pocket on his laptop case and slid out his cell phone. No signal. Well, it freaking figured, didn't it? He just couldn't catch a break on this assignment.

He climbed up on a sink and held the phone near the single window, high up on the wall, trying to catch a satellite beam.

The door creaked open, admitting an elderly man. He gave Clark a startled glance, then shuffled over to a urinal and unzipped his pants.

The phone beeped. Yes! Clark punched in a number and waited grimly for an answer.

"Hello?"

He didn't beat around the bush. "Diana. You've got to help me."

"Clark? Is that you?" Diana's breathless little laugh wafted over the wireless connection. "I thought you were on assignment."

"I am. And it was going fine. But now Bruce is in town and he's going to blow it for me. He's going to have Blossom in bed before dinner."

The old codger at the urinals looked up from his business and shot Clark an interested glance.

Clark lowered his voice, trying to keep his footing on the edge of the sink. "You've got to help me, Diana."

He could almost see her inspecting her long, red fingernails for flaws. "I don't know, Clark..."

He wasn't in the mood for her games. "Come on. You know you owe me."

The old man zipped up.

"Owe you? For what?"

"Programming your DVD player, for one thing. Updating the virus protection on your PC. And what about last spring when I reset every clock in your house for Daylight Savings Time? What are you going to do in October when you have to set them all back again?"

A long silence, broken only by the flush of the urinal.

"Diana..."

She gave a little sigh. "Oh, all right. I guess I can help you out, if it doesn't take too long. I'm in the middle of something."

"What?"

"Shopping. In downtown Megalopolis. And you know how hard it is for a superheroine to get a free afternoon."

"Megalopolis?" Clark laughed out loud. Finally, a break. "Perfect. How far are you from MPI?"

"About ten minutes," Diana said. "Why? What do you want me to do?"

The old man shuffled up to the sink next to Clark's and cocked his eyebrows.

"Get lost," Clark told him. "No, not you, Diana."

"Hmph," Diana said.

Clark waited while the old man dried his hands and creaked out the door.

"Clark? Are you still there? I haven't got all day, you know. I have a facial at four."

"You'll be done way before then," Clark assured her, and proceeded to outline his plan.

* * * *

Saturday, 12:57 p.m.

Eleven hours, three minutes, and counting...

Clark had to admit, Diana really had a flair for the dramatic. And she showed up right on cue, just as the Burger Shack waitress brought Bruce the check. She'd outdone herself with the costume. Clark barely recognized her.

He watched as Diana, garbed in a shapeless, colorless housecoat, waddled through the restaurant. He wasn't sure what she'd stuffed under her dress to simulate an eight-and-a-half month pregnancy, but from his position at the door to the men's room, her round stomach looked pretty damn convincing. Pink foam rollers stuck out all over her head and fuzzy pink slippers encased her feet.

Clark had lusted after Diana for years, but in all that time, he'd never seen her without makeup. Amazingly, without cosmetic assistance, Diana's looks hovered around average. Blossom's fresh, unadorned complexion was much more appealing. Clark mused over the discovery. Who would have guessed it?

Diana, clearly enjoying herself, waltzed halfway down the aisle. She stopped, made a big show of spotting Bruce and Blossom, and let out an earsplitting shriek.

Every head in the place turned.

"You!" she cried, marching up to Bruce and jabbing him on the shoulder with one finger. "You ... you ... worthless, low-life, two-timing excuse for a man!"

"Diana?" Bruce said.

Clark chuckled. Old Bruce was pretty slow on the uptake. He didn't even have the presence of mind to pretend ignorance.

Blossom gasped. "You know this woman?"

"Know me?" Diana yelled. She smoothed her hands over her impressive girth, arching her back and thrusting her belly in Bruce's face. "I'd say my husband knows me pretty damn well, wouldn't you?"

A purple-haired lady at the next table looked up from her lemon meringue pie. "I'd say so, honey."

Bruce's eyes bugged out. "What the hell--"

"Oh. My. God." Blossom scooted down to the end of booth seat. "You're married?"

"No," said Bruce, grabbing her wrist. "I'm not. Don't go. I don't have anything to do with this." He glared at Diana. "It's a set up."

"Don't you believe him, girlfriend," the lady with the purple hair advised.

"Right. Whatever." Blossom slapped Bruce's arm with her backpack. "Let me go."

Shit. Clark grabbed his laptop and jogged up the aisle. He hadn't counted on Bruce getting physical.

"Blossom, I--" Bruce started.

Clark staggered to a stop at the table and whipped out his cell phone. "You better do what she says," he puffed. "Or I'm calling the cops."

"Clark--" Blossom said.

"You," Bruce said, sending Clark a look that could vaporize. "I should have known. Go to hell. She's mine."

"See what I have to put up with?" Diana complained to the gathering crowd.

"What an asshole." The purple haired lady climbed onto her seat, straining for a better view. "Honey," she said to Blossom. "Get out while the getting's good. Guys like him are no damn picnic. They boink you once and think they own you."

"No," Bruce said, re-anchoring his grip on Blossom's wrist. "It's not like that. I can explain."

"Let ... me ... go," repeated Blossom, landing three more backpack blows to Bruce's arm.

Clark grabbed hold of Bruce's arm and pulled, using his laptop for leverage. He didn't move the hard muscles an inch. "You heard her," he said. "Let go."

"Not until she listens to me." He winced as Blossom's backpack whacked him upside the head. "What have you got in that thing?"

"You can forget me ever listening to you," Blossom said, angling for another blow. "Let me go!"

"No, I--"

Clark looped his arm around Bruce's neck and yanked as hard as he could. Nothing.

"That's it." Diana reached through the tangle of arms and put the supersqueeze on Bruce's wrist. "You're a sexist clod, Bruce. I don't know what I ever saw in you. We're through."

"Aaaaahh--" Bruce clawed at Diana's fingers with one hand. The other arm fended off Blossom's next attack.

Diana gave him an elbow under the chin.

"Ooof." Bruce fell back on the booth seat.

"You go, girlfriend," the purple-haired woman yelled.

The crowd pressed forward. "Come on," Clark said, tugging Blossom out of Bruce's limp grasp. "Let's get out of here."

"Noooo!" cried Bruce, lunging after them.

Diana crossed her wrists in front of her chest. She spun around once, fake stomach bouncing, and kicked out a leg. Bruce tried to vault it, aimed too low, and landed face first in the aisle.

Diana scooped up the purple-haired woman's lemon meringue pie and dumped it on Bruce's head. Bruce heaved himself to his knees. Diana jumped him.

"Ooof!" Bruce's lungs deflated.

They went down, limbs flailing, rolling down the aisle. The crowd parted. Someone called for the cops. The waitress shoved her way to the register and grabbed a phone. The lady with the purple hair jumped up on her booth table and shouted a play-by-play.

Clark grabbed Blossom around the waist. He shoved her through the crowd, angling for the back door. His laptop banged against his leg as they scurried around a smelly dumpster, up an alley, and across Main Street. They veered right on Broad. Sirens sounded in the distance.

They didn't stop until they reached Blossom's apartment. Clark doubled over in front of the door, trying to catch his breath. A sharp pain sliced through his right side. He was out of shape, no doubt about it. Too many damn hours in front of the computer. He really should do something about that. Take up jogging, maybe.

Beside him, Blossom was shaking. Ah, hell. Bruce's cave man tactics must have traumatized her. Anger surged into Clark's veins. He'd get Bruce back for this one. The next time Bruce Wynn, Superjerk, tried to log onto his HI user account, he'd better be prepared for a fight.

His network connection was going down, down, down.

Blossom shuddered again. Her hands covered her face and her shoulders heaved. Clark shifted uneasily, passing his laptop from one hand to the other. Hell. He'd rather confront twenty Evil Maniacal Geniuses than face a single feminine tear. He didn't know the first thing about pulling a hysterical woman together.

He reached out and put a timid hand on Blossom's shoulder. "It's ... uh ... all right."

Her shoulders only shook harder. He took a deep breath and stepped a little closer, patting her awkwardly on the arm. "Blossom. Please don't..."

She looked up and laughed in his face.

Clark gaped at her. "You're not crying."

"Crying?" she gasped. "God, no." She dissolved in a fit of giggles. "I've never ... seen anything ... so funny." She doubled over again, fighting for breath. "As when that guy hit the ground." She hiccupped.

Clark let out a relieved snort. "Me neither." He sobered a little. "I'm sorry I was late. The whole thing was my fault."

"No it wasn't," Blossom said quickly. "It was mine. I should have waited for you. I should have known things wouldn't work out with Bruce."

"Why not?"

She sighed. "He was too good to be true."

"He's not good at all," Clark pointed out. "He's a jerk. A totally ripped, phenomenally handsome jerk, but still."

"You're right," Blossom said. "I know you are. And I really try to like regular guys. I do. But the truth is, they just don't turn me on. I mean, take you for example."

Clark winced.

"You're great. You're smart, nice, and you have a good sense of humor. You really seem to like me--"

"I do," Clark put in.

"--but I just can't get excited about you. It would make life a whole heck of a lot easier if I could." Her voice rose, trembling dangerously. "I'm an idiot." She started blinking furiously.

Damn. Looked like those tears might materialize after all.

"Uh, Blossom--"

"I'm a loser, Clark. A geeky loser."

"No, you're not," he said. "You're just--"

"Don't tell me what I am."

"Uh, okay. Listen, Blossom--"

"Do you want to hear something really pathetic?" She couldn't seem to meet his gaze.

"No, I--"

"I've never had an orgasm."

"I know. That's why--"

Blossom's head snapped up. "You know? How the hell could you know? I just met you two days ago."

"Uh, I mean, I guessed," Clark said, backpedaling as fast as he could. "I can tell you're a woman who..."

"Who what?"

"Um... You're somebody that wouldn't..."

"Wouldn't what?"

"Sleep around," Clark finished feebly.

"Sleep around? I don't sleep around! Heck, I'm practically a virgin! How can you say that?"

"I didn't," Clark pointed out swiftly. "I was just trying to say--"

"I'm a mess." Blossom's eyes filled with tears.

"No," Clark said. He put down his laptop, inched closer, and draped one arm over her shoulders. "You're great. Fantastic. And very sexy."

"I'm frigid."

"You're not. I'm sure you'll have an orgasm when the right man comes along."

She sniffed. "You really think so?"

"Yes," Clark said. "All you have to do is close your eyes."

"Close my eyes?"

"Yeah. Close your eyes and listen to your heart."

Blossom sighed. "That's easier said than done. I'm a very visually oriented person, in case you hadn't noticed."

"I had," Clark said dryly. He maneuvered his free hand into his laptop zipper compartment. "But you know, if you're willing, I could help you overcome that."

Blossom's brows drew together. "How?"

He lifted a narrow swath of black satin. A blindfold. One of the purchases he'd made an hour ago. He dangled it in front of her.

"First," he said, "you tie this over your eyes."

Blossom stared at the thing. "You want me to put on a blindfold?"

"Yes," Clark said. "I do." She closed her eyes, as if imagining it. He felt a little shudder race through her.

He started getting hard.

She opened her eyes. "First I put on the blindfold," she repeated. She frowned a little. "And then what happens?"

"Then," Clark said, "you trust me."

Chapter Seven

Saturday, 1:39 p.m.
Ten hours, twenty-one minutes, and counting...

Clark's blindfold was black, soft, and utterly tantalizing. Blossom closed her eyes and tried to imagine how it would feel draped over her face. Blocking her vision. The bottom glided out of her belly and a soft tingling sprang to life between her thighs.

Clark's low, rich voice washed over her, sending little ripples of pleasure across her skin. "What do you say?"

Silence stretched between them for one heartbeat, two, three. "I don't know," Blossom said finally.

He ran the blindfold down her bare arm. It was cool, soft, and oh-so-smooth. "Just try it. I'll stop whenever you say."

She believed him. He was too nice of a guy to lie to her.

She took the long swath of material in her hands. The center was wide, and double thickness. The ends narrowed into long ties. She held it up to her eyes, pressing the fabric flat, trying to see through it.

Nothing.

Only inky darkness.

She jumped when Clark's warm hand descended on her nape. "Put it on," he whispered. His breath was moist on her neck. The tingling between her thighs started up again, more urgent this time. "Go on."

With shaking hands, she smoothed the blindfold over her eyes and crossed the laces behind her head.

"Here," Clark said, easing the ties from her fingers. "Let me help you." With swift, sure strokes, he secured the blindfold.

When she reached up to touch it, he trapped her hands in his. "Just relax."

"All right. I'll try." It was a blatant lie. Having her sight taken away had started her heart jack-hammering in her chest. No way could she relax.

She felt Clark shift behind her. He bent, as if retrieving something from the ground. His laptop, she thought, a little smile touching her lips. He was such a geek. But for the first time, the thought didn't disturb her.

He turned her, exerting a gentle pressure with his hand at the small of her back.

"Wait," she said. "First I want to know what else you've got in that bag."

He gave a low laugh. A rather sexy laugh, she thought. Funny how she hadn't noticed that about him before. She heard the scritch of a zipper. "You mean in here?"

"Yes."

"Just a few things I picked up on Spring Street."

"Spring Street?" she said. "But that's--"

"--a very, let's say, 'colorful' part of town." He laughed again. The sound made her want to lean back and melt into him. "I went shopping in a little store called Lavish Love."

She giggled. "It sounds like a porno flick."

"I think they shoot those in the back," Clark said. "In the front ... well, you'll just have to wait and see. I mean feel," he corrected himself.

He kissed her neck, just below the ear. She hadn't expected it, and the suddenness doubled the sweetness of the caress. He nipped his way up to her ear and swirled his tongue around the shell.

"Oh, God," she whispered. "That feels incredible."

"It's only the start," Clark whispered. He pushed her gently forward. "Now will you start walking?"

She nodded. He guided her to her apartment, pausing to extract the keys from her backpack. Then the door clicked shut behind them. His laptop case thudded to the floor.

Clark's arm dipped behind her knees. She clutched his shoulders as her feet left the ground. He carried her through black space. It was a strange feeling. Like being adrift on an endless sea. She heard him kick a door open.

Her bedroom. She tried to remember if she'd left the bed unmade. No. When she landed on the bed, it was on top of the comforter. It puffed around her like a cloud, with a little whoosh as it settled.

Clark came down on top of her, the weight of his lower body pressing her into the mattress, his upper body supported on rigid arms. She ran her hands up his arms, along his shoulder, across his chest. Funny. In darkness he seemed bigger, more muscular than she had thought. And so much more solid.

He smelled nice. A hint of aftershave overlying a scent of plain soap. She could hear his breathing--fast intakes of breath. She spread her palm over his heart. It was beating almost as fast as hers.

He kissed her. His lips were firm, mobile. They tasted of mint. They coaxed hers apart, and she sighed, letting him in. Who'd have thought that a geek would know how to kiss so well? It seemed Clark was full of surprises.

His tongue plunged and receded. She clung to him, enjoying the sensation. It ended too soon, but she didn't have time to miss it. Her attention snapped to his fingers, which were undoing the buttons on her blouse.

Sudden fear stabbed her. She couldn't see him, but he didn't have the same handicap. Would he like what he saw when he undressed her? How would she know what he thought if she couldn't look into his eyes?

Her hand rose to stop him, but her blouse was already undone. His fingers stroked along the edges of her bra, then found the front closure.

"Clark, I--"

"Shh..." he said. "Don't worry. Everything's fine."

"I don't know. I'm not sure I want you looking at me."

His hands paused. "Why not?"

"Because ... I'm not much to look at. No curves."

He chuckled. "Oh, I don't know about that." Her bra fell open and his palms cupped her breasts. "Looks to me like your curves are just fine. Perfect, in fact."

She felt his breath on her skin, then his mouth closed, hot and intense, on her nipple. She moaned, arching her back. Her fingers threaded into his thick hair, holding his head to her breast. He nipped and suckled, then licked a wet line to the other side and started all over again. Each tug of his lips and teeth shot a line of erotic fire straight to her groin. She moaned and wriggled, trying to ease the pressure building there.

After a few minutes, he eased away. "I'm going to undress you the rest of the way now." His voice trembled. "Is that all right?"

Blossom's heart pounded into her throat. "Yes."

He eased her arms out of her blouse and bra, and then they were gone. He unsnapped her jeans and drew the zipper down, link by link. His hands were unsteady. Shaking. Cool air wafted over her as he moved to the end of the bed to slip off her shoes and socks. Then her jeans slid over her hips and down her legs.

Had her panties gone with them? No. He rose over her, easing his fingers around the elastic at her hips and thighs, brushing his thumbs over the swollen mound beneath. She groaned a little, pushing upward into his hand. He slipped his hands around her hips and cradled her buttocks in his hands. He drew her panties down her legs, inch by excruciating inch.

He moved away from the bed, leaving her naked, blind, and vulnerable.

"What about your clothes?" she asked. "I want them off, too."

"Soon," he told her. His voice didn't seem too steady, and that made her feel a little bit better. She heard his footsteps retreat from the room.

She shifted, trying to get comfortable on the bed, turning her head so as to better catch the sounds coming from the living room. She heard the scruff of Velcro separating.

The laptop case again. She listened more carefully. She heard a tiny cracking sound, then a click, a snap, and another click.

A gentle whirring told her he'd started a CD spinning in her player. A moment later, strains of lush music enveloped her. In the background, an ocean broke on an invisible shoreline. She heard a birdcall, then the rush of the wind. The surf pounded again, hard and sure. Blossom's body responded. Her arousal coiled a little tighter and she shifted, unsettled.

"Do you like it?" Clark whispered.

"Yes." She held out her arms in the direction of his voice. "Come here and I'll show you how much."

"In a minute," he replied. He moved around the bed again. She heard the laptop zipper. Another purchase from Lavish Love?

She heard a clink, then the strike of a match. The faint smell of sulfur drifted past, then a richer, spicier scent.

"Cinnamon," she whispered. "I love cinnamon. How did you know?"

"I didn't," said Clark. "I got it because it reminded me of your hair."

She smiled at that.

"What else do you have in that bag?"

More Velcro. Blossom ran her hands down her body, excitement rising.

The Velcro stopped. "Do that again," Clark said.

"What?"

"That thing with your hands."

"You mean this?" She let her palms drift down her torso, slower this time. She brushed the sides of her breasts, her stomach, her hips, then threaded her fingers through the curls at the apex of her thighs.

"Yeah," Clark breathed. "That."

"You like it?"

"Oh, yeah."

She did it again, starting from the top, this time lingering long enough to circle her nipples and stroke between her legs.

Clark groaned. She chuckled, enjoying his distress.

"You like tormenting me, don't you?" he said.

She smiled. "It's fun. I only wish I could see you suffering."

"It's not a pretty sight," he said with a soft laugh. He shifted off the bed, and again she heard the laptop zipper. "Here's something that will distract you." He returned to the bed. The mattress dipped a little, rolling her toward him.

"Taste this." He brushed something cool and firm against her lips.

She opened her mouth. He dipped a rounded object inside. She skimmed it with the tip of her tongue. Ummm... Something chocolate. Delightful.

"Suck on it." His voice was husky. Low.

She obeyed, pursing her lips and sucking. An explosion of flavor burst into her mouth. A cool, ripe strawberry. Covered with a layer of thick, dark chocolate.

Heaven.

She ate it all, licking every bit from his fingers, and even sucking them a little afterwards. Clark groaned again, and leaned forward to kiss her.

"Please don't tell me that strawberry came from a porn shop," she said when she came up for air.

He snorted. "God, no. I got them at the gourmet grocer on Main Street." He reached across the bed, his arm brushing her legs as he retrieved something she could only guess at. "But I did get this at Lavish Love."

A soft tantalizing touch brushed her forehead, her cheeks, her lips. "What is it?"

"You tell me." He swept the unseen instrument down her arms, across her breasts, and over her stomach.

"A feather?"

"A long one," he said, stroking the crease at the top of one leg, then moving around to stroke the inside of her thighs. He lingered there, teasing. "Open your legs," he breathed.

She obeyed.

"Wider."

She did that too, quivering as the feather touched her again. Her inner muscles contracted, sending a faint glimpse of bliss shooting through her body. Clark ran the tip of the feather over her swollen folds, then played it over her tight nub. The sensation was too fleeting, too light. She groaned, as the coil in her belly tightened.

The feather vanished. Her hips moved, wanting it back. The ocean music from the CD player surged and receded. Then the laptop's Velcro parted again, and her body went on high alert. What was coming next?

She heard Clark moving around--undressing, she thought. After a moment, he settled back onto the bed, down near the end. His warm hands lifted her feet and cradled them in his lap. His bare lap.

Blossom caught her breath. He was naked, in her bed. She wanted very much to see him. So what if he didn't have the body of a superhero? He had the heart of one. And he wanted her. She was beginning to discover what a turn on that was.

He began massaging her foot. He wore some kind of glove on one hand. It was slightly scratchy, but not unpleasantly so. Like a loofah sponge. "What are you wearing?"

He laughed. "I think it's called a bath glove. It's purple."

"Really?" She tried to imagine Clark, sitting on the edge of her bed, wearing a purple glove. And nothing else.

Her mind boggled.

He worked his way up her legs, his gloved hand leaving a tingling path in its wake, his bare hand soothing over the same path almost immediately. He avoided her breasts, and the slick, sensitive folds between her legs, moving close, teasing, then retreating without satisfying. The ocean music surged and ebbed in the background, a floating accompaniment to his attentions.

As he moved up her body, she reached for him, exploring him with her hands like a blind woman. He was surprisingly firm muscled. Not bulky like the superhero posters on her walls, but not soft, either, as she expected a geek to be. He must get away from that laptop occasionally, she thought.

Her hands slid across his flat belly and dipped between his legs. He sucked in a breath as she gripped his cock. Her fingers ran the long, firm length of it, all the way down, then all the way up again. The head was wide and warm. She cupped it in her palm, squeezing a little.

His breathing went ragged. He groaned a little as he leaned in and kissed her.

"You took off your glasses," she said. She tried to imagine it.

"Yeah," he said. "I can't see a thing."

She laughed at that. Her arms went around his neck, holding him tight. "Are we really going to do this?"

"If you'll let me."

"Do you have condoms in that black bag?"

"Only a couple dozen."

She smiled against his lips. "We can always go out for more later."

He levered himself away, until they were no longer touching. She thought she heard him strip off the glove, then tear a foil packet. She waited for him to return, but the seconds ticked by and he waited, not moving, not speaking.

"Clark?"

No answer. She lay still, waiting, listening. She couldn't hear anything beyond the ocean music--no movement, no breathing. Had he left her? Why?

The seconds ticked by. Blossom lay still at first, not wanting to break the magic of the game. But when endless moments passed and still he didn't return, she sat up, her hands reaching for the ties on the blindfold.

"Leave it on," Clark said.

Her hands stilled on the laces. "I thought you had gone."

"No," he said. "I'm here, watching you."

"Why?"

He gave a wry laugh. "I don't know. I guess I just like looking at you, knowing you can't see me. I'm not sure you would be so eager to make love if your eyes were open."

A glimmer of shame flashed through her. "My posters bother you, don't they? I'm sorry. I know it's silly of me, obsessing about superheroes. About men who don't exist."

"No," he said. His voice sounded strange. Uncertain. "It's not that. It's just..."

She wished she could see his face. "What?"

"I've dreamed of a woman like you," Clark said.

Blossom gave a shaky laugh. "You've dreamed of woman with freckles and frizzy red hair, who didn't want to date you because you drag a laptop around?"

He shifted on the mattress. "Well, not that, exactly. I've dreamed of one who trusted me enough to let herself go in my arms."

Blossom kept her voice steady. "And you think I could do that?"

"I know you can," he said.

"I wish I could believe you," she said. "But the truth is, I'm not sure it's possible for me. I've never had an orgasm. I can't even imagine it."

In lieu of an answer, she felt his lips on her stomach, her breast, her neck. His body moved, fitting itself to hers. She parted her legs, cradling his arousal.

And then he was inside, filling her, stroking, moving. "You know what I'm imagining right now?" he whispered in her ear.

"What?" she whispered back.

"The two of us on a beach, alone. Doing this." He thrust in.

"Someone would see us," she said. He eased out.

"No. We're alone. On a deserted island." He surged forward, harder than before.

Blossom sucked in a breath. "Are there palm trees?"

"As many as you want," he said, his hips flexing under her hands. "All around us. Swaying gently in the warm breeze."

"What does the ocean look like?"

He quickened his pace. "Pale green and sparkling. You can see clear through the water to the sand."

She felt herself slip toward something she desperately wanted to reach. "The sky. Is it blue?"

"It's brilliant." He was loving her hard now, with long, deep strokes, mingled with the scent of his sweat and the ragged sound of his breath in her ears. She opened her mouth on his shoulder and tasted the salty, slick flavor of him.

"The sand is warm," he murmured. "Warm and soft. You can feel it beneath you."

His hands ran along the backs of her thighs, lifting them as he angled her body for a deeper thrust. She knotted her hands in the comforter. So close. She could feel the moist breeze on her face, smell the salt in the air.

"Let go," Clark breathed. "Now. Do it for me." He gripped her hips and surged forward.

Shattering light burst inside her. She felt her body fling outward, as if exploded into a million, glittering pieces, each one an eternal fragment of bliss. She clung to Clark's shoulders as his body pistoned against hers. She felt him go even harder inside her.

He cried her name as he came. His orgasm triggered aftershocks of her own release. They pulsed like the ocean, waves and waves of bliss, carrying her gently back to earth. When it was over, she melted into the warm sand, her mouth seeking Clark's lips. He kissed her deeply, his breath slowing until it matched the rhythm of the ocean in the background. A soft spray of water misted over her.

Wait a minute. Sand? Water?

She jackknifed to a sitting position. Her head hit Clark's chin.

"Ouch!"

She tore off the blindfold.

And glimpsed wide ocean and white sand. The sparkling sunlight forced her eyes shut again. She wasn't in her bedroom. Oh my God. "Clark?" Her voice wavered.

He grabbed her arms and yanked her to her feet. "Hooooyaaah," he yelled, swinging her around. Her bare feet fought for balance on the soft sand. "We did it!"

She cracked her eyes open and focused on his face, struck by how handsome he was without his glasses. "Did what?"

He shoved a springy dark curl out of his eyes and grinned at her. "We teleported."

"That's impossible."

He laughed and swung her around again. This time, Blossom had the presence of mind to be embarrassed. They were both naked, for God's sake. Out in the open.

"Look around you," Clark said. "We're here. It's possible." He dropped her hand and punched a victorious fist in the air.

She couldn't deny he had a point. "But how?" she asked. "What did you do?"

"It wasn't me," Clark said. "You did this."

"No, I didn't."

"Yes," he said, "you did." He caught her hand and tugged her back down on the sand. "Let me explain."

By the time he had, she was stunned, bewildered, and seething mad. And wishing she had some clothes to put on. It was beyond awkward sitting here on the beach, naked, while Clark explained how he'd been acting under orders to talk her into bed.

"Let me get this straight," she said. "You're some kind of psychic superhero secret agent. I needed an orgasm to turn me into a superheroine. And you volunteered to give it to me? So I could help you save the world?"

He looked away. "Yeah. Something like that. You know, I think that's why you're so visually oriented. It's part of your talent. You have to see where you're going in your mind in order to teleport there."

Tears stung her eyes. She blinked hard, willing them not to fall. She'd thought she'd attracted Clark on her own. She thought he cared for her. Now she'd discovered she was nothing but an assignment to him. She scrambled to her feet and started marching across the sand.

"You can just take your save-the-world problem and shove it, Clark. I'm not helping."

He jogged up behind her. "What do you mean? You have to help. Or else everyone in the world, including us, will be dead in--" He checked his bare wrist. "Shit. I left my watch in your apartment."

She came to a halt. "Can't some other superhero stop Lex Loser?"

"If that were possible, Heroes Incorporated would have handled it by now." He shook his head. "No. The fate of humanity rests in our hands. You have to get us into Lex's lair. I'll do the rest."

"How am I supposed to do that? I don't even know how I got us here." She bit her lip. "What if I can't get us back? We could be stuck here for weeks. Naked. With no food."

"There are coconuts, probably," Clark said. "But that's beside the point. You can get us back. I know you can. Just picture it."

Blossom sighed. "Okay, what do I have to do?"

Clark blinked. "I don't know. What were you doing when you teleported us here?"

Blossom frowned, trying to remember. "Nothing special."

"Thanks a lot," Clark said.

Blossom blushed. "I mean, I was just picturing the beach you were talking about, then, when I came, here we were."

"Okay," said Clark. "We can work with that. I'll describe HI headquarters, give you a mental image. You grab my hand, concentrate, and we'll be there."

"Uh, Clark."

"Yes?"

"There's only one problem."

"What's that?"

"We can't go to headquarters."

He gave her a puzzled look. "Why not?"

"We're naked, remember?"

He looked down. "Oh. Yeah. I forgot."

Blossom rolled her eyes. "Geeks."

Chapter Eight

Saturday, 3:52 p.m.
Eight hours, eight minutes, and counting...

They landed in the bathtub, limbs tangled.

Clark lifted Blossom over the rim of the tub, trying not to get distracted by all the soft skin in his hands.

"That's strange," she said. "I was picturing the bedroom."

"That's not good," Clark told her. "We could have rematerialized in a wall or something. Or in mid-air. Your father was killed by an error like that."

Blossom shivered. "Oh, God. I had no idea."

Clark strode into the bedroom. "Ideally, you should practice. Do some safe, little jumps. Get the hang of it." He glanced at the clock on the nightstand. "But there's not time for much. We've got to get to headquarters as soon as possible." He grabbed his clothes, then scooped up hers and tossed them to her.

She caught them and dressed while he placed a cell call to Captain Marvelous. He updated the Captain as to Blossom's... uh... progress.

The Captain chuckled. "Good for you, son. I knew you had it in you."

Clark stood a little taller. "Thank you, Captain."

Blossom practiced teleporting from the bedroom to the kitchen several times, then into the hall. First alone, then with Clark in tow.

"I can never get to the exact spot I want," she grumbled.

Clark wasn't too thrilled about that, but he didn't want to alarm Blossom by telling her so. She was already freaked out enough as it was.

"We can't delay much longer," he said. "The Captain wants us to report ASAP. Lex's bomb is set to blow in--" He checked his watch. "Six hours, forty-nine minutes, and counting."

* * * *

Saturday, 5:17 p.m.
Six hours, forty-three minutes, and counting...

Blossom grasped Clark's hand, closed her eyes, and tried to teleport into the HI ready room.

They landed in the dumpster behind the fake sub shop.

"Great," Blossom muttered, pulling unidentifiable muck out of her hair. "Just great. At this rate, all I'm going to do is get us killed."

Clark lowered his laptop to the asphalt, then jumped over the side of the dumpster and offered Blossom a hand. "No, you won't," he told her, but she could tell he was worried. "You'll do just fine. You're only a little off. The briefing room is directly below us."

"How far?"

Clark hesitated. "Thirty-six feet."

"Oh, God." Blossom's knees buckled.

Clark caught her before she could hit the ground. "Your long-distance accuracy is improving, you know." He steadied her on her feet, keeping one hand on her elbow and the other on the handle of his laptop case. "Come on. Try again. Thirty-six feet. Straight down." He described Captain Marvelous' briefing room.

Blossom sighed. "Hold on." She shut her eyes and pictured it.

They landed right outside the door. "Not bad," Clark said, but Blossom wasn't so sure. There was more to this teleporting business than one would think. It required a heck of a lot of concentration.

Clark guided her across the threshold. The room was small, just big enough for a round table and a few chairs. A tall, elderly man with a shock of white hair rose to greet them.

"Clark. You're right on time, son. Good work with the ... ah ... recovery of Ms. Breeze."

Good work. Sheesh. Blossom rolled her eyes. As if taking her to bed had been some kind of chore.

Her stomach twisted a little. Maybe it had been.

After all, Clark was a superhero. Oh, he may be a little on the underdeveloped side physically, but a lot of women wouldn't care about that. They'd be looking for the prestige of dating a superhero. Clark probably slept with a different woman every night.

Her stomach twisted some more. She didn't like thinking about that.

"Ah, Blossom," Captain Marvelous was saying. "Good to meet you, my girl." He wrinkled his nose. "What is that smell?"

"We had a small mishap, sir," Clark explained. "Nothing to get alarmed about."

"I see. Well, get cleaned up. The faster you get into Lex's lair, the safer the world will be."

* * * *

Saturday, 6:22 p.m.
Five hours, thirty-eight minutes, and counting...

"I don't know if I can do this," Blossom told Clark. They were standing in the middle of a very closed Megalopolis Museum of Natural History, in front of an enormous Tyrannosaurus Rex skeleton. "I was supposed to land us next to the Triceratops."

"That's only a few feet away," Clark pointed out. "And it could have been worse. You might have teleported us into the men's room."

She frowned at him. "Don't joke. We've been practicing for hours, and the best I've done is three feet from the target. According to the Captain, Lex Loser's underground lair is a twisting maze of narrow passages. I'll never hit one. We'll materialize right in bedrock."

"His central lab is a large room. We'll go for that."

"And lose the element of surprise," Blossom grumbled. "He'll see us coming and blast us before you get a chance to defuse the bomb."

"Jeez," said Clark. "Are you always this pessimistic?"

"I don't know," admitted Blossom. "I've never done anything this important before."

"Welcome to the wonderful world of superheroes," Clark said.

* * * *

Saturday, 8:30 p.m.
Three hours, thirty minutes, and counting...

"Ready?" Captain Marvelous asked.

Clark glanced at Blossom. She didn't look the least bit ready, but unfortunately, their time had run out.

"Ready," Clark said.

"Go," the Captain said.

* * * *

Saturday, 8:33 p.m.
Three hours, twenty-seven minutes, and counting...

Well, the good news was, Blossom didn't teleport them into bedrock. The bad news was, Clark had no idea where they were. They'd materialized in a narrow channel enclosed by rocky walls. He raised his flashlight and shone the beam first in one direction, then the other. Nothing.

A drop of water splashed onto his nose. He sneezed. The sound echoed like a thunderclap.

"I hope Lex didn't hear that," Blossom said.

Clark unzipped his laptop case and powered up the machine. If he could get a satellite signal, he could triangulate their location with his GPS receiver. He punched in the required keystrokes. "Come on..."

A "no service" message flashed onto the screen.

"Damn," Clark said. "I guess we're on our own."

"Not what I wanted to hear," Blossom said. She'd found out during her practice sessions that if she didn't know where she was, it was much harder to get where she wanted to go.

Clark zipped up his laptop, then swung his flashlight to the front and rear. "Which way do you think?"

Blossom closed her eyes and pointed. "That way."

Clark clipped the flashlight onto his belt and put his arm around her waist. "Ready when you are," he said.

* * * *

Saturday, 11:46 p.m.
Fourteen minutes, and counting...

"Ah, Clark. I knew they would send you."

Lex's voice was casual, but the way his fingers stroked the buttons and levers on his futuristic-looking control panel was anything but. Clark swallowed hard. He'd hoped to defuse the bomb before Lex noticed anything was amiss. Unfortunately, after three frustrating hours of bouncing through caves and tunnels like human ping pong balls, Blossom had finally landed them right at Lex's feet. Within seconds, they'd found their arms stretched overhead, restrained by robotically controlled shackles. And not just your regular, everyday, run of the mill titanium shackles, either. No. Lex had imprisoned Clark with...

"Magnets," Lex said, sounding inordinately pleased with himself. "Your one weakness. Your psychic computer tampering powers are useless, Clark."

Clark supposed it was better than materializing in bedrock, but not by much.

"Only a few minutes until detonation," Lex said, squinting up at the foot-high digital clock on the wall above his head.

11:48:23 Eleven minutes, thirty-seven seconds and counting. And Clark was strung up like a side of beef, powerless to stop humanity's destruction.

Lex chuckled as his fingers danced over the control panel. "We'll want to watch, of course." He pushed a button and a picture appeared on the flat screen overhead. Downtown Megalopolis, bustling with nighttime activity.

"You don't want to go through with this, Lex," Clark said.

Lex ran a hand over his bald head. "Why not?" He seemed genuinely puzzled.

Clark eyed his laptop, lying useless on the floor at his feet. "Say your scheme is successful. Say you kill everyone in the world. What will you do for fun when there's no one left to terrorize?"

Lex's brows drew in. "A good point," he said, tapping his finger against his lips. "I didn't consider that." He laughed. "I guess I'll have to keep your girlfriend. That should be amusing."

Clark felt Blossom go stiff beside him. "Not an option," he told Lex. "You'd have to kill me first."

Lex smiled broadly. "That can be arranged." He reached under the counter and drew out a small caliber pistol. He leveled it at a point midway between Clark's eyes.

Beads of sweat broke out on Clark's forehead.

The trigger cocked.

"No," Blossom whispered.

"Oh, yes, yes, yes!" Lex said with an evil, maniacal laugh.

Clark's closed his eyes and braced for the end, a sharp sense of failure slicing through him. Some superhero he turned out to be. He should have let Bruce handle this one. Maybe then, humanity would've had a chance.

The gun's blast sounded in his ears. Clark's body went rigid, waiting for the pain.

It didn't come.

What the...?

He opened his eyes, then blinked to clear his vision. Lex Loser was sprawled on the ground, unconscious, his gun loose in his fingers. Blossom sat on his back, a startled look on her face.

"I did it," she said. "I really did it. I hit my target."

"Hit it hard, it looks like," Clark said.

"He smashed his head on the way down," Blossom said. "That part was pure luck."

Clark rattled his shackles. "The key," he said. "Find it. We've only got--" He checked the digital clock. Shit. "Nine minutes, seventeen seconds."

Blossom sifted frantically through Lex's pockets. "Got it." She lunged to Clark's side. Going up on her toes, she slid the key home--first one wrist, then the other.

Clark stumbled forward. "Thanks."

"There's only eight minutes left," Blossom said nervously. "Is it enough?"

"It'll have to be," Clark said. Bracing his hands on Lex's control panel, he closed his eyes and sank his mind into the neutron bomb's computer trigger.

<password?>

"Crap," Clark said. "Lex's account isn't logged on. The system's asking for a password." He dove for his laptop.

"Can you hack it?" Blossom asked, watching him power up his code-cracking program.

He linked it to Lex's computer, using his mind as a network bridge. "Of course," Clark said. "Given enough time. But can I do it in--" he looked at the clock, "--six and a half minutes? I don't know."

He urged the program to run faster. "Lex's password is ten alphanumeric digits," he said.

"That's 8.4×10^{17} possible combinations," Blossom said. "That could take hours."

She was right, but there wasn't much Clark could do about it. Except pray. He watched the list of possible passwords flash through the login screen. So far, nothing.

"Three minutes," Blossom said. "Maybe you should try a few manual combinations."

"Like what?" Clark asked, exasperated.

She bit her lip. "I don't know. He's your nemesis, isn't he? You should have an idea what he might pick."

"Birthday? Hometown? Mother's maiden name?" Clark tried them all. No luck.

"1-2-3-4-5-6-7-8-9-0?" Blossom suggested.

Nope.

Clark glanced at the clock. Seventeen seconds. Come on. What would Lex have picked?

An idea hit him. Mentally, he typed it in.

Hot damn!

"We're in," he shouted.

"What did you put in?" Blossom asked.

"C-l-a-r-k-s-u-c-k-s."

His mind raced through Lex's system, picking up information. The bomb itself was hidden in one of the lair's upper passageways. Ironically, not far from Blossom and Clark's first teleport location. It was controlled by wireless pulse.

"Eight seconds," Blossom breathed.

Clark's brain rocketed through the directories on Lex's hard drive, searching for the bomb execution program.

"Six," Blossom said.

He found the document.

<C:\documents\lexdocs\evilplan\bomb\bang.exe>

Originality had never been Lex's strong point, Clark mused. Luckily for humanity.

"Five seconds," Blossom squeaked. "Four, three..."

Clark dove into the system manager and executed a delete command. "Got it," he said, slumping into Lex's leather upholstered command chair.

Blossom squinted at the readout on the control panel screen. "Are you sure?"

Clark looked up at the plasma image of Megalopolis at midnight. A couple strolled by, hand in hand, laughing, blissfully unaware of their narrow escape.

"Yep," Clark told her.

Blossom blinked. "Then we really did it? We saved the day?"

Clark exhaled a shaky laugh. "With two-point-four seconds to spare."

"Wow," Blossom said. "Who would have thought it?"

Chapter Nine

Friday, 10:35 p.m.

You'd think she'd be ecstatic.

Blossom leaned against the bar in the HI lounge, worrying the swizzle stick in her Long Island iced tea as she watched the free flow of testosterone all around her. The room belched muscle. Corded pecs, bulging biceps, buns of steel--you name it, it was here.

And a good portion of it was trying to impress her.

"So then I swung through the window," Peter Parkington was saying. "And knocked the kidnapper on his butt."

Pete was kind of cute, Blossom thought, but he seemed a bit immature.

"That's nothing," Dr. Banning said with a scowl. "Just last week I knocked a hole in a concrete wall with my bare fist and discovered a secret weapons cache."

A handsome man, Blossom reflected, but the green tinge to his skin was a bit disconcerting.

"Hey, babe. How's it going?"

She looked up, startled to find Bruce Wynn gazing down at her. Diana Price clung to his perfect tricep.

"I didn't know you two were still..." She drew a breath. "I mean after the Burger Shack..." She tried again. "I thought after Bruce ended up on the floor..."

Ah, hell. She took a gulp of her drink.

Diana laughed. "We're fine," she said. She leaned in close and lowered her voice. "Bruce likes things rough once in a while. You should try it with Clark."

"Clark?" Blossom squeaked. She couldn't imagine it.

Bruce's moody gaze scanned the room. "Yeah. Where is Geek Man, anyway?"

"Not here," Blossom said in a small voice. And she didn't know where he was, either. It had been six days since she'd last seen him, during the mission debriefing with Captain Marvelous. She had a sneaky feeling he was avoiding her.

Diana confirmed it. "It's not like Clark to miss his own victory party. Or a free buffet," she added thoughtfully.

"He's a geek," Bruce said. "He probably got wrapped up in a Star Trek marathon or something."

They laughed and moved off.

Blossom set her drink on the bar, feeling suddenly sick. It was true, then. She'd been just an assignment to Clark, and now that the world was safe, he didn't want anything to do with her. Probably, he was out on the town, one tall, anorexic supermodel draped over each arm. Probably, he'd spend the night with them. Probably, he wouldn't give Blossom a thought while he was doing it. Probably...

Probably he couldn't care less that she was in love with him.

The bar phone rang. The bartender snagged it. "Yo... Yeah, sure thing, Clark. It'll be down in fifteen."

Blossom's eyes widened. "Excuse me," she said. "But . was that Clark Kendall on the line?"

"Yep," the muscle-bound bartender said. "He's in the computer lab. He wants me to send him a sandwich."

* * * *

Saturday, 10:59 p.m.

Clark clicked aimlessly on the Internet browser window, not even caring what popped up. It hardly mattered. He couldn't think of anything but Blossom, anyway.

He'd known it couldn't last, of course. But somehow, rather than being a comfort, the knowledge only made his heart ache. Blossom was everything he ever wanted in a woman--she was cute, smart, and brave. She didn't give up when things got tough. And she was sexy as hell. He closed his eyes, reliving the moment she'd reached her first orgasm. In his arms. Her inner muscles had tightened so hard on him that he'd seen stars. That's when he'd realized he loved her. And when she'd saved him from taking Lex's bullet, the emotion intensified exponentially.

Then they'd returned to HI headquarters, where Blossom had been swamped by every superhero on the payroll. They all wanted to meet her. He'd stayed close, and heard five invitations to dinner in the space of seven minutes. Laughing, she'd accepted them all.

In that moment, Clark knew he wouldn't be able to compete. Blossom couldn't help her visual orientation--it was part of her superpower. And Clark just didn't look like a superhero. He never would. He wasn't even going to try.

He pushed his glasses up the bridge of his nose and clicked over to digital TV streaming. There was an all-night Star Trek marathon starting at eleven. At least it would get his mind off his troubles.

A knock sounded at the door. His sandwich from the bar, most likely. "Come on in," he called. "Door's unlocked."

Footsteps, then a soft hand on his shoulder.

He swallowed hard and swiveled his chair around. "Blossom. What are you doing down here?"

"I brought you this." She placed a Styrofoam take-out container and a large soda on his desk. "So. This is where you've been hiding all week."

"I spend most of my time here," he told her. "I'm a geek, remember?"

She gave a soft laugh at that. "Yeah. I remember." Then, more softly, "How could I forget?"

Clark popped the lid of his sandwich container. "You should go back to the party. Everyone will miss you."

"It's your party, too," Blossom said. "Come with me."

"No," said Clark abruptly. "I've got work to do."

Blossom sidled in closer. "Work? That looks like Star Trek."

He hit the minimize button. "So what?"

"So turn it off. Come to the party."

He couldn't stand being the object of her pity. "I know what you're doing," he said. "And I appreciate it, but you really don't have to. The assignment's over. Let's just try to forget it." He took a bite of his turkey club.

She inhaled a sharp intake of breath. "So that's all I am to you, then. A completed assignment. Someone you fucked--"

Clark nearly choked.

"--in the name of duty."

"Is that what you think?" He grabbed his soda and took a gulp.

"It's true, isn't it?"

He coughed. "God, no."

"Then why are you avoiding me?"

He looked up at her, slightly dizzy from lack of air. "I'm not avoiding you." Well, okay, maybe he was, but he didn't like admitting it. "I'm giving you a chance to get what you want. A real superhero. Like the ones hanging all over your apartment walls."

"But I don't want a man like that anymore," she said softly.

"You don't?"

"No. I don't. You're my hero now."

Clark gaped at her.

She looked away, her cheeks turning pink. "I didn't mean to say that," she said. "Look. Just forget I mentioned it." She inched toward the door. "I'm going back to the party now."

He leaped out of his seat and grabbed her arm. "I can't forget it," he told her. "I need to know. Is it true?"

She hesitated.

"Blossom..."

"Yes," she said irritably. "Okay? Are you satisfied? Yes. I love you. Now let me go."

She loved him?

"No," said Clark. "Not until you say that again."

"Let me go."

"No." He grinned. "Not that part. The other thing. About how you love me."

"Clark..."

"Because I love you, too, you know."

She blinked up at him. "You do?"

"Yeah," he said softly, gathering her into his arms. She fit just right. A reckless, joyful feeling crept over him. "Marry me, Blossom."

"What?!" She tried to twist out of his arms, but he didn't let her. "Are you nuts? You're kidding, right? You can't possibly want to get married. Marriage means car payments, kids, a mortgage, life insurance..."

"And sex," Clark said. "Don't forget the sex. Lots of it. Night and day. In every room in the house. Even the closets. In every position you can think of."

She blushed. "Oh. Well. When you put it like that, I don't know what to say."

"Say yes."

Blossom looked into his eyes and laughed. "All right. Yes."

"Great," Clark said, taking off his glasses. He set them on the desk next to his laptop and reached for her.

"Hey," she said. "What are you doing?"

"This," he said, and kissed her.

The End

SILK

Michelle M. Pillow

Prologue

His touch burned into her skin like liquid fire, as he clutched her arms in what must have been desperation and panic. It was more memory than any grown woman should have of her father. Everything she had been was lost in that moment of betrayal--a violation worse than death because it could never end, could never be escaped.

The father gave her life, but the scientist took it back. She had been sixteen, in the prime of her youth. He killed her that day. Her father--genius, patriot, madman, scientist--had been given no choice and in turn didn't give her one. He was dying. It was her or the enemy. And so he chose the impossible. He chose the death of his child in exchange for the birth of a new elite superhero.

That is why Silk could never hate her killer.

Chapter One

Quinlan St. James gasped as coffee spilled over her dark designer pantsuit. Blinking, she glared after the hoverboarders who trailed by, laughing rudely at her. Their boards glided noiselessly over the uneven sidewalks of Pierson Park, carrying the spike-haired lads to their next victim.

She clutched her newspaper under her arm as she leaned over to pick up the cup and throw it in the trash. She didn't mind the kids, not really. They were just being young and obnoxious. She should have been watching for them, but her mind was clouded with other things. Brushing the brown droplets off her suit with the back of her hand, she sighed. The suit was stained, but it wasn't like she needed to be anywhere that it would matter.

Quinlan turned around and headed straight back to the quaint little sidewalk coffee vendor. The man behind the counter wiped his hands on his twenty-first century green apron and automatically handed her another cup. As she made a move to reach for her card, but he smiled and waved her away. Quinlan nodded at him and walked back over to her customary bench beneath the shade of a tall oak tree.

She took a small sip before setting the cup down. Coffee was better in the old district. They still ground it by hand and brewed it in refurbished coffee machines. Flipping to the science section of the New Pierson City Times, her face fell as she saw her father's cheery expression staring at her. Quietly, she scanned the feature article on him.

Ten years after his unexplained death, Dr. William St. James, renowned genetic engineer, will be inducted into the Scientific Achievement Hall of Fame this weekend. Dr. St. James spent the last two decades of his life fighting the war against genetic diseases ... work that is the foundation of modern genetic study....

Quinlan narrowed her gray-green eyes, refusing to cry about things she could not change. She looked silently up at the bright blue sky. Clouds peeked down from behind the tree limbs and the dark skyscrapers of the oldest section of the city. Nearby, the motor of a 1950 Chevy Fastback revved as it gave tourist rides around the historical section of the park.

Quinlan frowned. The newspaper wasn't telling her anything she didn't already know. Sighing, she turned back to the article anyway.

The official induction will be held at the St. James Estate in East Bend this Friday. It is the first time since Dr. St. James' death that the home will be opened to guests. Dr. St. James' daughter, Quinlan St. James, owns the estate, a renovated castle from England.... Miss St. James is ... a reclusive billionaire. An invitation only cocktail party will follow the official induction, where some of the scientist's papers will be on display for the first time, along with some of his earlier inventions. All items are being donated to the Genetic Science Museum.

Even now caterers and decorators invaded her home. It was the whole reason she'd come into the city. The giant photograph the museum had sent over of her father had been staring down at her for days, bringing up a myriad of emotions she didn't want to feel.

Quinlan's eyes skimmed the rest of the article before carefully folding it up. It didn't even come close to describing the full truth of her father's work--the strange late night visitors they'd had while she was growing up, the coded messages he received at all hours. She didn't care. Let the public have their fairy tale version.

Grabbing her coffee, she stood and walked over to the trashcan. William St. James' face stared up at her from the paper she held, smiling in a crooked way she still remembered. She didn't smile back. Hesitating slightly, she threw the article away.

* * * *

Nikandros Grant pulled his hands from the pockets of his blue jeans as he pushed off an old fashioned light post. He liked the historical park. It reminded him of a simpler time in human evolution--before technology advanced so far that even walking across a city or stopping to flip a light switch became unnecessary.

Trailing over the uneven cement path, he followed the slender beauty he was watching. She stood, walking over to a trashcan as she finished her paper. Looking down at the small leather wallet in his hands, he smiled. The hoverboarders had been a perfect distraction. Although, when Miss St. James had dropped her coffee and went to retrieve a new one, he'd been worried she'd discover it was missing.

Passing the trash, he glanced over to the side. He saw the article she'd been reading neatly folded on the top of the pile. His old friend's face smiled up from the black and white photograph. Nikandros let loose a quick, humorless chuckle at William's 2-D expression. Silently, he nodded at the photo. William had been a good man.

Quinlan hardly looked as he had imagined her when he first found out about her plan to make William's personal documents public. She didn't take after her father at all. William had been a squat, short man with a sunny smile and laughing blue eyes hidden beneath spectacles. His daughter was a tall, slender woman with a serious face and wide gray-green eyes that pierced silently as she studied everything around her.

His gaze automatically strayed to her hips and thighs. Wicked thoughts danced in his head and he wanted to groan his sudden wave of sexual frustration to the world. Nikandros grinned in his wickedness. He was a man after all and it was his assignment to 'watch' her. She was beautiful, which would make his job of seducing her all the more pleasurable--and all the more dangerous.

After studying her case file, it was determined that a new love interest is just what a woman like her might need. Seduction was always a dangerous game and Nikandros knew he would have to be careful and not get too involved. It wouldn't be hard. He had never gotten too involved before. Besides, he had to find out exactly where her sympathies lay. He only hoped William would forgive him for anything he had to do.

Quinlan was a recluse that kept to herself. She didn't have a job, as she was independently wealthy, thanks to her inheritance. She didn't have any close friends, no serious boyfriends or known lovers. She didn't own a pleasure droid like most rich women. She didn't go to sex clubs or belong to sexual consent groups. Although, he had been able to uncover the fact that she did have a subscription to some pretty risqué magazine-discs. It at least proved that she wasn't completely made of ice.

With an inward groan, he watched the flexing muscles of her backside. His hand twitched. With a figure like that, it would be a sin for her not to use her body to its full potential.

Quinlan took a corner, rounding slowly away from the park to a more private section of the historic district. She seemed more intent at staring at her coffee cup than looking around at the shrubbery landscape. Taking the opportunity to approach, Nikandros began to jog after her.

"Miss!" he called lightly. "Miss, wait! I believe you dropped this."

Quinlan blinked at the sound, but kept walking. She was lost in thoughts of the past and the speech she would have to give to her father's old colleagues. Some of the old men had been hounding her for weeks, ever since the announcement that she was donating a large portion of her father's work to the museum. It seemed they all wanted a piece of it first.

It wasn't her idea to get rid of the boxes of old stuff. When Henry Thompson, the museum's head coordinator, first contacted her with the news of her father's induction, she thought it a very fitting place for his life's work to go. Besides, with the added publicity of her father's career and death, old skeletons would come out of the closet to play.

Feeling a hand on her arm, she jolted in surprise.

"Miss," Nikandros said, smiling brightly for her.

Quinlan turned at the sound, blinking to see who'd stopped her. Her wide eyes moved up to a face. She was startled to see such a handsome man trying to get her attention. For a moment, she stood, just staring at him. His teeth were white and straight, hidden beneath the most gorgeous mouth she'd ever seen.

His body was in fine shape, if the strength of his hand was any indication. His eyes were dark, almost black in their solid piercing depths, framed by the slashing of his masculine eyebrows. His dark brown hair was a perfect match to his steady gaze, combed back into a short easy style that fit well with the blue jeans and T-shirt he wore. He smiled at her, but she could feel there was more to him than that heart-stopping look.

Quinlan shivered. She could feel a potent heat coming from him and it disturbed her. Glancing down at where he touched her arm, she watched him slowly draw his hand away.

"Miss?" Nikandros said, wondering at her distrustful look. Did she suspect him? Her eyes traveled gradually over him and he felt his body begin to stir at the feminine interest. Quinlan blinked. Nikandros' grin widened in masculine invitation and he added, "Your wallet."

Quinlan looked at his offered hand, frowning. Feeling her pocket, she did indeed find her wallet to be missing.

"Ah, thanks, Mr. ah...?" she inquired, taking it from him. She clutched the thin wallet in her hand, taking pains to put

it into her breast pocket for safer keeping. She must really
be distracted today.

"Nick Grant," he answered, holding his hand out for her
to take. Quinlan took his warm palm in hers. He watched
her face to see if she recognized the name. If she did, she
didn't show it.

A memory pulled at Quinlan, but she blinked it away.
Nick was a common enough name, as was Grant. She gave
him a kind, distracted smile. When he didn't let go right
away, she pulled her hand back and said, "Thank you, Mr.
Grant."

Her voice was soft, unintentionally sultry to his senses.
Nikandros glanced down at his palm. Her hand had been as
smooth as silk--almost too smooth. He rubbed his fingers
absently over his palm, wondering at it.

"No problem," he murmured, his tone dipping ever so
slightly. As he looked at her strikingly alluring face, he
almost forgot what he was doing. Her light brown hair
blew in layers over her shoulder and she absently pushed it
back as she turned from him. She began to walk away.
Rushing, he again stopped her, this time with words.
"Would you like to go get some coffee, or something?"

Quinlan gave him a small smile. At the playful pull of her
look, desire shot through his stomach like a spark. He
swallowed and his throat suddenly went dry. She slowly
lifted up her coffee cup at him, and said, "Thanks anyway,
but I'm good."

Nikandros swallowed down his disappointment as she
walked away. Although, he knew that it was better that she
left him. The Protectors would expect a report. The first
contact had been made. That was enough for now.

Nikandros sighed heavily. He was old enough to know
when a woman's look held more than passing curiosity.
There was a cunning mind hiding behind her eyes. Quinlan
St. James was definitely up to something. It was his job to
figure out what. If she planned on selling her late father's
formula, as they suspected she might be, it would be his job
to stop her.

Quinlan kept her pace slow as she crossed the street and
made her way to the long transport limo that waited for her.
The driver nodded at her as he opened the door. Her home
was about thirty miles outside the city, but with the new

transit system in place, it would only take her about ten minutes to get there.

Once alone, she slid across the seat to look out the tinted window. She felt the tires jolt as the limo's wheels pulled from the street and folded under the car. The car floated soundlessly over the road.

She didn't realize the slight smile of interest that came to her face as she saw Nick Grant walking along a side path. Her lips parted with a heavy sigh, even as her eyes took in the muscles playing along his firm backside. It had been a long time since she felt a jolt like that when first meeting someone.

It was a good thing she hadn't struck up a conversation with him. She had seen the heated cast of interest in his eyes when he looked at her. The last thing she needed was a man complicating her already complex life--especially now of all times.

Her home was usually locked up tighter than a maximum-security prison complex. Whoever wanted her father's formula wouldn't be able to resist coming to the celebration, particularly with all his papers going for public display. It was quite possible the man responsible for her father's death would be there. It was up to her to discover who, out of all his colleagues, had betrayed him. Then, she could finally put her father's memory to rest. After all, it had been ten long years of waiting.

The limo sped up and Nick was blurred out of her life. Quinlan doubted she would ever see him again. Sighing, she leaned back and sipped at her coffee. It was just as well. A woman like her could never keep a relationship.

* * * *

East Bend was a small suburb of Pierson City. The St. James Estate sat just on the edge, far away from the neighbors. Quinlan's father had bought the ancient family home and moved it from England in his youth. He'd built a stone wall around the edge of the property. It looked serene, but if anyone tried to scale it, they would be in for a stunning electrical shock that would leave them paralyzed for days.

The only way in was through the front gate. The wrought iron bars were well guarded by robotic security. The guards never slept and they never left their post. They hardly even moved to acknowledge the limo, but Quinlan knew their eyes scanned the vehicle to identify all passengers. They would only find her. The robotic driver would register a pulse that the guards recognized.

The yard surrounding her home was green with spring grass. Flowers were beginning to bloom on the landscaped lawn. Little cobblestone trails weaved over the garden, intermingled with statues and benches. In the center was a tiered water fountain with no water. Its old stone was cracked ever so slightly and it was overgrown with vines. Quinlan didn't have the heart to fix it.

The square castellated home stood tall against the sky. It wasn't a full castle, just the part that could be restored after so many centuries of decay. It had a narrow stained glass window in the front by the thick oak front door and smaller, framed windows spread throughout the sidewalls. The old stones seemed to have a life of their own and as a child Quinlan loved to touch them, claiming she could feel their energy.

Coming to a stop, the limo door opened automatically. Quinlan stepped out and the limo drove off to the garage. Sighing, she walked up the round sweep of steps leading to the front door of her home.

Her butler was there to greet her in his very formal uniform. He bowed low over his waist and said, "Welcome home, Miss."

Quinlan handed him the empty coffee cup. He was mechanical like the rest of her staff, so she didn't bother with pleasantries. "Any messages?"

"Fifty-two, Miss," said the butler.

"Any not pertaining to my father?" Quinlan asked wryly.

"No, Miss," answered the butler/giant answering machine.

"Send the standard replies," ordered Quinlan quietly.

"Very good, Miss," answered the butler. Going to his post by the door, he plugged himself into his adaptor. His eyes closed and Quinlan could hear the faint sound of a ring as he began to call back her pre-recorded messages.

A long sweep of stairs went up the right side, carpeted with a plush red down the center. The banister crossed along the second story to leave a top section open to the front hall's view. Quinlan ignored the giant portrait of her father staring down at her from the top handrail. The ceiling was high in this section of the home, reaching up to the top of the second floor and arching with picturesque stone cornices. White satin sashes crossed over the walls and roses wrapped around over the stone handrail leading upstairs.

Taking the steps two at a time, Quinlan reached the top of the stairs. She ignored the mechanical maid units as they bustled about at lightening speed. She had them programmed to work, never acknowledging her. She might be lonely, but she would not lower herself to programming herself some company.

Crossing over the opened area, she turned down a long hall and opened the thick oak of her bedroom door. She stripped the stained jacket from her shoulders as she walked across the luxurious rug covering the stone floor. Her shirt was soon to follow. A maid unit clicked on in the corner and went to retrieve the clothing. Quinlan tossed her slacks at the unit and the maid caught them.

"Menu six," Quinlan said, ordering her food for the evening. "Privacy."

The unit scurried off with the clothes, taking them to laundry and shutting the door behind her.

"Fire," Quinlan murmured, flinging herself onto the oversized poster bed. She lay against the silk of her sheets, turning her head to watch the flames dancing in the large marble fireplace. The orange glow flickered over the stone walls, caressing her nearly naked flesh with its softness. Thick velvet curtains were opened over long floor-to-ceiling windows overlooking the side garden. Quinlan ordered them closed. The room was instantly shrouded in a softened darkness.

She pulled all four pillows to her body, curling around them as she closed her eyes. Unbidden, the image of Nick Grant came to mind. She was alone. She would never see him again. There was no one to watch her fantasize. She imagined the pillow beside her was his naked chest. She ran her hand over it and snuggled deeper. For a brief moment, right before she fell asleep, she didn't feel so alone.

Chapter Two

Silk wrapped her black cape around her body, concealing herself in darkness beneath the draping hood. Her hardened gaze narrowed as she peered through the eye slits of her all-concealing mask. She was as motionless as a statue, watching the quiet courtyard from above.

The moon was half full, but the tall trees kept its blue light from revealing her. She blended perfectly into the shadows. A bird perched near her foot, only to get a quick jolt from the gate's security system. The bird flapped away. Silk remained, unharmed.

Her ears focused for sound, trying to listen for the soft hum of an invisible security laser. Picking up a noise so faint that mere humans couldn't hear it, she smiled. She quickly mapped the haphazard pattern of lasers in her mind, marking a route to the home's front door.

With unyielding precision, she hopped from the high gate and onto a tree branch. Spinnerets on the tips of her fingers cocooned a soft silk mass to the limb. Her hands clutched together, pulled above her head, as she lowered herself slowly down to the courtyard ground.

The strands of silk growing from her fingers twisted together to keep her from falling. Her knee high boots landed soundlessly in the grass. With a tug of her hands, the silk released itself from the branch and drifted off into the night, floating on the breeze, no heavier than a spider's web.

* * * *

Nikandros glanced up from the electron microscope and grimaced. This wasn't good. Running his hands through his hair, he mussed the dark locks in his frustration. He then leaned back in his chair to flex his tired neck muscles. If the little sample he'd been able to collect off of Quinlan's hand was any indication, she was dabbling in the Bombyx project or knew someone who was.

He reached into the large pocket of his white lab coat and pulled out his video phone. Flipping it open, he set it on the desk atop a stack of papers and pushed redial. After several rings a man's face appeared on the small screen.

"Korbin," Nikandros said. Dark circles marred the skin beneath Korbin's sleepy eyes and Nikandros watched him rub at them tiredly. "It's confirmed."

That woke Korbin up. Blinking blue eyes that seemed to drive women crazy, he stared out from the video display. His voice hard, he asked, "You're sure?"

"Fairly," Nikandros answered, though he wished he didn't have to. "It could be why she's going public after so many years."

"Do you think she's found the missing part of the formula?" Korbin asked.

"I can't tell from the sample," replied Nikandros. He scratched the back of his head, before smoothing down his hair. "But, if she has, this celebration could be a veritable seller's market. Have you seen the copy of the guest list I · sent you?"

Korbin nodded. "It's a genuine who's who of the scientific underworld. You made contact with her. Do you think she's up to something?"

"It's hard to tell. Her eyes are cunning," Nikandros replied, thinking of Quinlan's lovely green gaze. It had been haunting him ever since that playful smile she'd given him earlier in the park. Feeling his lower extremities becoming uncomfortably full at the memory, he cleared his throat and his head. "I can't tell if it's because she is eccentric or because she is a conspirator."

"You need to get closer," Korbin put forth. He nodded thoughtfully. "I think you should seduce her."

Korbin had mentioned the idea before. Nikandros had toyed with it himself, especially after seeing what she looked like. He planned on taking it no further than his personal fantasies. Although, to seduce someone didn't mean you took them to your bed necessarily. It just meant you made them want to be in it.

As if reading Nikandros' thoughts, Korbin said, "And this time, I don't just mean romance her. Get her into your bed and screw her--"

"I understand," Nikandros interrupted with a deepening frown.

"What?" Korbin asked, sensing his friend's hesitance. He almost looked as if he felt sorry for Nikandros' situation, as he asked, "Is she that appalling?"

The answering scowl deepened.

"Ahh," Korbin began to laugh and pounded his fist on his nightstand so that his video phone bounced. Nikandros detected a woman to moan sleepily from behind his friend's back. Sniffing in merriment, Korbin lowered his tone to say, "She's not, is she? Hell, man, it's about time you got laid. Go get her, tiger."

"I'm hanging up now," Nikandros said, his tone dry.

"No, wait, Nick," Korbin demanded. "I have to tell you something. It's important."

"What?"

"Do you still know how to do it? If not, I--" Korbin's laughing voice was cut off as Nikandros shut the video phone.

All right, so it had been awhile since he was attracted to someone enough to sleep with them. He lowered his head onto his hands and groaned. Even know he could smell the erotic perfume of her body. As far as attraction went, Quinlan St. James had all the right equipment.

* * * *

Silk pulled low over the balcony. Scaling the side of the old Victorian hadn't been too hard. Seeing a soft light in the window, she crept under it on her stomach. Then, coming to the edge of the balcony, she climbed over the rail. Weaving a strand from her spinnerets, she jumped off the side and swung herself from one balcony to another. Her cape flapped around her, displaying the tight gray body suit underneath.

Within moments, she worked her way to an opened window and slipped inside, headfirst over a windowsill. Standing, she saw she was in a small bathroom. The decontaminator unit was made to look like an old fashioned shower. She crouched underneath the moving light sensors, not wanting them to detect her. Hitting the black leather pouch on her belt, she again stood. The box would emit a pulse that scrambled any household droids or contraptions, keeping them from alerting their owners as they tried to 'serve her'.

Opening the bathroom door, she stepped out into the hall and stealthily tried to make her way to the stairwell at the far end. Suddenly, a door opened and she froze. Her eyes widened as she pressed into the wall. She was too far from the bathroom to duck back in. Her heart began to pound.

She heard a woman's voice giggle from within the bedroom. Silk looked all around for a place to hide. About to reach up and jump to the ceiling, she noticed movement by her side. A large, naked man came from the bedroom. His muscles rippled like an Olympian God and his member was still very much erect and vibrating. Sniffing, Silk grimaced. It was a pleasure droid and he reeked of sex.

Holding very still, she watched as the naked robot passed right next to her. She couldn't help the curious glance over its backside. She grinned naughtily. For a machine, it was certainly a work of art. A darker face flashed through her head and her smile faded. Why was she thinking of Nick Grant at a time like this?

Hurrying down the stairs before the droid made the return trip back to his mistress' bedroom, Silk rushed across the dark house. She barely noted the antique furniture, or the endless lace and frippery draping all over of it.

Taking a scanner from her belt, she held it up and began to search around, examining behind the walls. She stopped as she found the inner working of a time lock safe hidden behind some paneling. With a push of a button, she looked inside it. Only a packet of money and some family jewels flashed on her screen so she ignored it. Working her way from room to room, she suddenly stopped as she found what she was looking for. It was the entrance to Dr. Nathaniel's laboratory.

Pulling back a fake wall, she pushed her pointer finger to the lock and filled it with a hard tissue, packing it full. Then, turning her hand, she unlocked the door and slipped downstairs to the basement.

The laboratory was as long as the courtyard outside. Bright light flooded the metal structure. Silk stealthily made her way over the walkway, pulling her cape over her shoulder so it could not tangle amongst her feet. Holding onto the rail, she hopped over the side. Her fingers wrapped their silken cords over the metal bar and she slowly lowered herself down, her arms directly over her head. Then, stopping, she grimaced.

A full head of dark hair was beneath her, lying on top of a messy desk. If she let go, she would land right on top of the late working scientist. Silk frowned. The lab was supposed to be empty. Dr. Nathaniel was out of town for business and his very lovely trophy wife was enjoying her rental upstairs. As she looked back up, her body began to twist and she turned slightly in the air.

Ah, hell!

Silk released the gossamer strands from her fingers and flipped through the air, dropping to the ground with a heavy thud behind the scientist's body.

Nikandros felt the presence above him. He didn't move, pretending to sleep on the desk. The hairs on the back of his neck stood on end. His senses peaked, ready to do battle. As he heard the thud behind him, he swung around, ready to strike.

Nikandros stiffened, not moving as the lovely creature before him held his fist in her hand. A silver clasp of a stylized butterfly kept a hood to her forehead. He couldn't see her features beneath the tight mask and the cloak shaded the color of her eyes.

A tight gray body suit hugged every one of her curves, leaving nothing to the imagination but the texture of her skin. A black weapons belt hung low on her hips. Her waist was slender, curving delightfully up. The cape hid her upper body from view. The sexiest vinyl boots he had ever seen in his centuries of living molded over her calves. Nikandros smiled in manly appreciation.

He'd never been so turned on in his life--or, at least since earlier in the park. The woman blinked, looking more fully at him. He swore her eyes were flecked with purple.

Silk grabbed the hand that flew at her, surprised that the scientist would attack. Usually such men didn't have it in them. Without warning, she froze, recognizing the handsome face. Her breath caught in her throat.

Silk looked the attractive man over, from his firm parted lips to his solid dark eyes that studied her. He had been in her thoughts since their meeting in the park. She desperately wanted to kiss him, wanted to fulfill the strange fantasies she had of him. But then, something odd happened. His eyes began to shift and change with red, just a tinting. If she hadn't have seen him out during the day, she would have thought him a vampire.

Silk shook herself from the depths of his sultry dark gaze. The image of the naked pleasure droid came to mind to taunt her, as did her dreams of this man earlier in the day. She had the strangest urge to see if his body could even compare to the robot upstairs or to the fantasies in her head.

Unable to stop herself, she released his hand and twirled. The silk from her fingers pulled his arm around. In one swift motion, she had his wrist pinned behind his back in a silken web.

Nikandros froze, knowing he could get out of her trap if he wanted to. He'd have to reveal his powers to do it, but he could. He didn't move. He didn't want to. The action had brought her body close to him and she was pressed fully along his frame. Though her eyes were hard, the body molding into him was anything but.

Silk allowed herself to feel him, never knowing why she let temptation overcome her. Beneath the lab coat, she could feel that he was all solid man--from the definition of his abs to the rock-hard feel of his thighs against hers. To her amazement, she felt his body twitch and rise between her legs. His manhood pressed full into her, giving away its master's thoughts.

Fear, she would have expected from him. But this?

"This is private property," he whispered, his voice dipping low to send chills over her. He felt her reaction, smelled it in her. His lips brushed forward to where her mouth would have been under her disguise.

"Then I guess I'm trespassing," she murmured back.

Nikandros swore he saw her mask shift with a smile. He knew she felt his body's response to her and yet she didn't back away.

"What do you want?" he asked. Vivid images of conquering her over every surface of the laboratory came to mind. "Why are you here?"

Feeling the insistent shove of his rising center as it burned firmly into her hip, she collapsed her body against him and whispered, "Not for this, sweetheart."

Silk swung her hand around him, cocooning him faster than he could think to protest. Grabbing a handheld computer off the desk, she turned at a full run, leaping into the air as she flipped onto the top walkway.

Nikandros broke his arms free just in time to see her body swinging over the side rail. Giving chase, he leapt behind her. His lab coat fluttered to the ground as he stripped of it in midair.

Silk dashed through the living room. With a press of a button, she disarmed the front lawn security and was out the front door. Nikandros cursed as he came from the lab. Dr. Nathaniel's maid unit sensed his presence and switched on. With a press of her cleavage beneath a skimpy French maid uniform, she tried to get in his way to offer him a drink.

Nikandros pushed her aside. The maid gasped. Her mouth widened with affront. His eyes growing molten with red outrage, he ignored the machine as he ran out the front door. His vision pierced through the darkness with ease, only to stop at the cloaked figure hiding in the shadows. He growled, running up the side of the tree to soar over the fence. Seeing her blurring body, he went after her.

Silk detected the moment he saw her hiding and jumped down from the gate. With a supernatural speed, she began to take off down the quiet residential street. She tired to lose him, jumping down an impossible side cliff with the aid of her gossamer threads. He was right behind her, springing without fear as if he could glide through the air with ease. Seeing a hover bus, she hopped on top of it, clinging to the roof as it sped down the street. Attaching herself with the thread from her fingers, she turned over onto her back to ease herself down the side.

Nikandros, his red gaze flashing fire, landed on top of her. Silk jolted. Nikandros' body came hard against her as the bus hastened forward over the city streets. Everything blurred along their sides until trees and houses were no longer recognizable.

Silk didn't dare let her fingers go, lest she lose her grip. If she did, they would both go flying to their deaths. Nikandros' fingers curled strong and sure around her wrists. She tried to buck him off of her, but he merely bounced. She struggled against him, grunting to be free.

Nikandros growled. It was a horrific noise meant to drive fear into her. The woman merely continued to fight him. In her efforts, his hips worked between her thighs until his body pressed intimately into her.

Feeling the hard length of him digging and grinding as the bus bounced in the air, she froze. Desire swam into her racing blood, heating her with a liquid excitement she had never felt before. Her heart thundered wildly in her chest with the thrill of the fight, the adrenaline of his chase, the passion in his loins pressed thoroughly into hers.

"Who are you?" he asked in a frustrated growl.

"Silk," she answered simply, not stopping to think.

Nikandros sensed her body heating. Unable to help himself, masculine hunger overtook him and he dropped a hand to her covered breast. He pressed his lips to her masked mouth. Silk moaned in surprise. His lips parted, as if he could taste her through her disguise. His fingers boldly caressed her, as if they could part her from her clothing. He could find no seam in her outfit from which to liberate her.

Suddenly, the bus jolted to a stop. Nikandros flew forward, flipping over, off her body. They were in the city, next to an abandoned bus stop. Silk didn't wait. She rolled off the side and disappeared into the night. When Nikandros sat back up, he gripped his computer in his hand and watched the last fluttering of her cape.

"We will meet again, Silk," he swore, his body flowing with a potent, animalistic hunger. His hair was tousled from the windy ride.

As he rolled over the side, the bus passengers gasped to see him. They hadn't heard a thing while in the soundproofed interior.

Clearing his throat, Nikandros smoothed his hair and patted down his clothes. Giving the onlookers a crooked smile, he shrugged and stated, "Almost missed the bus."

* * * *

Silk ran until her lungs nearly exploded. The bus had taken her miles away from home. Glowering, she reached into her pocket and grabbed a video phone. Covering the camera lens, she called home for a ride. Minutes later, her limo pulled up to take her back to the St. James Estate. She climbed inside before the robotic driver could get out to open her door.

Pulling off her mask, Quinlan frowned. Her hair was matted to her head from her excursion. What was Nick Grant doing at Dr. Nathaniel's laboratory? And what exactly was he anyway? Who was he?

Thinking of him, her body trembled. Oh, but he had felt wickedly sinful against her. Even now she could feel the hard press of him. Quinlan was sure she'd be up for the rest of the night feeling him in her memory.

Why hadn't she just bought a pleasure droid? She'd been tempted a few times. But in the end she knew that, though it might soothe the ache in her body, it wouldn't be able to soothe the loneliness in her heart.

Nick Grant was a mystery. Did he know who she was? Was their chance encounter in the park just a coincidence? Quinlan didn't believe in coincidences and wasn't about to start now. Nick was up to something, she just couldn't figure out what.

Smiling, she thought, But I know how to find out.

Quinlan reached to her side to pull out the handheld computer. It wasn't there. Cursing, her eyes narrowed. Even as she hated him, he intrigued her. It had been a long time since anyone or anything had quickened her blood like he did when he touched her. "Damn you, Nick Grant. If you want to play, oh, we'll play."

Chapter Three

"This collection is superb, Quinlan," said Henry Thompson, head of the Genetic Science Museum. Henry was an older, balding gentleman with beady little eyes that gave Quinlan the chills. Right now those eyes were looking over the glass cases that lined the front hall of the castellated mansion home.

Musicians played old ballroom dances--waltzes, merengues, allemandes. Some couples danced, others strolled out into the lit gardens. Quinlan had robotic guards at every door and several between the large main hall and her father's laboratory. The robots, however, were programmed to respond only to hostility so that whoever wanted to break in would have an easy time of it. What everyone didn't know was that her father's laboratory was completely empty--except for some bogus documents she had written herself.

Continuing, Henry said, "They will be a great addition to the museum's collection. Your father would have been proud."

Quinlan smiled for the man, slowly holding up her glass of champagne. Her home was filled with the most elite members of the scientific community--all of them clamoring to get a look at the famous scientist's daughter.

"Miss St. James, a photograph, please!"

Quinlan turned her back as a man pulled a camera from his jacket. A flash went off, getting only the long line of her naked back in a sleek red silk dress. Henry Thompson frowned as a robotic security guard grabbed the guest and forcibly escorted him out. He stepped a little too close to Quinlan's back, lifting his arm to belatedly protect her from the cameraman.

Quinlan pulled artfully away from Henry and kept her face pleasant as if nothing had happened.

"This collection looks incomplete. Have some of the papers been lost?" asked a man Quinlan recognized instantly. She looked into his cool brown eyes, trying to gauge him. There was nothing in the vacuous depths-- nothing but greed and an overabundance of pride.

"I'm sorry, you are?" Quinlan asked, pretending she didn't know.

"Dr. Thomas Nathaniel," he said.

"Oh," said a woman with a shrill, grating voice. "Weren't you the man whose home was broken into?"

"My laboratory actually," said Dr. Nathaniel.

"Did they discover who?" asked the loud woman with a flick of her richly decorated fingers.

"Just a criminal in need of a microscope," he laughed pretentiously. The surrounding group joined in. "My wife was alone at the time and didn't see a thing."

"How dreadful for her!" gasped the woman.

Quinlan hid her face into her glass, remembering just how 'alone' the doctor's wife had been. Looking over Dr. Nathaniel's excessively thin frame, she guessed Mrs. Nathaniel much preferred to be alone with her Adonis model pleasure droid.

Quinlan tried not to blush. She had looked him up in a catalog late the night before as she considered buying one. Only, as she flipped through the pages, none of the droids struck her fancy. She kept thinking of Nick Grant. A flesh and blood man sounded much more appealing than a bloodless machine.

"I worked with your father right before his death, Miss St. James," said Dr. Nathaniel. "I don't see some of his later projects here."

"You are right, of course," Quinlan said, noticing how ears perked up at the admission. "I didn't think it necessary to display his incomplete works. They are no good to anyone."

"But, maybe his research could be continued," said Henry, his eyes lighting with interest at the thought. "What better testament to your father than to see his work finished?"

"My father's later years were spent on fanciful dreams, Dr. Thompson. I believe he would like to be remembered for the advances he made in genetic engineering. It is that work which I have given to the public he tried to serve," Quinlan said. A murmur of appreciation went up from around the group and she quietly excused herself with a gracious bow of her coiffed head.

"I've been waiting for you to drop something all night, so that I may come to your service, Miss St. James."

That voice! Quinlan shivered, stopping mid-stride. Of all places, this is not where she thought to see Nick again. Turning around to look at him, she affected an air of confusion.

"I'm sorry?" she asked, cocking her head to the side as she met his steady dark eyes. "I believe you have me confused with someone else."

Quinlan had to focus to keep her eyes from traveling over his deliciously formed body. He was handsome in his dashing black tuxedo. A dark red rose, a perfect match to her dress, was pinned on his lapel. All too well did she remember the press of him to her body--especially into her thighs.

"Quinlan," said Henry, eager to come to her assistance. He'd been hovering over her like a mother hen all night. It was driving her to distraction. "May I introduce you to Dr. Nikandros Grant?"

"Nikandros?" Quinlan asked, a memory pulling at the side of her brain. Her brows furrowed in confusion. She slowly began to nod. "You look like your father."

It was Nikandros' turn to be surprised. "My father?"

"Yes," Quinlan said. "He used to come around when I was a very young girl--maybe six. I remember him because he always arrived at the oddest hours and he was so mysterious...."

Nikandros barely remembered her as the young, ratty-haired girl that would sneak into her father's laboratory to play with the butterflies and caterpillars. He was surprised that she would remember him at all--er, his father at all.

Now looking at her, in the stunningly sleek gown of blood red silk, he couldn't see the annoying youngster she had been at all. He'd almost lost himself when he first found her from across the room. The strong lines of her bared back were showcased in a dipping sweep of material that teased the male eyes with a full view of her muscular lower back. A band dipped around the nape of her neck and crossed over the base of her throat to hold the front of the gown around her breasts. The material again swept to tease. Licking his lips, Nikandros would bet his life she wore nothing beneath the alluring silk.

"I believe my father mentioned you to me," he said gallantly. Henry eyed him suspiciously. He didn't like the possessive way the man stood too close to Quinlan. "He only had nice things to say."

"Hum, maybe I am thinking of the wrong man." Quinlan laughed. "The Nikandros Grant I'm thinking about use to call me a spoiled brat. I don't think he cared for me at all--or the fact that I gave all my father's butterflies names."

Henry laughed, trying to draw her attention. Quinlan felt the man take up her arm. He was trying to lead her away from the breathtakingly handsome gentleman she was flirting with.

Was she flirting with him? Quinlan inwardly grimaced.

"So, Dr. G--," she began.

"Please," Nikandros murmured in a voice that sent chills over her flesh. "Call me Nick."

"All right, Nick," she smiled up at him. Henry's sweaty hand began to rub. "What is this about me dropping something for you?"

"Ah, you don't remember?" he asked, affecting a properly injured disposition. "Your wallet? In the park a few days ago?"

"Oh, how silly of me to forget," she affected. Henry began to pull. From the corner of her eye she saw his mouth open as if he would speak. Rushing, she said to Nikandros, "I believe I said I owed you a dance for the favor."

Nikandros saw the pleading in her gaze and instantly smiled. He reached for her. Quinlan gladly lifted her arm away from Henry, who was trying to think of a way to protest. She placed her fingers in Nikandros' offered hand. His fingers were warmth to her flesh, very unlike the sweaty grip of the museum coordinator. Gracefully, he placed her hand on his forearm.

Watching his eyes for a sign of change, she smiled at him and sighed prettily. His eyes stayed the same dark brown, solid and spine-tinglingly handsome. If she hadn't seen the shift to red for herself, she would have never believed it. She wondered if he knew who she was. Her heart beat a little faster, thoroughly enjoying the dangerous game.

"Thank you," she murmured coyly when he had taken her out of earshot. "If I had to stand around with those stuffy scientists and doctors any longer, I was going to start screaming."

Nikandros smiled down at her, not letting her see any of his thoughts. He had overheard her comments about her father's later work. It was good she didn't have it for public display, but it didn't mean she wasn't fishing for buyers.

When Quinlan tried to pull away from him, his arm tightened on her hand.

"What about my dance?" he said in a low tone that neared upon a growl. Nikandros knew that seducing her would be the sweetest assignment he'd ever had and possibly the most disastrous for both of them. It didn't stop him as he drew her around into his arms. Her mouth opened in surprise, as her body came near his. She could smell the strong lure of his cologne. "I would hate to make you a liar."

Quinlan watched him carefully, intrigued. His smile was all charm--very uncharacteristic of the man who had broken into Dr. Nathaniel's laboratory to borrow a microscope, and then proceeded to jump over cliffs and onto buses with barely a scratch to show for it. She didn't trust him. But, she was intrigued and most assuredly aroused.

His hand dropped down over her lower back as he drew her closer. His eyes dared her to pull away as his fingers settled boldly on her naked flesh--almost caressing in their possessive hold against her skin. Gradually, he brought her closer to his chest. He drew his fingers over her shoulder. A trail of fire ignited on her arm as his touch dipped to cup her hand into his. The corner of his lips lifted, unwittingly tempting her to taste him. The musicians started a new piece and Nikandros took a step back and then another, automatically joining the other couples on the floor.

"You have a beautiful home," he said lightly, easily leading her further onto the floor.

Quinlan just smiled, not answering. Her gaze moved over his shoulder and she saw the portrait of her father staring down at her. Nikandros felt her tense. He knew where her eyes went.

"Tango?" he asked.

Quinlan blinked, drawing her wide gray-green gaze back to him. Nikandros was surprised to see pain there. She quickly hid the emotion.

"Do you tango?" he inquired softly, drawing his head down near her ear. She felt the brush of his breath against her cheek.

Instead of answering, she took an aggressive move toward him, making him back up as she stalked him. He grabbed her arm, a wide smile on his face, as he swirled her around on the floor. A path cleared and couples stopped to watch. Quinlan was captured in the spell of him and didn't notice. It was as if they were the only two in the room.

They danced. Their movements were more like a battle of wills than a seduction. But the battle was seducing, heating their blood, impassioning their bodies. Quinlan felt his hands brushing over her back, her waist, barely stroking the silk along the side of her breast. When he touched her, she felt as if he undressed her.

Nikandros' body was firm beneath her palms. She felt the hard press of his arms and chest beneath the tuxedo he wore. In what seemed like only a second, the dance ended.

The gathered crowd began to clap. Nikandros pulled her up to face him, setting her tight along his body. The silk was no match to his heat.

Quinlan blinked. Her father's portrait was looking at them, watching, smiling down from above. Her head moved to the crowd. Henry was there, his face red with jealousy. She swallowed, artfully dipping away from her handsome dance partner. As the musicians started anew, she turned to walk away without a sound.

Nikandros started to go after her, wondering at the sudden chill he'd felt in her toward him. Surely a woman, who danced as confidently as she, did not embarrass easily at the attention of the crowd. He reminded himself that she was a recluse. Maybe she didn't like crowds.

"Dr. Grant," said Henry, blocking his way. Nikandros watched Quinlan work through the throng, smiling politely at those she passed but not lingering. She slipped up the side stairwell. "I had no idea you were coming tonight. The invitation was for your father."

"My father is dead," Nikandros said easily. He eyed the little man, wanting nothing more than to push past him and go after the red covered goddess. She might not beckon him with words, but her body screamed her attraction loud and clear. "We buried him a few years back. I came to pay my respects to Dr. St. James' daughter. My father always spoke highly of the good doctor."

"I know what you've come for," said Henry in a low growl. Nikandros finally turned his attention away from the stairwell to study Henry fully, thinking he meant to possessively mark Quinlan as his own. To his surprise, the man said, "You'll not get her father's notes. They belong to the museum."

"What do you know about it?" he asked, keeping his smile light, though his eyes bore down to intimidate the little man.

"I know plenty," said Henry, not backing down. A snarl formed on his lips and he didn't seem so much the simple little man Nikandros had easily dismissed him as. "I know that Quinlan won't give them to you--no matter how much you try and seduce her with your charm. She is a smart woman. She won't be swayed by charm. She might humor you, but she will not be swayed. Besides, the collection is already donated."

"Then what about money?" Nikandros asked, gauging the man. "I take it you're her...broker?"

Henry smiled. "What I am to her, you don't need to know."

Nikandros frowned at the obvious implication the man tried to get across. He didn't buy for a moment that Henry Thompson was Quinlan's lover. He'd sensed more than saw her repulsion when the man had touched her arm. Her eyes had begged him to get her away from him.

"Look around you, dear boy," said Henry, very condescending. "She doesn't need your money. Anything she does will be done out of loyalty."

Nikandros didn't move. His blood slowed in his veins, leaving him cold.

Henry sniffed, looking him up and down. "You will never be able to have her loyalty."

Henry turned away as someone vied for his attention, a wide grin of victory on his lips. Nikandros silently watched him, before walking out one of the side doors leading to the garden. It was worse than he thought. If Quinlan was selling the formula, then he could have easily come up with the money to buy it from her, if she wouldn't hand it over to him willingly.

However, loyalty was something else altogether. Henry was right. She was a billionaire. Her loyalty would not be easily purchased. Besides, he sensed a great amount of pride in her. Even if she weren't rich, she wouldn't be easily turned from a cause she believed in.

* * * *

Quinlan's body was on fire. The thin red silk was no match for Nikandros' hands on her body. If anything, it had made his touch all the more erotic. She swallowed, knowing he was a distraction to her. She had a duty to her father to find out who killed him. She had a duty to herself to put an end to the whole formula mess once and for all. No one would be getting the formula. No one. Not even a handsome stranger with the body of a God and the dance moves to match.

It didn't take Quinlan long to realize Nikandros seduced her for her father's formula. Everyone at the party had hinted at its existence in one subtle way or another. Finding the murderer was proving harder than she first imagined. She'd just have to wait for that one person who would threaten her. She'd dangle hints of it all around until whoever burned badly enough with greed would come forward.

Nikandros would have been too young when her father died to be a big part of the conspiracy, but what of his father? Did he come to fulfill a family legacy? She would have to be very cautious of him.

The blood in her veins was still heavy with desire and the persistent throb in her stomach that only grew each passing moment until she thought she might explode. Quinlan knew she would also have to be very cautious of herself. She wanted Nikandros like she had never wanted anyone-- much more than she had wanted that fumbling idiot who'd taken her virginity after her father died. She'd been on a self-destructive path of self-loathing at the time, hating her father and herself for what she had become.

But that was then, before she had discovered the true depths of her gift and her curse. Her father's formula had made it one and the same. She was cursed to be alone, blessed to be a heroine. She'd done a lot of good in the last ten years. She'd saved lives, helped the helpless. And not once did anyone discover their helper. Her life was a complicated secret and she preferred to keep it that way.

Crossing over to her bedroom fireplace, she pushed a brick. A small door slid open and she ducked into the secret passage. Ignoring Silk's bodysuit hanging on the wall of the small den, she walked quickly past it into a narrow hall that led out into the garden. When she emerged, she was behind a rose bush. She closed her eyes, listening, taking quick stock of her surroundings with her sensitive hearing. The closest person she could detect was fifty yards to her right.

Quinlan straightened, walking out into the moonlit garden as if she had been there all along.

"That was an interesting trick. You'll have to show me how you did that."

She shivered. A smile came unbidden to her excited, panting lips at the sound of his voice. Turning, she watched

Nikandros alight from the shadows. She hadn't sensed him there.

Cocking her head to the side, she shot him a sultry smile and asked, "Are you stalking me, Dr. Grant?"

Chapter Four

Nikandros watched the blue moonlight play across Quinlan's lovely features. He'd sensed more than saw her coming from the side of the home. Unable to help himself, he went to her. He tried to tell himself that it was his duty to go to her. But as he felt the burning desire in his loins, he knew that it was something else altogether that spurred him on.

"I should have you thrown out for this," Quinlan said after a long moment of impassioned silence. Sparks flew between them and they each knew it.

Instead of answering, he smiled.

"I have a feeling you are a dangerous man, Nick Grant," Quinlan said. They were hidden by the shadows of a tree from the rest of the guests. The feel of him dancing with her had not lessened and she wanted to go eagerly back into his arms.

Nikandros took the low, sultry words as an invitation to go forward.

"And you, my dear, are a mystery," he returned. His hand lifted to her cheek. Her eyes dreamily closed at his touch. There was no point denying the desire between them. It blazed on the night like stars shooting across the heavens.

"So we're agreed?" she sighed, letting him feel her. She was too weak to protest. He had taken up too many of her thought as of late. "We don't trust each other."

Her lips parted, begging him to taste her.

"Not in the slightest," he whispered back, leaning to claim her mouth with his. His fingers glided to her slender neck, holding her steady and light, as he felt the pulse racing beneath her flesh.

Quinlan moaned to feel him. The contact felt odd after being alone and untouched for so long. His lips were tender, persuasive, teasing. When his tongue edged forward, tasting the champagne on her lips, she gasped in excitement.

Nikandros nearly groaned to hear the soft, feminine plea. In that moment, she almost sounded helpless, vulnerable. He drew back to study her face. Her eyes were closed to him, her lips still parted.

Quinlan felt as if she was in a cloud. She wanted him to keep touching her. She wanted him to kiss her, to make love to her. His hand was so gentle against her body. His lips were so firm and commanding, yet giving. She'd felt his kiss all the way to her curling toes. Her body burned. She felt ... she felt a vibrating at her throat?

"Quinlan?" Nikandros said when she didn't move.

"The lab," she whispered, blinking to awareness. Her hand went to her throat. Beneath the crossing of silk, the silent alarm vibrated against her skin. Someone was breaking into her father's laboratory. Jolting into action, she began to run to a servant's entrance to the house.

Nikandros had heard her soft whisper and moved to follow behind her as she darted away. Quinlan ignored him, intent on finding out who was trying to steal her father's formula.

She tore through the servant hall and through the kitchen, ignored by the robotic staff as she whipped past them. They continued working, loading trays full of champagne and wine, caviar and toast points.

With a push of a button, a stone wall moved and shifted, creating an entrance into a separate hall. Nikandros grabbed her arm as she tried to rush forward. The door shut, sealing them in the passageway. Dim red lights switched on to part the darkness.

"Quinlan, wait," he commanded. His gaze easily detected her in the darkened light. Her skin glowed eerie in the red and her gown looked as if it bled from her body. "You don't know who--"

"I can take care of myself," she growled, jerking her arm away. With a few narrow turns, she opened the secret entrance into the laboratory.

The room was dusty, almost exactly like her father had left it all those years ago--aside from what she had moved out for the museum display. Stiffening, she stopped and listened. She felt Nikandros take up her elbow, as if he would push her behind his back to protect her. She would have laughed at the chivalry, if the situation weren't so serious.

Quinlan knitted her brow in concentration, hearing a noise on the far side where her father's thinking couch still sat. William had spent many hours lying on the old piece of worn furniture as he figured out scientific equations.

Suddenly, a giggling rose and a woman's voice said, "Oh, but you're programmed to be a quiet one, aren't you?"

Quinlan frowned, glancing over at Nikandros. He too studied the couch.

"Now, where's your control panel?" the woman murmured. "I know you've got to have one here some...oh, here it is. Let's see...yellow and red make erection."

Quinlan instantly stepped forward. She grimaced. On her father's old couch was Mrs. Nathaniel with the butler unit. She had his uniform lifted off his slightly rounded stomach was trying to reprogram the unresponsive unit to....

"Excuse me," Quinlan said. "This room is off limits. And I would appreciate it if you didn't reprogram the help."

Nikandros hid his chuckle at the wryness of her tone. Mrs. Nathaniel blinked, nearly screaming in surprise at being found out.

"Get back to the party before I tell your husband you have a robot fetish," Quinlan ordered. The woman nodded her head and scurried off, her face coloring in horror and mortification.

Quinlan sighed in frustration. She had been so sure she was going to solve the mystery. Disappointment was hard to swallow. She went to the unit and began rerouting the wires to their original settings.

"How did you know she had a robot fetish?" Nikandros asked, a suspicion forming in the back of his mind.

"Lucky guess," she murmured in distraction. She righted the uniform. "Only a woman with a robot fetish would know which wires to cross."

The butler unit blinked and sat up. "Welcome home, Miss."

"Restart program," ordered Quinlan. The butler nodded and blinked. He stood before her. "Back to your post."

The butler silently walked out the laboratory door.

"So, this is your father's lab?" Nikandros asked, looking around when they were alone. He remembered the place well. He had spent many hours with William in it. William had been a good man with a truly pure heart and had treated him like a son.

"It was," Quinlan said, a hard edge to her tone.

Nikandros studied her. Her eyes were no longer soft or dreamy when she looked at him. She moved, glancing around to see if anything was disturbed. His body still burned for her, wanting to draw her back into his arms.

With that in mind, he went to her and ran the backs of his fingers over her bare back, from her neck to her side. He lightly let his fingers dip beneath the silk to land on her waist in a most intimate caress. She trembled beneath his hand. Nikandros leaned into her, letting her feel the hard length of his desire against her hip.

Nikandros wanted nothing more than to pull up her gown and passionately take her right there in the laboratory. His mind came up with many splendid options--the desk, the couch, the floor, backed up against a wall. He dipped his head near her neck, intent on kissing her nape and exploring the soft skin of her body further.

"Can we pick up where we left off?" he hushed, sending a wave of tremors over her spine at the thought.

Quinlan pulled away and walked to the door. His hard body had burned her through the silk of her gown and she became nervous. "I can't. I have guests I must attend to and a speech to give."

Nikandros sighed. As he moved to follow her, his hand darted to a table and pulled a sheet from a dusty file. Deftly, he tucked it into his pocket. When she turned around to glance at him, he smiled angelically at her.

Quinlan frowned in suspicion, nodding her head to indicate he should leave first. Nikandros walked boldly past, stopping long enough to send her a heated look of tempered desire. Quinlan shivered, watching him walk down the hall. Then, looking back over the laboratory, she whispered, "Sorry, dad. Don't worry. I'll get them next time."

* * * *

Quinlan's speech was short and sweet. She sung praises about her father's earlier works and alluded enigmatically to his later ones. Mrs. Nathaniel was next to her husband, looking properly mortified as she refused to meet Quinlan's eyes. During her speech, she felt Nikandros' dark gaze on her from the back of the crowd, stabbing into her with his denied passion. No doubt he was upset by her dismissal of him.

"Very lovely," said Henry to her as she stepped back down from the podium to rejoin the party. His hand lifted, as if to touch her back, but hesitated and merely hovered as he tried to guide her into the crowd.

"Thank you," acknowledged Quinlan. She saw Nikandros watching her from the distance, his eye alighting possessively on her. His jaw stiffened and he didn't make a move to come to her.

Quinlan shivered.

"Is something wrong?" Henry asked.

Quinlan blinked in surprise and turned to him.

"You look pale," he continued.

"I'm just tired. It's been a long night," she answered.

Henry nodded, seeming to understand.

* * * *

Nikandros watched Quinlan's face stiffen as she talked to Henry. He wondered what they could have been discussing that would make her skin turn pale like that. Her eyes darted to the man as she answered him, before moving around the crowd. Nikandros dipped back into the shadows, slipping out of sight.

* * * *

Quinlan heaved a sigh of relief as the guests left. She was glad the party was finally over. Henry had been the last to leave, promising to send over movers first thing in the morning to take the glass cases and oversized photograph to their permanent new home in the museum. His eyes had looked her over as if he wanted to ask her something, but she yawned heavily for show and bid him goodnight before he could speak.

Leaving the maid units to clean up the mess, she grimaced to discover someone had thrown up in her broken water fountain. It only served as a reminder of why she hated throwing these functions. If she never did it again, she'd be happy.

After ordering the security droids to search and scan the entire premises, Quinlan slowly made her way to her bedroom. The house was quiet again, just as she liked it. The droids ignored everything but their task at hand.

Her bedroom was dark and she called for fire, not bothering to ask for more light. With a pull of two hairpins, her hair spilled down over her shoulders. She dropped the clips on her vanity and kicked off her shoes. The maid unit switched on, picking up after her.

"Shower," Quinlan called, crossing over next to the fireplace to where her bathroom door was.

"Mind if I join you?"

For a moment, Quinlan thought it was her fantasy coming to life. Her hands dropped from the back of her neck. She'd been almost ready to unclasp the straps to her dress. Spinning on her heels, she saw Nikandros lounging on her bed, a wide smile on his face as he watched her.

"Please, don't stop what you were doing on my account." His words were low and sultry. His eyes glowed with meaning as he looked at her dress. His gaze turned seductive in the orange glow of the firelight.

"Privacy," Quinlan demanded.

Nikandros blinked in confusion at the order until she saw the maid unit leaving.

"What are you doing in here?" she asked when they were alone, a little too weakly for her liking.

"I thought you might like to see me," he said, bringing his feet around the edge of the bed. His tuxedo jacket was off, lying across one of her chairs. "Since we were interrupted last time."

Quinlan swallowed. It was more than her erotically charged brain could take in, seeing him next to her bed--a place where the naughtiest thoughts of him had occurred.

"I didn't invite you in here," she said, taking an unwitting step back. Her legs shook, as she debated what to do. Did she take him up on his offer and let him shower with her? Or did she call for her droid guards and have him dragged out of her home?

"I think you should let me stay," he murmured, as if he read her thoughts easily on her face.

"What do you want?" she whispered, her eyes taking him into their wide green depths.

At that, he smiled, coming forward until he towered above her. His hand lightly touched her throat, running down over her breast in a tender stroke. Quinlan gasped as her nipple budded to instant attention against a circling thumb. He smiled a devilishly wicked smile.

"That, my darling," he whispered, his eyes daring her to run. "I would think was most obvious."

Quinlan gasped as he seized her hand firmly in his and pulled it onto his full arousal. He was rigid and hard beneath her palm, thick and ready for impaling.

"I want you," he said with a manly growl.

Quinlan shivered at the admission. His mouth dipped forward to swallow anything she might say. She trembled at the onslaught of his lips. This searing kiss wasn't tender like the one in the garden. It was hard and demanding--just like the rest of him. His teeth devoured her, biting. His tongue soothed the wounds, licking and teasing, stealing her breath.

Before she knew what was happening, his tongue was dipping into her mouth and his hands were on her thigh, lifting her silk covered leg up to his waist. Quinlan's hands were all over him, pulling at the white linen of his shirt to bare his chest to her. Buttons snapped off at her eager exploration.

Their panting moans rose up between them. His chest was smooth, molded in hot perfection. Each muscle was toned and rippled when he pressed himself against her. The doorframe dug into her tender back. She didn't care. The silk of her gown was no match for his branding heat.

With a groan, Nikandros pulled away. His hot eyes tinged with red as he looked her over. Her leg dropped to the ground.

"Remove the dress," he ordered fervently.

Quinlan could not disobey. He was every fantasy she had ever had rolled into one man of flesh and bone. At the moment, she didn't care who he was or that he might be using her. She couldn't care, not when her body burned with such passionate ardor.

Taking her hands to her neck, she pulled her dress free. The material whispered over her skin, pooling on the floor at her feet. She was completely naked under the gown, just as he had expected. His eyes narrowed as he took her in--

her round breasts, the pleasant shading of her nether region. His lips parted. He was pleased, very pleased.

His hands at his waist, he noticed the steam from the water shower was beginning to fog the bathroom. He licked his lips.

"I want to make love to you," he said boldly. His managed to unbutton his pants and they slipped from his waist. Kicking out of his clothes, he stood naked before her.

Quinlan's eyes widened as she looked him over. Not an ounce of fat marred his thick frame. The wide base of his desire stood tall, frightfully persuasive in its large size. Not even in her dreams had he been this delectable. She couldn't speak.

"You're exquisite," he continued to stare. "I want to make love to you in the shower."

Quinlan's mouth went dry. She slowly started to back away from him into the shower stall. She opened the door and stepped inside. Before she could even turn around, she felt his hands on her naked back.

Nikandros shut the door as he stepped in behind her. His hands glided over her flesh, at once finding hold on her chest. Insistently, he pushed her forward until her body was pressed against the unforgiving tile wall. His lips dipped to drink from her wet flesh, kissing and licking her delectable skin.

"You taste so good," he said between sips. She gasped, her hand reaching behind her to feel for him. Her fingers met with flexing muscular hips.

Nikandros groaned, pressing his risen manhood into her tender backside. Quinlan whimpered, gasping loudly as he began to rub himself into the sensitive flesh of her cleft. She knew the house was empty, knew that the robot staff wouldn't care if she screamed in pleasure.

"You like that, don't you?" he demanded hotly. His teeth bit into the tender lobe of her ear. "You want me inside you, don't you?"

"Yes," she panted, liking the sound of his voice, the feel of him. His hands were doing delightful things to her breasts, tweaking and teasing them to hard points.

At her admission, Nikandros turned her in the shower to face him. He kissed her softly, passionately. His fingers glided over her hot, wet skin, sending wave after wave of desire through her.

Quinlan was on fire. She felt cream pooling between her thighs, wet and hot and so very ready for him. When he lifted her legs to wrap around his waist, she didn't protest. His hands supported her. His weight pressed her back into the wall.

Nikandros guided himself forward. Her wet heat called to him. He stroked himself lightly along her opening, parting her velvet lips with his hard shaft, testing to see if she was ready to accept him. He'd waited for so long, had been tormented by the sound of her voice. He had been haunted in dreams and in wakefulness.

To her surprise, he took her slowly, entering her with a gentleness that made her body weak and strong at the same time. Quinlan had never felt anything like him. He tested her, probing as he stretched her to fit around him. The shower made their skin glide easily, just as her wetness made his claiming all the sweeter.

Nikandros groaned as she fitted around him. She was tight, but her muscles surrendered to his solid heat. Not stopping until he was fully embedded, he growled loudly.

"Oh," she breathed, wiggling against him. Her fingernails dug into his shoulders. "Yes. Yes."

Grabbing onto her hips, he began to move, pulling out only to delve back inside. Nikandros grunted. Quinlan screamed. Their bodies slammed together in a primal rhythm.

"Oh, ye-es, Nick," she gasped, urging him on. Her head fell forward to bite at his neck. He continued to move, picking up the tempo of his possession.

"Ah, Quinlan, you feel so good, so tight," he growled, trying to control her hips and touch all of her at the same time. The movements of his body quickened, sparking a reaction deep inside her.

When he pulled back, her eyes were staring into him, wide and trusting. Something inside of him broke in that moment. He saw her loneliness--so deep and raw. He knew she was innocent of everything they thought her capable of. He couldn't explain it, but he knew it as sure as he knew himself.

The swiftness with which her body peaked amazed her as she tensed against him, arching violently into the tile. Nikandros almost lost his footing on the slick stone beneath his feet. And, as her body tightened around him with forceful tremors, clenching him hard, it was all he could do to hold on as he jerked his release into her.

Chapter Five

Nikandros lowered Quinlan down from the wall. At first, he didn't move away, keeping her pressed against him, trapped to him. The feel of her soft body beneath him made him want to stand there forever, protecting her.

She quivered against the solid mass of his flesh, feeling secure in his strong arms. She couldn't explain it, but she knew she was falling for him. She knew it wasn't completely due to the sensations she'd just experienced-- though they had shattered her world. It was like she knew him, like she'd known him all her life.

Nikandros slowly pulled back, only to kiss her in an effort to cut off anything she might try to say. Whatever she thought, he didn't want to hear it. Yet again, she moaned lightly against him, easily melting into his passion. At the soft sound, he was surprised to find his body eager to claim her all over again.

"Turn off the shower," he murmured to her panting lips.

"Shower off," she breathed, sucking his tongue into her mouth. The water instantly stopped spraying.

"Invite me to your bed," he urged.

Quinlan nodded, her finger wound up into his soft wet hair, as she whispered, "Mm-hum. Come to my bed."

His hand found its way over her hip. His fingers moved to touch her intimately, bolding circling around her until she felt her hips jerk in response.

"Invite me to come inside you," he whispered.

"Yes," she breathed, growing hot under his touch. Her eyes closed in pleasure. She didn't know how he managed it, but with a few simple words he'd heated her back past the point of reasoning. "Oh! Come inside me."

Nikandros growled. Quinlan giggled as he swung her up into his arms and rushed her across her bedroom. Her body glided onto the silk sheets of her bed as he laid her down.

"You feel just like this silk," he confessed, running his hands over her as he came to lay half way on top of her moist body. Her gray-green eyes widened at the admission. His large thigh pressed her legs down, trapping her beneath him, not that she had anywhere else she wanted to go.

His nose nudged near her ear, pushing her cheek over so he could place hot kisses along her neck. Her body was still wet from the shower and it aided his lips as they slid to envelop the base of her throat, moving along her collarbone. Quinlan shivered, arching slightly into him.

"Where did you come from?" she whispered in awe, panting as he kissed her. Surely he had emerged from her dreams. Reality was never like this.

Nikandros wanted to tell her the truth, but couldn't. When his lips stilled in their journey, she pulled back to study him.

"Who are you, really?" she asked, her eyes searching and vulnerable. She swallowed. She had been alone for so long, that she never imagined that anything could take away the ache she felt. But, with him, she didn't feel the emptiness.

Nikandros closed his eyes, fighting the truth that tried to spill forth from him. He'd never realized until that moment of ecstasy in her arms how alone his centuries had truly been. He was old enough to know his feelings for what they were. He was old enough to know his own heart. He was old enough to know he couldn't blow his cover until he had solid proof that she wasn't guilty. Taking a deep breath, he said the only truth he could. "I am a man you shouldn't trust just yet."

Her eyes fell. He felt her sadness as if it was his own.

"But I am also a man who wants nothing more than to be here right now, making love to you," he whispered.

Quinlan took the answer for what it was, knowing that was all he would or could say. She was familiar with secrets. Slowly, she nodded, offering her neck up to him so he could resume his pleasurable torture of her skin.

Nikandros was awed by how easily she accepted his response. She did not scream or try to coax answers from him. She did not demand anything from him at all, except what he would readily give her. He again kissed her throat, licking at her pulse until it began to speed up at his rapt attention.

His hand found her breast, ripening a nipple with his thumb. His lips found the other peak, nipping at it with his teeth only to soothe it the next instant with a deep kiss. Quinlan moaned, loving the feel of his strong body. His kisses trailed over her stomach, to her hips, only to center on her most intimate need.

He was surprised to find her ready for him as his fingers dipped inside to stroke her. Her leg rubbed restlessly against him, her foot working its way to lie against his arousal, stroking him in return the only way she could reach.

Quinlan thought she died when his lips latched onto her moistened center. His fingers began to move more insistently, urging her to climax against his hand. She began to tremble. Nikandros felt the response and sucked her deeper into his mouth. His fingers quickened until her hands were in his hair smothering his lips into her softness. Her head thrashed wildly against her pillows.

"Nick," she screamed, jerking and tensing against him. It was the most beautiful sound he'd ever heard. He didn't let up until he milked every last quiver her body had to offer him. A dominant smile on his lips, he released her and crawled up over her weakened body.

He moved as if he would enter her, but Quinlan tightened her thighs on his waist and flung him onto his back with a surprising strength. A sultry vixen's smile came to her mouth as she eyed his naked and readied body.

"I must have you," he growled, reaching to grab her hips. She met his hands and pressed them over his head, pinning him down. The moisture from her body slid between them as she sat on his hard stomach.

"It's my turn to play," she whispered.

Nikandros was glad that her head dipped to kiss his chest, because his mouth fell open in amazement at the bold statement. Her lips were on his hot flesh, tracing a pattern over the ridges of his muscles. Her mouth was light, dropping little feathery caresses along him until he squirmed to be free of her torture.

She was amazedly strong, but he knew that if really wanted to, he could buck her off him. But, as she sat up, he saw the lowered lids of her impassioned gaze and he wouldn't have stopped her torture for the world. She leaned over to explore his neck and throat, biting him as he had her and then soothing the same way.

"Do you like this?" she asked, licking her way to his earlobe. She was answered by a husky growl.

"Yes," he groaned. The loudness of his response pleased her.

She kissed up his jaw to claim his mouth. She sucked at his eager tongue, massaging it with her own. His hips jerked and her body slid back along his waist so that her backside was flush against his heavy erection. She could feel him against her, large and powerful. The smooth skin of him rubbed insistently into her as he thrust his hips up, searching for his release that could not come unless she took him deep inside.

"I must have you now," he urged against her mouth, not letting her up from his all-consuming kiss. "Let me inside you, Quinlan, please. I need to feel your silken depths before I explode."

Quinlan released his arms. He growled, his hands automatically finding her hips to raise her up. With a potent force, he guided himself directly inside of her, hitting hard upon her heated core. Quinlan jerked in surprise.

Nikandros howled with delight at the feel of her on top of him. His stomach tensed and he sat up, rocking her thighs against his hips. The action caused him to go deeper still. His fingers dug into the silk sheets as he braced his arms back. Her hips began to move, controlling the motion of their thrusts. His knees bent and his heels dug into the bed for leverage. His body jerked, impatient to meet the down stroke of her hips, slamming his body up into hers.

"Ah, faster," he begged her, breathless and gasping for air. "Harder."

Quinlan began to move faster, instantly discovering the delight of claiming him hard.

"Harder," he growled, pumping up into her, his whole body tensing and flexing.

She could not deny him. Watching his face, contorted in what seemed like agony, she gave him what he begged for.

Her body squeezed him, colliding against him, forcing him to come inside her as she rode him hard. Her body began to peak with desire. Sweat glistened on their skin. She tried to hold back from her climax, wanting to give him his first.

"Oh, yeah, sweetheart," he implored demandingly. "That's it. Ah, that's it. Don't stop. Just ... like ... that, darling. Don't stop ... ah. Keep it hard. Oh, you feel so good on me."

Quinlan couldn't deny herself any longer as his words washed over her. She pushed him back. She braced her hands onto his chest as he fell over in surprise. Her fingers dug into his nipples. She circled her hips while still pounding into his flesh. Her body began to tense, she could feel it coming, she needed it to come, she needed him to release her....

"Aahh!" she screamed, shaking ferociously as she peaked. Her hands clawed viciously into him.

Nikandros' head fell back as he arched into her. He never felt anything like it. It was as if her body sucked the life out of him and he willingly gave it to her. His mouth opened, his eyes sought to look at her, wanting the memory of her climaxing pose to forever be with him. He was stunned to see her eyes shifted to the subtlest purple.

"Silk," he whispered.

Quinlan collapsed on top of him, breathless. She couldn't move. "What did you say?"

"I said you feel like silk," he murmured into her hair. She was too spent to move. His lips trailed to her temple to give her a gentle kiss. She fell asleep on his body, his member still embedded within her.

* * * *

Nikandros didn't know how long he dozed, but sometime during his rest, Quinlan had slid off to his side and now lay nestled next to him on the bed. She was achingly beautiful in her nakedness and his body stirred, wanting to take possession of her again. Her lips parted and she moaned in her sleep, tempting him to a kiss. He held back. He didn't dare wake her.

Thinking of her shifting eyes, he slowly stood and went to look for the formula he'd stolen from her father's laboratory. It angered him slightly that she would just leave it lying out like that. He didn't dream for a moment that a scientist's daughter wouldn't know what it was--especially William's daughter.

Guilt overwhelmed him as he pulled the paper out. Slowly, he read over the encoded documentation. It was part of William's research. He knew because William had used part of his DNA coding in his research and Nikandros recognized the sequencing.

Getting to the end, he frowned. The work was incomplete and, in the corner, in a tight script that looked just like William's, it read, All attempts to produce genetic enhancements a complete failure. All subjects unstable and die within twelve hours before any genetic altering can even take hold. Am regretfully calling an end to the project.

It was dated the day before William died.

Nikandros glanced at the bed to the sleeping woman. The smooth curve of her backside was to him. The documents were fakes--good fakes, but fakes nonetheless. He knew because he had seen the real research. Where this paper claimed to hit a dead end, they had surpassed by leaps and bounds.

He sighed, knowing he would be expected to report in. Taking a leap of faith, he grabbed a pen from his pocket and scrolled quick note onto the back of the page. Then, laying it by her head, he placed the rose from his lapel on top of it. He wanted to kiss her again, but didn't dare until this nasty business was done for good.

Quietly, he dressed and snuck from her bedroom window, leaping down the way he'd gotten in. His body blended completely with the darkness, blurring as he moved, turning into a fine, undetectable mist as he went easily past her security.

* * * *

Quinlan awoke the next morning with a smile forming on her lips before she even opened her eyes. She was thoroughly rested. Yawning, she reached across her large bed, searching for Nikandros. To her disappointment, he wasn't there. Still grinning like a fool, her fingers hit a flower. She grabbed the bud, sitting up to look around. The fire still burned golden. Save for her, the room was empty.

"Nick?" she called lightly, her head leaning over to look into the bathroom as she smelled the red rose. There was no answer. She frowned in disappointment. Then, seeing a white piece of paper on her pillow, she picked it up.

I know the truth about your father's formula. Meet me tonight. Pierson Park. Midnight. Nikandros.

Quinlan's hand trembled as she turned the paper over. It was the fake sheet she'd put in her father's office and carefully sprinkled with dust to make it look like an original. Her hands trembled and a tear slid down her face. If Nikandros knew the truth, then others might know it as well. She couldn't let the secret out. She couldn't let them make more like her. She had to stop him.

"No," she whispered, looking down at her naked body in bittersweet dejection. "Silk has to stop him."

* * * *

Nikandros frowned into the video phone. "I don't think she is trying to sell the formula."

Korbin's eyes narrowed. "What makes you think that?"

"I just do," Nikandros said. He rolled a little piece of silk residue in his fingers. He'd found it on his chest when he got back to his hotel room, next to the scratch marks from Quinlan's fingers. He'd also seen the way her eyes changed to a most familiar purple.

"Are you sure you're not thinking with your--" began Korbin.

"William figured out the formula," Nikandros broke in. "It's complete."

"No," Korbin whispered, with an expression akin to horror. "Then you know what we must do. We have to get that formula. If it fell into the wrong hands, just imagine the evil we'd be dealing with."

"I don't think she's going to give it out," Nikandros said, wondering what made him so sure of that fact.

"You're not thinking straight," Korbin said. "I know you like her, but--"

"I think I love her," Nikandros said. Korbin paled. He knew his friend would never say anything like that lightly.

"Nick," Korbin began, almost mournful.

"All I ask is that you give me time to talk to her before you send in the other Protectors. If she is trying to give out the formula, I'll take her down myself--on my honor." Nikandros stared boldly in the phone.

"All right," Korbin said. After hundreds of years of working together, he knew to take Nikandros at his word. But, from experience, he also knew that love clouded the mind. He didn't know what was going on down in Pierson City, but he was sure he didn't like it. "I'll give you till tomorrow. But if the formula's completed, she could already have a buyer lined up for it. I can't think of a single man at that party I would want to have it."

"I know," Nikandros said. "I won't let you down. Trust me."

"I do, old friend," Korbin said. "Just don't forget who you are ... what we are. We are the Protectors and we must do just that."

Nikandros nodded, switching off the phone. His eyes drifted down to the silk ball he had rolled in his hands. Slowly, he lifted his fingers and threw it at the trashcan. It was time to end this.

Chapter Six

It was a half an hour until midnight and Silk wasn't sure what made her go to her father's laboratory instead of straight to Pierson Park. The tight, familiar fit of her clothes was comforting to her skin as she walked silently through the secret passageways.

Henry Thompson had sent a crew to pick up her father's collection earlier in the day and she was a little sad to see the big portrait go. With it there, so big and commanding, she had felt like he was with her again, watching over her. Then Nikandros had come and she felt the loneliness leaving her for a sweet moment of ecstasy.

It had been so hard the last ten years--alone and isolated from the world. No one had been there to help her understand her new powers. She couldn't let anyone in, lest they discover her secret. She would not be exposed for a freak--prodded and tested and torn apart until there was nothing left. And, most importantly, she would not see anyone else burdened with her curse.

Taking a deep breath, she pushed open the secret door to the laboratory. For a moment, she let herself remember what it was like to be a young girl, sneaking away from her nanny to go to her father's lab. He'd always scold her, but never once did he send her away.

Clutching her teddy bear, she'd watch him look into his microscope. He always took the time to show her what he worked on, doing his best to explain complex concepts to a young daughter who didn't understand them. All Quinlan had known at the time was that her father was a good man and he was trying to save and improve lives. Dr. William St. James had done just that time and time again. But the two lives he couldn't save, were his own and his daughter's.

"I'm sorry, Dad," she whispered, feeling like a failure. All she ever wanted was to avenge him and put an end to the reality of his formula.

Suddenly, two strong arms clamped around her from behind. Silk had been so lost in thought, that she didn't hear anyone else in the room. Glancing down through the red fog of the security lights, she saw two very strong, pale masculine hands on her arms.

Silk didn't scream, biding her time.

"I'm sorry, Daddy," came a mocking feminine whine.

Silk blinked, narrowing her eyes through the mask as she peered out into the darkness. To her amazement, Mrs. Nathaniel walked out from behind her father's antique filing cabinet.

"Ah, great," Silk said, giving a heavy sigh of frustration. "You're not trying to seduce the robotic help again are you?"

Mrs. Nathaniel grimaced, storming forward to slap Silk across the face with the flat of her palm. "Shut up! I was rewiring to listen to your messages."

Silk just laughed. It occurred to her that the hands on her arms more than likely belonged to the Adonis model pleasure droid.

"Uh-huh," chuckled Silk, mocking. "The last time I checked, robotic droids didn't store their message files in their erections."

"Hurt her, Adonis," cried Mrs. Nathaniel, pulling at her blonde hair.

The pleasure droid squeezed ever so slightly, but didn't really do her skin any harm. Pleasure droids were not programmed for pain. They were like any other droid. If they tried to really hurt a human, they would self-destruct instantly. Silk, an idea forming in her head, gritted her teeth as if she were in pain.

"That's better," said Mrs. Nathaniel. "Now, tell me where you've hidden your father's formula."

"Formula?" spat Silk, giving a pretend jerk in the android's arms. "What formula?"

"Argh!" the woman screeched, slapping Silk again.

Silk frowned. This was quickly getting old.

"Did your husband send you here?" Silk asked.

"My husband?" the woman asked, laughing.

Silk held perfectly still, watching her wild eyes roll in her head.

"My husband," Mrs. Nathaniel spat with venom, "is too busy with his lecture tours and publicity trips to even dream of such a thing."

"Oh, so you're just a poor little victim?" mocked Silk.

"Where is the formula?!" the woman demanded.

"There is no formula. It doesn't work," Silk said.

"Then why are you all dressed up in your Halloween costume?" the woman challenged.

"I'm rich," Silk said, "and eccentric. Don't you read the papers?"

"I know the formula exists! I've seen it," screamed Mrs. Nathaniel. She began to run her hands into her hair, pulling at the tender strands. Her lips curled in anger as she huffed, "I've felt the power of it inside me. I've got to have it again."

"You lie," Silk said. "If you'd of felt it, you'd still have it and wouldn't need the formula."

"You know it doesn't last!" the woman cried. "Now tell me where it is."

Silk knew that the woman was insane. Her wild eyes rolled back in her blonde head.

"Prove it," Silk said. "Tell me how."

"I've felt it," said the woman. Greed lit in her gaze. "I came to visit your father to have him build me a biomechanical droid--you know something that feels more real. That was before I developed a taste for synthetic.

Anyway, your father wouldn't help me and in my anger I cut my finger on a piece of glass. His formula spilled on me. And I know he gave it to you. I've seen you. I saw how you leapt over my fence the night you broke into my house. Now, tell me where it is!"

Silk's lips tightened, letting the woman hang herself with her own words. Adonis' hands stayed strong, binding her. She was too angry to move. If this woman saw her, than she saw Nikandros too. It all started to make sense. This woman knew Nikandros was in her lab. Maybe the woman paid him to duplicate her father's work. It would explain how he knew her document was a fake.

"Come on," Mrs. Nathaniel begged. "Please. I have to have it. I have to feel the power of it again. You're father wouldn't give it to me and I showed him. But, you'll give it to me. If you don't, I'll kill you too. You're not going to stop--"

"You killed my father," Silk said, her tone low. She never would have suspected this woman.

"What of it?" she growled. "Now you're going to join him if you don't give me what I want!"

"Adonis," Silk said unexpectedly. "Pleasure your mistress."

Instantly Adonis' hands let her go and he began to move around to grab his owner. Mrs. Nathaniel's lips puckered in surprise before she began screeching in protest. Silk grabbed Adonis' head and twisted it to the side, shutting him off. The droid froze in mid-stride like a statue.

Mrs. Nathaniel screamed in protest as Silk came after her. She tried to run, but Silk caught the back of her hair. She wanted to kill her, wanted to maim her for what she had taken away from her. But Silk was above this woman. Justice would prevail.

With a call to her security, Silk dragged the woman from the laboratory kicking and screaming behind her.

"Take her prisoner," Silk said to the guard. "Call the police. And get her damned pleasure droid out of my house!"

* * * *

The police came and arrested Mrs. Nathaniel, taking the security tapes from the laboratory as evidence against her. They never once spoke directly to the mistress of the estate, only stopped at the gate where the robotic guard had Mrs. Nathaniel and her pleasure droid detained. The guard handed them the tape and sent them on their way.

With the newer, faster judicial system in place, she was convicted of the murder by her own confession and sentenced to life imprisonment in a maximum-security complex. Adonis wasn't allowed to go with her.

* * * *

Nikandros frowned, looking down at his digital watch. Quinlan was late--very late. He began to pace, looking over at the bench where he'd first saw her. His body ached to hold her again, just as his soul ached to clear her of any suspicion.

He didn't know why he continued to wait for her as the clock neared half past twelve. He only hoped that she'd come to her senses and show. Leaning against the thick trunk of a tree, he sighed. All of a sudden, his video phone beeped. Slowly, he drew it out of his pocket. It was time to go. He could wait no longer.

* * * *

Silk frowned as she wrapped her cape around her body. Pierson Park was quiet this time of night. The vendors were all locked up. The expansive lawn was empty. She was late for her meeting with Nikandros. Closing her eyes, she listened. She couldn't hear him.

Her legs sprang forward as she jumped off her post into the night. Walking, she strode over the darkened grass, her senses peeked. For all she knew it could be a trap.

Then, she heard a soft beep. Silk froze. Her head twitched to the side. Her purple gaze narrowed as she focused on the sound. There, behind a tree.

Darting forward, she kicked out legs first. Her fingers found the rough bark. Her spinnerets automatically attached themselves to the trunk as she flew around the side. She trapped Nikandros to the tree's base, as she wound her silk around him like rope.

"Silk," he whispered in surprise to see her. His phone dropped to the ground before he could answer it.

Silk flew full circle around the tree before landing in front of him. Nikandros took in her mask, able to recognize her alluring body easily.

"You came," he began. Relief overwhelmed him until he realized she had trapped him.

"Of course I came," she said under her breath. "What do you want?"

"I need to speak to you about the Bombyx project your father was working on," he said. "I need you to give me the formula."

"Why should I give it to you?" she snarled. "I've been offered a lot of money for it. Do you think you can offer me something better?"

"Quinlan, please." His eyes dipped over her face and body, taking her in. She could feel the hidden plea coming from his dark eyes. His look stung and she snarled.

Bitterly, she lied, "Sorry, lover boy. I've had that already and don't have any desire to taste it again. You'll have to come up with a better offer."

"You want money?" he asked, dejected by her heated words and the hard glint to her eyes.

"I have money--more than I will ever spend," she returned. "What else you got?"

"What about doing what is right?" he inquired.

"And you're what's right?" she asked, laughing callously.

"Quinl--," he began, her unsympathetic words hitting him like a brick.

Silk took her fingers and ran them over his mouth, trapping his lips shut beneath a veil of silken threads. His words were muffled as he tried to speak.

"Quiet," she commanded. Her purple gaze deepened in her anger. She felt betrayed by him. She knew she shouldn't. He had warned her not to trust him, but like a fool she had. "I know who you are. I know what you're up to."

Again he mumbled.

"Listen to me very carefully. The formula is gone." She spoke slowly, so there could be no misunderstanding her words. "I am all that is left of the Bombyx project and I will kill myself before I let you, or anyone else, have the formula. All my father's notes are destroyed--all of them. I will not let another be turned like me."

Nikandros' jaw broke free of her gag. His eyes lit with fire at her admission. He had been right. She was innocent. "Quinlan, listen to me ... mmupf."

Silk swiped both her hands over his mouth this time, making the gag thicker as she pulled her fingers back to the tree trunk to secure his head into place. Slowly, she crossed her hands over his chest to make her trap stronger--just in case.

"Haven't you been paying attention?" she hissed into his face.

Nikandros searched her eyes for a sign of affection and found nothing. Oh, how he wished she'd take off her mask and let him kiss her.

"Quinlan St. James is dead. Her father killed her. He injected her ... me with the serum to keep it away from men like you. I became a human silkworm."

He groaned a word that sounded suspiciously like, no.

"I will only tell you this one more time. The serum is gone. The formula for it is destroyed," she said. His eyes brightened and she thought he was thinking about Mrs. Nathaniel. "Sorry, lover. Your cohort has failed. Mrs. Nathaniel is being transported to maximum security for the murder of my father. It's over. Do you understand me? It ... is ... over. If you ever come around me again, I will kill you."

Before he knew what was happening, Silk took off running. Nikandros' eyes flickered red as his body dissolved into a soft mist. He came out of her silken ropes, turning to give chase. But, as he came around the tree, she was gone.

"Nick!" came a call.

Nikandros blinked, looking around.

"Nick! Where are you?"

Nikandros looked at his feet. His video phone had fallen open and a miniature display of Korbin's face stared at him. Picking up the phone, he carried it as he walked, searching the distance for Quinlan.

"Nick?" Korbin asked.

"She's innocent," he said, his heart feeling like it was ripped out of his chest.

"I know. I heard everything," Korbin admitted. "You were right."

"What do we do now?" he asked, his eyes desperate.

"I need you to come back here," Korbin said. "We've got to tell the other Protectors what we know."

Nikandros nodded. Quinlan was gone. His voice hoarse, he asked, "What about Quinlan? What will happen to her?"

"It is not for us to decide," Korbin said sadly. "She's no longer human."

* * * *

Quinlan didn't care if she never left her room again. It had been weeks since she last left Nikandros in the park. Her heart still ached as if it was yesterday. She knew he had used her and betrayed her, but try telling that to an organ that only beat for the memory of his name.

She knew that Nikandros was in on the plot to steal her father's formula. It all fell together perfectly. Mrs. Nathaniel let him use her husband's lab while her husband was gone on various business trips--even going so far as to cover it up when attention was drawn to his presence.

Then, Nikandros had been sent to seduce the reclusive billionaire, gaining her trust. After that, he was to have lured her away to the park while Mrs. Nathaniel had free reign of her father's laboratory to look for the notes. Oh, it had been a good plan too--so simple. And she had fallen for it. If not for her sudden wave of longing for the council of her father, she'd never have suspected his connection to the woman.

She knew the facts, fitted them together so nicely. But then, why did her heart continue to scream at her like she was the one guilty of betrayal? Why did her body ache and sweat until she could hardly move? Why did her eyes leak damnable tears until she couldn't see for the redness of them? The loneliness was worse than before.

Burying her head in her pillow, she screamed her frustration at the world. She couldn't even throw herself into crime fighting like before. Helping the world held no appeal for her. She wasn't much sure she liked the world right now.

"Let them fend for themselves," she muttered in despondency.

Suddenly, her maid unit switched on and walked over to the bed. Her eyes staring straight, she said, "Pardon me, Miss. You have a call."

"Who?" Quinlan sniffed. For a moment, she wished it were Nikandros. Her heart sped ever so slightly at the faint hope. Oh, what she would give to just hear his soothing voice!

"Henry Thompson," said the maid. "Shall I answer?"

Quinlan frowned. Henry had been calling almost every day for the last three weeks, ever since news of Dr. Nathaniel's wife surfaced in the papers. Dr. Nathaniel, out of embarrassment, severed all ties with the woman and had moved out of the district. Rumor had it that he was courting a new piece of eye-candy.

"Yes," Quinlan said. "But, no video feed."

"Quinlan?" came Henry's voice. He sounded relieved. "What's happening? I can't see you."

"I'm not decent," she lied. "I just got out of the shower."

"Oh," he said, sounding mildly interested, before clearing his throat with a lower sounding, "Oh, sorry. Didn't mean to disturb you."

Quinlan gave a small laugh at that.

"Are you all right?" he asked. "I've been trying to get a hold of you for days."

"I know, sorry," Quinlan answered. "I've been preoccupied. I didn't feel like talking to anyone and the reporters have been calling my house like mad."

"I can well imagine," said Henry.

Quinlan just bet he could. She'd seen personal quotes from him in almost all the papers.

"I wanted to let you know that your father's collection is a huge success," said Henry. "It is our most popular display to date."

"I'm glad to hear it," Quinlan said. Her father would have liked that.

"Now, about this formula business," said Henry. "Is it true?"

"No," answered Quinlan without hesitation. "My father was working on it when he died. He said the properties were too unstable. The DNA mutations it caused would liquefy anyone who tried to use it. The whole project was a failure. It was my father's only failure as a scientist. That is why I don't want the record of it released."

"I understand," said Henry. He took her at her word. "As a leader in the scientific community, I will tell everyone that his work wasn't even started into the field. Your father's secret is safe with me."

"I know, Henry," Quinlan said. "You're a good friend."

"I was hoping to be more," said Henry. There was an optimism to his tone that she couldn't ignore.

"I know, Henry," repeated Quinlan softly, not encouraging him and not wanting to hurt him. Deep down, under all his bluffing and posturing, he was a good man.

"Well," said Henry, knowing his bid for a suitor was denied. "You can't blame a man for trying, can you, Quinlan?"

Quinlan chuckled. "Good-bye, Henry."

"Bye. I'll check on you later."

"Hang up," Quinlan said, turning over on her stomach. The maid unit disconnected the call. With a sigh, she said to the unit, "Make it menu one tonight."

Chapter Seven

Two weeks after Henry called, Quinlan finally made it off her bed, away from her bedroom, and out of her house--as far as the broken water fountain.

Looking around the quiet garden, she sighed. She rested her head against the hard stone of the fountain's base as she stared up at the stars. Quinlan frowned at the beautiful night. The old saying wasn't true. Time did not heal all wounds. Sometimes, time only made them worse.

"This is no way for a superhero to act."

Quinlan frowned, her head darting up at the noise to look around. She blinked to make sure her vision was clear. She was alone.

"Hello?" she called. The hairs on the back of her neck stood on end as if an endless presence was around her. She could see nothing. "Is someone there?"

Quinlan's breath caught in her throat. Right before her eyes a man materialized out of thin air. He was wearing a loose black shirt with a strange symbol on the chest. His dark pants fit snugly to his legs. His long, blonde hair blew in the wind as he watched her from the bluest eyes she'd ever seen. Scurrying to her feet, she stood, examining him through her awe. His gaze seemed to laugh good-naturedly at her open-mouthed amazement.

"Who are you?" she asked carefully. Her jaw hardened at his obvious humor. She was in no mood for the company of cheerful people. "This is private property. You can't be here."

"I am like you," the man answered her first question, ignoring her second.

"You're a woman beneath your clothes?" she asked, sarcastically.

"I am gifted," he said. His body glimmered and he disappeared into thin air, only to materialize by her side, his hand on her shoulders.

Quinlan jumped, jerking away as if stung. "What do you want?"

"I want to offer you a job," he answered.

"I'm not interested," she dismissed immediately. "Now go away."

"That is no way for a lady to treat a guest."

Quinlan flinched as a woman materialized from a surrounding bush. Her chameleon body mirrored her surroundings, making her move as if she were air. Slowly, her body filled in with a pleasing peach color as she made herself known. She too wore a matching black uniform.

"Who are you?" Quinlan demanded. Her eyes shifted with purple, as she prepared to fight them.

"So it is true, Korbin" said the chameleon to the blue-eyed man at her side.

Korbin nodded. His smile widened.

"They are the Protectors," answered a third voice. Quinlan turned. A third man walked up to her, his blue skin glimmering beneath silver flowing robes. His white hair parted down the center and hung nearly to his feet. Blinking, Quinlan saw that his eyes were so light a blue they were nearly white. "And I am the oracle who guides them."

Quinlan glanced at the man and woman at her side. They bowed before the oracle. Quinlan nodded her head in suit, but as she did so, she took a hesitant step away from them.

"How many of you are there?" she asked, looking around in fright.

"Show yourselves," ordered the oracle.

Quinlan tensed. It was like superheroes rained from the sky. All of them were different--some coming from behind trees, some appearing from thin air, some running in a blur to join the group. When nearly twenty of them were before her, their eyes shining, their bodies all clad in black uniforms, she gasped.

"What are you doing here?" she demanded, worried.

The group stood to watch as Korbin moved to face her. "It is as I said. We come to offer you a place within our family."

"But, you don't know me," Quinlan said. "You...?"

"We know of you," said the oracle. "I have looked into the future and have seen the possibility of your deeds. I have looked into your past and have seen what you have done, never asking for praise or reward. The only thing clouded is your present. You have a choice to make."

"Choice?" she asked, her strength leaving her as she grew weary. "What choice?"

"You can continue to pine for your lost love," said the oracle. His eyes shifted to complete white as he read her. "Or you can become an immortal, dedicating your years into doing that which you have already begun--helping the world be rid of evil forces."

"There is a battle," explained Korbin. "It's good against evil. We'd like you to join us. Help us keep the scales tipped for the side of good. It is what your father was working on when he died. It is what he intended his formula to be used for."

Quinlan began to shake her head, wishing she could deny their words. She could read the truth in their eyes, feel it in her. To become an immortal would mean she'd spend an eternity of her years longing for something she could never have--Nikandros.

"Yes, Silk," said the oracle. "It will not be an easy task. You will lose much. You will sacrifice many things. The years will eat at you until you no longer know why you do it. But, in the end, you will make a difference. You're father's gift to you will not have been in vain."

Quinlan swallowed.

"The moon wanes, Silk," said the oracle. "I need an answer. We will not ask you this again."

Quinlan looked around her. They were offering her an endless lifetime of serving others, of living alone as she did now. Seeing their faces, she knew she'd have them as her family. But, they were strangers. She started to shake her head, but something deep inside her stopped her. She thought of her father. She could not let his last scientific discovery go to waste.

"Yes," she said. Without Nikandros, she didn't have anything else to live for anyway.

The oracle smiled. "Come to me."

She stepped forward, glancing nervously around.

The oracle placed a blue hand on her cheek. His eyes darkened in their blue. "I give you the gift."

Quinlan tensed. He leaned over to kiss her and a soft mist drew out of his lips, coming inside her. She felt her limbs strengthen with a great force. She felt the knowledge of old being passed into her, teaching her of her duty, forcing an oath of loyalty from her mind. His lips were soft and passionless against her. She closed her eyes to his brightness. In the next instant, the lips were gone.

Quinlan blinked. The yard was empty.

"Welcome," came a voice from behind her.

Quinlan jolted, turning to look at Korbin. He was the only one left with her. She swallowed, a little frightened by what had just happened.

"What now?" she whispered, feeling very strange.

Korbin merely smiled, motioning over her shoulder as he disappeared into thin air.

Quinlan turned. Her limbs shook as a soft mist began to travel over the yard. She held very still, watching it gather as it drew before her. The mist rose, forming into a man.

"Nick?" she breathed, seeing his face. "What ... how?"

"Quinlan," he smiled, reaching for her.

Tears entered her eyes and she backed away. "You can't be here, Nick. You have to go."

"I can't be anywhere else," he whispered.

"What's going on? Who are you? What are you?" she demanded, shaking. This was all too much. Her eyes took him in, telling her that he was very real. But she couldn't go to him. She was afraid he would disappear from her like a dream, as he did every morning when she awoke.

"I am an immortal," Nikandros said, his eyes slowly drifting to red as he looked at her. "Nearly five hundred years ago I was born human, like the others. My town was attacked by a vampire. I fought him and was bitten. Before I turned, I killed him. The oracle found me and gave me the same choice he gave you."

"You're a vampire?" she asked weakly. "But, I've seen you in sunlight."

"Half-vampire," he murmured, again trying to step for her. "The change wasn't completed. The oracle saved me in time."

"You're supposed to help people. Why were you trying to steal my father's formula?" she inquired. This time when he came for her, she couldn't run. The sweetness of his voice made her will crumble.

"I was trying to stop you from selling it," he answered. She could read the truth of it in his expression.

"It was you, wasn't it?" she whispered. "It was you who worked with my father when I was a child."

"Yes," he admitted. "I did."

Suddenly, Quinlan couldn't take it. She rushed forward, her arms wrapping around his sturdy neck. Tears streamed down her face, as she said, "I thought I'd never see you again. I was so scared."

Nikandros' chest convulsed with relief. He pulled her tightly against him and began to kiss her, never wanting to take his lips away.

"Why did you stay away so long?" she panted, running her hands all over his delectable body to make sure he was real.

"I had to convince the council to test you," he said. "It's the only way we could be together."

"What test?" she sighed, pulling back to look into the solid dark depths of his eyes.

"To see if you would selflessly choose to serve others, regardless of the personal cost," he answered. "The oracle knew you would think you had nothing to gain by saying yes."

"I almost refused," she admitted. "What would have happened if I did?"

"You would have never seen me again," he replied. "You would have lived out your life as you have been."

Quinlan, hating the thought, pressed her body into his. She kissed him fervently, knocking him over to the ground in her passion for him. Nikandros chuckled in surprise at her ardor, but only pulled her closer.

"Never leave me again," she demanded, grasping his face in her hands. "I love you. I need you."

"I love you, too," he whispered.

As Quinlan leaned over to kiss him, Nikandros saw Korbin standing over them, grinning like a fool. Korbin winked at him, nodding his head as he shot him a thumb's up. Nikandros frowned, waving his hand for his friend to get lost. Korbin disappeared as Quinlan broke the kiss and glanced over her shoulder.

"What...?" she began.

Nikandros rolled her swiftly onto her back. When she looked up at him, his head was surrounded by stars. "It's nothing, just a pest."

At his comment, Nikandros felt an invisible kick to his backside, pushing him down fully onto Quinlan. Her body jolted in surprise. In the next instant, Nikandros knew Korbin had finally gone.

Quinlan smiled brightly, happiness flooding out of her onto him. Moaning, leaning up to capture his lips, nothing else mattered. He was hers and she was his. With tenderness in their hearts, they proceeded to make love right there on the lawn.

The End

Printed in the United States
35517LVS00001B/37-51